BLOOD OF THE INNOCENT

BEYOND THE ETHER

BOOK ONE

MYRANDA RAE

ONE

My fingers tap anxiously on the windowsill as I sit idly, waiting. I have so much nervous energy in my body that I can't stop moving. My toes tap, my knee bounces, and I'm chewing the inside of my lip raw.

Maybe the fact that it's already dark and they still haven't returned is a good thing. Maybe they found her.

Just as that naive, optimistic thought pops into my head, headlights illuminate the street. One car, then another, and another.

Jumping up, I run as fast as my legs will carry me. Losing my footing, I stumble down the stairs. I can't get to them fast enough.

I reach them as they are stepping out of their cars.

My hopes are immediately dashed when I see their faces. They didn't find her. She's still out there somewhere.

"Oh, Kiah ." Her mom falls apart when we make eye contact. "Where is she?"

"I'm so sorry." My voice cracks. "I don't know. Don't lose hope; we'll find her."

Holding her as she sobs, the familiar feeling of guilt burns up my insides. It's like acid, slowly corroding everything it touches. I should have gone with her. If I had, she might be here right now.

Deep, in the places I ignore, I know this isn't my fault but fuck it feels like it.

My legs feel wobbly and unsteady as I support her weight. A wet spot, all of her tears and anguish pouring out onto my shirt.

Behind us, a police car pulls to a stop on the street.

Officer Diller and Detective Salinger.

It could just be my own impatience; I don't know police procedures, and I've never found a missing person before, but I feel like they are fucking it up.

"Sunrise is at five fifty-eight tomorrow morning. We will begin searching again at first light." Officer Diller hands them a map. "We are going to be on the red grid."

"Then we will take the green area." Cheyenne's dad nods, looking at the map. "We'll cover more ground that way."

He looks like he's aged ten years in the past three days. A haggard, hard-hearted kind of tiredness is etched into his face. The suffering is like a physical feature as clear as his nose or lips.

"Kiah," Detective Salinger says, turning his beady eyes to me as Chey's parents pore over the map with the rest of the group. His voice is as grating as ever, each syllable dragging like nails on a chalkboard. "I was wondering if you would come down to the station for another interview."

"Sure." I force the word out, biting back the groan that's lodged in my throat. I want to be helpful; I really do. But helping should mean joining the search parties or hanging up flyers, not sitting in a stuffy police station with this jackass, while he asks the same question for four agonizing hours.

"Great, I'll drive you down."

"Great," I keep my tone and my expression as flat as I possibly can. I want him to know how much I don't like him. If they had taken us seriously on day one, if they hadn't brushed us off, maybe she would be warm and safe in her house right now. But they didn't take it seriously.

"She's twenty-one. She's an adult. Adults are allowed to leave."

But *she* wouldn't leave. Not without a word, not without telling us where she was going. She wouldn't just vanish. Yet, instead of believing the people who have known her all her life, he decided to wait until she'd been missing for forty-eight hours before getting involved.

I will never stop hating his guts.

Sitting in the back of his squad car, I pull out my phone and text my mom. If I'm outside for more than two minutes without checking in, she's ready to send out a search party after me. She's on edge, just like everyone else. I'm trying my best to be a good daughter—to reassure her, to keep myself safe—but it's starting to feel impossible.

But I have to help with the searches. Sitting inside, safe, comfortable, dry—all the things she might not be—is not an option anymore. Not when every fiber of my being is screaming at me to find her, to bring her home.

The single country road leading us from our isolated neighborhood to the town we've wanted to escape since childhood, I stare out the window. The forest stretches on endlessly, an ocean of trees that seems to go on forever. Thousands of trees stretch from our middle-of-nowhere town to the next one.

An outsider could easily get lost here, swallowed up by the vastness of it all.

But not Cheyenne. She's not a stranger. She knows this place like the back of her hand. As kids, we explored every inch of it—the deserted roads, the streams that carved through the forest, the caves, and the long-abandoned railroad tracks that once carried logs from here to the rest of the country. Those memories feel like they belong to another lifetime now, a time when the world was safe and whole.

The image of her, injured but very much alive, waiting to be found, haunts me. It's an image I can't shake, no matter how hard I try. She's out there, somewhere, and I can't rest until she's home.

"What is your timeline for involving the FBI in the search?" I ask, breaking the silence.

He pulls into one of three designated officer parking slots in the small lot outside the station, taking his time as if the question doesn't warrant a quick answer.

"We are discussing it," he glances at me in the rearview mirror.

It's the kind of non-answer I've come to expect from him. A hollow, empty statement that means nothing. Just like everything else, he's done. Fucking useless.

I've watched enough True Crime documentaries to know that the smallest town police department bungles the investigation from the start, and it's often a victim's family that pays the price. They are great for petty crimes. If someone runs a stop sign, they're on the case. But something this serious—a missing person—they need help.

Following him into the station, I wave and smile at Vicky. Too bad she's only the dispatcher. She's more helpful than the actual officers.

Plopping down in the seat, I lean back, already annoyed to be here.

I told him everything I needed yesterday while he interviewed me for three and a half hours. What more could he possibly have to ask?

He sets up a tape recorder on the table between us.

"Please state your full name for the record."

"Kiah Campbell." I don't hide the bored disinterest in my voice. We're wasting time.

"The time is eight-twelve p.m. on Thursday, October seventeenth." He looks at me again, his lips forming a straight line, before he looks down at his notes.

"You're about to graduate from Gonzaga University over in Washington, right?"

Fighting the urge to roll my eyes, I lean forward, closer to the recorder. "Yes, in May."

"Has Cheyenne ever visited you there?"

"Were you not actually listening when you interviewed me yesterday? Yes, she's visited me three times in the three and a half years that I've been at school." I fold my arms. He asked me this question four different ways already.

It's starting to feel like he suspects me of doing something to her. I understand that he needs information, but she's been my best friend since before kindergarten. I think I know her pretty well.

"And to the best of your knowledge, she's not there now? Maybe visiting a boy she met there?"

"I would be willing to say that I'm a hundred percent certain she's not there right now. She didn't meet the guy there, but if she had, she would have told me about it. If she was going to go out there, she would have waited for two weeks to go with me. If I'm home for fall break, she has no reason to go there." I hope my expression shows how truly stupid I believe him to be.

"The reason I ask is that we've done some digging into her electronics. She has been exchanging text messages with a burner phone out of Washington. Her communication has been through an app that deletes the messages after they're sent, so we are unable to see what she's saying to this individual." His face looks almost smug. As if he thinks he caught me in a lie.

My first instinct is to call him a liar. I don't believe it. There's no way that she's been in communication with someone in Washington who isn't me and kept it from me.

"Look." I run my fingers through my tangled hair. "Even if what you're saying is true and she was talking to someone, I'm still telling you that there is absolutely no way she would leave town without telling anybody. She loves her parents. She loves her dog! She would never leave Porky! She is kind and considerate and wouldn't want everyone she loves worried sick about her!"

Talking to him is like talking to a brick wall.

"The fact that she has no record here and that you don't know her should be worth something, right? She's not a troublemaker!" I'm close to tears. I don't know what else to say to make him believe that something bad happened to her.

For the next hour, we go back and forth over the same questions he asked me yesterday. My answers are all the same. I've been racking my brain trying to think of anything that would be helpful.

There's nothing. There is no thread that I can follow that will lead me to her. She didn't leave any breadcrumbs behind. It's like she vanished into thin air.

Frustrated and emotionally exhausted, I slump against the window in the backseat of his car.

We pass through town on our way to the same lonely stretch of road I've been on a million times before. For some reason, it feels longer tonight. The road is darker, twistier, and the trees look menacing where they never did before.

As we pull into the small cluster of seven houses that I've always called home, my chest aches. This tiny neighborhood is like a beacon, surrounded by darkness. There is nothing but trees for miles in every direction.

My eyes immediately go up to her darkened bedroom window. I bet her mom is in there now, searching for the only comfort she can find by lying in her missing daughter's bed.

At that moment, everything became clear to me. I have to go find her. I'll lie to my mom if I have to. I can't spend one more night warm in my bed while she is out there, hurt, lost, or worse. I can't let myself think about the possible 'worse' for long. It's too horrifying.

Mom is sitting on the porch, waiting for me.

Her arms open wide, and I accept without hesitation. Curling up against her body on the old bench swing, I rest my head on her lap.

"Mom, I have to go look for her."

"Kiah." She sighs. "I know how this is going to sound. But what if this isn't just a case of her being hurt or lost? What if there is foul play involved? I don't want you out there. I love Cheyenne, but you're my child."

"Your adult child." I can't believe what I'm hearing. If it were me out there, she would be asking the whole town to be a part of the searches.

"I know I can't forbid it, but I'm asking you, as your mom, to please stay out of the woods."

Rolling my lips into my mouth, I rest my head on her lap again. I won't make a promise I have no intention of keeping.

Two

"Water, extra sweatshirt, first aid kit, whistle." I check off the things on my list as I put them in my backpack.

The sun is starting to rise outside, and Mom will be heading to the hospital for her shift. As soon as she is gone, so am I.

I barely slept last night. Nodding off for a few minutes at a time before waking up in a cold sweat is not my favorite way to spend an evening. Thoughts of her outside in the cold kept me up. Each time I would nod off, I would see her in my dreams and wake up ready to scream.

Shoving my backpack under my bed, I pull my blanket up over my shoulder and wait. Mom should peek her head in to check on me any minute now. I feel ridiculous. I'm an adult. I shouldn't have to sneak out like a teenager anymore.

But I know Mom can't afford to stay home today. And if I push the issue, she will.

Like clockwork, my door clicks open, and a sliver of light spreads across the carpet. A relieved huff of breath from her chest fills me with that fucking guilt again. I wonder if she expected to open the door and find my bed empty.

I'm in a lose-lose situation here. It feels like I'm betraying one of them, no matter what choice I make. But I know that if I were the one who was missing, Cheyenne would be out looking under every rock for me. She wouldn't leave the woods until I was safe at home.

I'll be back before mom gets home tonight. She'll never know I left.

Watching my window, I wait for her headlights. As soon as I see them cast light across my wall, I jump out of bed.

As I lock the front door behind me, a strange feeling washes over me. It crashes down on my head like a wave. My stomach churns with a nauseous kind of nervousness. It could be my guilty conscience telling me to stay. Or it's intuition.

Forcing it down, I adjust my bag over my shoulders and head out.

By the time I reach the well-worn path that cuts through the 'magic forest,' the sun is glowing orange in the sky.

Looking around, it dawns on me that I've never actually been here alone. Despite the hundreds of times I must have walked this trail through the woods, I've never done it by myself. I was always with her.

Moving with a sense of purpose, I trudge along the overgrown path, my boots sinking slightly into the mud. The woods are eerily quiet, the only sounds being the occasional rustle of leaves and the distant call of a bird. My eyes scan the dense underbrush, searching for any sign of her, any hint that she passed this way. The morning fog sits low to the ground, making the air feel wet and heavy around me.

When I spoke to her parents on the first day, I showed them on the map where she might have gone. They said there was nothing there, but I'm looking anyway. That's where she was headed, I'm sure of it. The place she always talked about, the one spot she believed held the purest of materials for her crafts.

With each step, my irritation grows, gnawing at the edges of my mind. Under the paralyzing fear, I feel a simmering rage starting to build. It's a low, steady burn, with tiny bubbles of anger flowing through my veins. Why would she do this? Why couldn't she just buy paint and dye at the store like a normal person?

Her hippy all-natural bullshit isn't just annoying now; it's dangerous. For years, she's been gathering wildflowers, leaves, and even red clay from the creek bed, crafting her own dyes to color the wool she spins and knits. It's a unique, if not obsessive, passion of hers—one that she's fiercely proud of. And sure, it's cool, I guess. Her work sells like crazy at the craft fair in Helena. But at this point, I don't think it's worth the risk. Not anymore.

When we find her, and we will find her, I'm going to give her a piece of my mind. I've told her a thousand times not to wander around the woods by herself. It's too easy to get lost, too easy for something to go wrong. My thoughts spiral, the words I've been holding back bubbling to the surface as if she's standing right in front of me.

"Cheyenne Louise Coleman, you are not to set foot in these woods alone again, do you hear me?" I practice scolding her. "You scared the shit out of everyone."

As I imagine the embarrassed blush that will cover her cheeks and how she'll hang her head, uncontrollable tears well up in my eyes. I can't stop them.

Deep down, in the part of my brain that I'm trying to ignore, I'm afraid that I won't be able to tell her anything. I'm afraid that she's gone. The anger is just a mask covering the fear that's been gnawing at me since we realized she was missing.

I'm terrified of what I'll find—or worse, what I won't find—out here.

The last time I saw her can't be the last time. It wasn't long enough. I didn't tell her how much I love her or that she is truly the sister I never had.

A series of loud caws erupts from the trees surrounding me, slicing through the stillness with a sudden, jarring intensity that sends shivers racing down my spine. My body trembles, my breath catching as I freeze in place, every muscle tensing. I strain to listen, my senses heightened, but the forest around me falls into an eerie silence.

The trees loom above me as my eyes dart around, searching. Where are they? Where is it coming from?

Then it happens again. It's like they are swarming all around me, the calls coming from all directions, one after the other. Squinting, I look between the trees, searching the branches. I don't see a single bird.

It feels like they're closing in. The calls overlap in a chaotic, deafening roar. My heart hammers in my chest as I search the branches, but there's nothing there.

Ignoring the pit in my stomach and the overwhelming urge to turn around and run, I force my lead feet forward. I've barely made it a few steps when the caws start up again, more insistent this time, more relentless. They seem to come from everywhere, and nowhere, all at once.

By the time I reach the old logging road, I'm sure they're following me. An invisible flock is stalking me.

I never see a bird. Not one.

The calls grow more rhythmic, more deliberate, each one echoing ominously between the trees. Five calls, a pause, then three more. The pattern repeats, over and over, a sound that digs into my mind like a pulse. The echoes bounce off the trees, distorting the direction, making it impossible to tell where they're coming from.

My pace unintentionally speeds up. Fear creeps up my spine, grabbing hold of my heart and squeezing it tight. It's spooky. I'm expecting someone to jump out from behind the trees.

Stepping off the road, I walk through the trees. Gnarled roots and leaves cover the ground as I slowly make my way through the densely packed brush.

I walk parallel with the road, making sure that I can see it to my left at all times.

This is a more difficult walk, but I'm hidden. Being out in the open is making me feel too vulnerable.

It's been at least three hours, and I haven't seen anything out of place. It's almost as if I'm the only person who's ever been here. It's untouched earth.

A flash of purple catches my eye.

Setting my bag down to guide me back to the road, I walk deeper into the trees.

In a small, perfectly round clearing, there are thousands of tiny purple flowers. This is definitely a place that Chey would be drawn to. This bright color would call to her. Sunlight beams down, illuminating the spot. It's so unbelievably pretty and unexpected. Little trails of mushrooms in tiny circular clusters grow like polka dots out of the ground.

It's so cute.

I lift my foot to step in, and the birds go berserk again. It sounds like a thousand crows at once. Stumbling back, I fall, slamming into the decaying trunk of a tree.

"What the fuck is happening?" I cover my ears with my hands until the screaming caws stop. I barely notice the pain from falling. Fear is the only thing I can focus my attention on. The deafening sound blares on for what feels like several minutes.

Pinching my eyes closed, I rock back and forth.

"Please," I beg to no one. "Please, stop!"

Blinking my eyes open, I notice something on the other side of the clearing.

Something pink. An unnatural color out here in the woods.

On the day she went missing, she was wearing a pink pullover sweater. That looks like a pink piece of plastic.

Like a pink barrette.

Jumping up without thinking, I rush to grab it. Studying the small, cheap piece of plastic. I'm positive that it's hers. It's the same pink hair barrette I've seen in my best friend's hair a million times before.

Clutching it like a piece of treasure, tight in my fist, I pull myself up from the ground.

In a chaotic whirlwind of confusion, I feel like I'm being pushed down, like someone shoved me hard from behind, and I'm falling.

THREE

S teadying myself on the ground, I spin around, expecting to find someone, but I'm alone.

The pink barrette is still in my trembling hand. I feel hazy, like being startled awake. But I was never asleep.

It's much darker than it was just a second ago. It's as if the sun began to set in fast-forward. Did I get knocked out when I fell?

It so distinctly felt like someone pushed me over. I'm not in pain. There is no blood, no injury, nothing. Aside from my confusion, there isn't anything to indicate that I'm hurt.

How did it get so dark?

Panic courses through me as I run through the trees. I have to grab my backpack and get back on the road.

There is no way I can get back before Mom comes home.

Fuck, I'm in so much trouble. I can already see the disappointment on her face.

Stumbling through the growing darkness, I can't shake this feeling of disorientation. How did I lose so much time?

There are sounds in the forest now—chirps and twitters—that weren't there before. At least the crows are gone. These new sounds aren't necessarily comforting, though. I don't recognize them.

"Where is my backpack?" I circle around again. It should be right here.

I'm lost. I've never seen these trees before. Turning around, I go back to the clearing to reorient myself, but even it has changed. The calmness that was here before is gone.

The trees are different, longer, and thinner. The trunks aren't thick or sturdy, they look wispy, like I could snap them. The leaves on the ground aren't the typical layer of decaying plants; they look fresh, like each one only just fell from the branch. Deep greens and blues—these leaves aren't from the sugar maples.

A manic kind of terror sets in. The more I try, the harder it becomes. The air is thicker, heavier, and wet, like a humid day. It feels like static in my lungs.

I don't recognize anything anymore. Each step is taking me farther from home, not closer.

When I burst through the tree line onto the road, it's not the logging road but something else entirely. Sure, it's a road, but not the one I just came from. This isn't just a case of things looking different in the dark. This is not my home.

Outside of the dense brush, I can see how truly lost I am. Every single detail is just a little bit off. Not quite right. Some things, like the sky or the leaves, are glaring and obvious, others, like the smell of the forest, are more subtle. It's not the earthy, soft, damp smell I'm used to.

Stopping in the middle of the road, I close my eyes. I'm acutely aware that even with my eyes closed, even without seeing where I am, it feels different. There is something palpable about the air.

The sky is a hazy shade of orange, dark but still bright enough to see. There are no moons or stars. The sky is empty. I've never seen so much nothing—a vast, open void.

I must have a head injury. That's the only thing that explains this. Or I'm unconscious, and this whole thing is a hallucination.

"Wake up, Kiah !" I pinch my arm. "Wake up, now!"

Peeking my eyes open, I'm still in the same place.

Taking a deep breath, I start to walk down the road. Aside from the very obvious wrongness of the whole situation, everything is fine. There is just enough light to see ahead of me. I'm not hurt anywhere that I can feel.

An intense helplessness settles into my chest.

Out of the corner of my eye, there is a flash of motion—like catching sight of your own shadow on the ground. When I jump, looking down, there is a dark figure on the ground, moving. Screaming, I take several steps away and look around.

There isn't anyone else here.

Standing still, my body frozen in fear, I watch the shadow move across the ground. It dances across the floor, not just moving, but it looks like it's alive all on its own.

I must be unconscious. Shadows don't move on their own. They simply don't. This is a nightmare.

I'm trapped here, in a made-up hell inside my head.

The shadow dances, almost whimsically, down the road. I follow it, unable to do anything else.

At the crest of a hill, the landscape sweeps downward into a crater. It stops me dead.

It's unlike anything I've ever seen. As far as the eye can see, there is nothing but meadow. It's grassland dotted with the most peculiar flowers. Glossy black petals that almost glow against the darkened sky.

The road cuts straight through, down one side and up the other like a bowl. From this height, the road appears to dissect a perfect line directly in the center. It looks strange—too perfect.

As I walk slowly down into the valley, following the road, a whisper floats on the wind, blowing through my hair.

It's a voice—quiet but as clear as day.

Spinning around, I frantically look for the person who spoke, but there is no one.

I'm going crazy. I'm hearing things. I'm seeing things.

The voice murmurs again. And just as before, there is nothing there when I turn around. I am just missing them, I can feel them there.

"Hello?" I call out, and my voice echoes through the valley. "Hello?"

With each echo, it changes, morphing from my voice into something unrecognizable.

Snapping my mouth closed, I don't speak again. Hearing my own voice mutate into something so distinctly different from me is terrifying.

Forcing myself forward, following the shadows that dance across the road, I hear the voice again. My hair moves, like someone's breath blows against it as they speak. Covering my ears with my hands, I fight the urge to turn around and look.

My mind is playing tricks on me. There's no one there. I'm utterly alone.

Gasping, I stand up straight, the realization hitting me. Mushrooms! The mushrooms in the little clearing must have been toxic! I breathed in the spores! That can happen, right? That is the only explanation for all of this. I'm drugged!

Feeling slightly relieved, I begin the journey up the other side of the crater.

Each step feels like a fight. I can't seem to make it to the top. Step after step, but I never get any closer.

Sitting down on the road to catch my breath, I turn to look out over the valley. There are wispy shadows coming up the road behind me. They don't seem to notice me, they just move across the ground.

Taking the barrette out of my pocket, I run my fingers over it. I didn't find Chey. Mom is going to be beside herself. I've completely failed today.

I've managed to stay strong up to this point, but sitting here, exhausted and defeated, I let the tears that have burned in my eyes finally fall.

I royally fucked up today.

While I cry, frustrated, disappointed, and afraid, I notice movement beside me. I don't want to look. I won't like whatever it is.

The black flowers are stretching, leaning toward me as if they were reaching out. It's not a subtle motion, the stems are parallel to the ground as they extend themselves to me.

Scooting away, I wave my hand, shooing them away. "Go," I whisper. "Leave me alone."

My hand touches one of the flowers, and it stops moving, the black color draining out of it like blood, dripping onto the road. It's yellow now.

Like a ripple spreading over water, all of the flowers fade from black to yellow. The whole field changes. The big, yellow petals radiate light that makes the valley glow.

I watch in stunned silence. It looks very different now --cheerful.

"Human." A voice from behind me makes me scream and nearly jump out of my skin.

I turn to look but lose my balance and tumble several full rotations down the slant I'm seated on.

With a rough jerk, a hand wraps around my arm, yanking me up.

His mouth is moving, but I can't hear him. There are two men. The one holding my arm and the other standing behind him.

My eyes can't seem to focus on one detail to look at.

Strikingly tall and eerily beautiful. Every new feature is captivating to me. The deepest black hair, sharp jawlines, and full lips—they're stunning, but the longer I look, the less human they appear.

Those lips hide sharp teeth that peek out, pressing into his lower lip as he speaks.

Nestled into their thick, dark hair, their ears come to a point near the top.

But most shocking are their eyes—piercing and bright but terrifying.

"How did you get here?" He shakes me slightly.

"I..." I have no answer to give. Where is here? I should be in my hometown. Is this private property?

"Human." His voice sounds angry, but I can't think past the fact that he has called me that multiple times now. Human.

Is he not one?

"Are there more of you?" He shakes me again, harder this time.

"I'm looking for my friend! She-"

Without a word, he turns and pulls me behind him.

"Wait! Please! I-"

He turns, looking over his shoulder and staring at me. He doesn't say anything, but I shrivel back. The look in his eyes speaks for him. My instincts completely fail me, shutting down and leaving me here with no idea what to do. I don't fight; I just let him drag me away.

FOUR

He pulls me with ease to the top of the hill. Beyond it, there is another field with a river running through it. Silver water that looks like melted metal.

I stop resisting and let him pull me toward it. It's mesmerizing.

Not just that it looks like liquid silver, but that it's here at all. There shouldn't be a river here. I guess I shouldn't be surprised, this place is all twisted around.

I have questions, but I'm afraid to ask them. The longer this goes on, the more I'm starting to doubt myself. Confusion and fear creep in and cloud my mind. Is this a dream? A hallucination brought on by mushrooms? I can't make up my mind. This cannot be real. But it feels real.

If I could just take a deep breath without this heavy feeling in my chest; I might be able to think more clearly. Everything is too real to be my imagination, but then it's too fantastical to explain.

As we approach the river, the ground turns from grassy fields to black sand. It's weird that things you focus on in moments like this. There are so many things that seem more important, but the sand is what has captured my attention. As we moved from dry to wet, I can't stop staring at it. It's soft under my shoes like regular sand, but it shimmers like trillions of specks of black glitter.

A boat floats on the water. It looks like black glass. The silver water creates a rippling reflection on the side.

Everything about this place is alluring in a dark, unsettling way. My gut is telling me I'm not safe, but it's so beautiful.

"Where are we?" I don't even mean to ask; the words just slip out.

The one yanking my arm out of the socket stops, smiling. "Welcome to Noctyra."

His smile is anything but welcoming. The long, fanged teeth on either side of his mouth press into his lower lip. I would venture to guess that menacing was the look he was going for. They don't need to try; they are menacing enough, naturally.

With one question answered and a thousand more floating around in my mind, he physically tosses me into the boat.

"Don't touch the water. Sit." He gestures with his chin to a row of seats.

This ill-fated rescue mission aside, I'm not generally rebellious. I was never a 'learn the hard way' type. For reasons I don't have, I have a guttural, bone-deep, all-consuming desire to touch the water. I want to touch it more than I've ever wanted anything in my life.

I feel myself leaning. I try to stop it, but it's like I'm being controlled by someone else.

"I forgot how feeble minded humans are." They both laugh, and one of them grabs me.

I have to distract myself, or I might try to dive in. It looks so refreshing. Silver and crisp, like I would just glide through it. I want to drink it. I want to let myself sink below the surface of it.

Shaking the thoughts out of my head, I turn to them. "What are you?"

They just called me feeble-minded, I don't think we need to fake niceties. I don't expect them to tell me or to suddenly start chatting.

I wasn't expecting them both to laugh.

"Feeble-minded with short memories, I guess." He licks his lips. "She smells good, though, doesn't she?"

My wide-eyed expression makes them laugh again. One of them sits in the chair beside mine, and I watch, horrified, as he brings his hand up to my face. I'm so uncomfortable, but I don't move. He brushes his fingertips over my cheek, then my lips.

"We're Fae, little human."

"Fae?"

"Fae." He repeats again, a flicker behind him catching my attention. Wings.

"Oh my god." A hideous sob bursts from my chest, and I'm instantly weeping. I'm overwhelmed. The prevailing emotions—fear and confusion—are starting to mix with frustration. This can't be real, but I can't make myself wake up. I want to scream and run—to escape —but I feel like a deer in the headlights. I'm so unsure of everything. I feel like a version of myself, but not really. It's like parts of me have been rearranged.

He lets out a disgusted huff. "I also forgot how emotional they are." He moves away from me like my tears are contagious.

Get your shit together, Kiah. I swallow down the painful ball of emotion in my throat. No more tears.

They have completely moved on. Whatever they are quietly discussing, I only catch little bits and pieces.

In an attempt at discretion, I put my head down and peek at them through my bangs.

This is a wild hallucination. I have to give my subconscious props for what I've been able to conjure up here.

Last year, I took a psychology course. There was a girl who would always bring the conversation to dreams and the unconscious mind. Cheyenne would have loved her. They have the same free-spirited thing going on.

Because of her, we spent more time on the subject. I learned that when we dream, we don't create faces. The people in our dreams are real, whether we know them or have passed them on the street and their image stuck.

Looking at these guys, I'm racking my brain trying to figure out where I might have seen them before. They are not familiar at all.

"Is this a dream?" I blurt out. Would dream beings tell you they are dream beings? I guess the only way to find out is to ask outright.

"Unfortunately for you, it's not."

"Why is it unfortunate?"

"Because whatever egregious errand brought you here, you will not succeed in it." He looks down at me over the tip of his perfect nose.

"I'm not here on an egregious errand. I am trying to find my friend."

He hums, raising his brows slightly with a clear attitude. For whatever reason, he doesn't like me—that much he's made clear.

"Ready?" A smirk tugs at his lips.

"Ready for what?"

"To meet your fate?" He gestures behind me.

"My fate..." My voice fades away as I turn. Anything I wanted to say is completely forgotten at the sight before us. The silver river winds ahead, through the fields, until it flows directly into a city. A city made of the same black glass as the boat we're sitting in.

The water forks into two separate paths around an island with a singular, sprawling cathedral in the center. It looks like a place for worshiping something dark—something cruel. Tall, spiked pinnacles stretch into the orange sky like reaching vines. Call it intuition or maybe good old-fashioned fear, but I don't want to go there.

There is something ominous about it, like if I enter, I might never walk out again.

The eeriness grows as we wind slowly toward it. The water pushes us forward, carrying me there against my will.

The closer we get, the more other boats dot the water. As we pass, the occupants look at me in stunned horror. By the third boat, I'm feeling like I've grown a third head. I've never caused such a negative reaction in people before. They hate me on sight.

With each ugly stare and look of disdain, my anger grows, too. They can hate me, and I don't like them either.

Equal parts beauty and evil created this place. As we float past the building, I feel small before them, like standing beside the ocean. The vastness is humbling. The black glass is haunting, reflecting a twisted picture back.

We seem to be making a beeline for the cathedral.

Two bridges connect the island to the city on either side. Black vines grow over them, dripping with black flowers. It is somehow ancient and modern.

There is a woman waiting there. She is as unearthly beautiful as the others, but there is something less cold about her. The sterile rage I've seen in every other face is not present on hers.

"Did she touch anything?" She asks, never even looking at me.

"The Hollow Valley. The flowers have changed." He side-eyes me with obvious irritation before bowing his head to hear.

Her shoulders slump slightly. "Come with me." She turns to me, looking like a disappointed parent picking up their child from the principal's office.

Walking behind her, I stare at her wings. They hardly look airworthy. Fragile and delicate, they could be blown apart by anything more forceful than a gentle breeze.

From a distance, they are black, but up close, woven in are patterns of intricate golden threads.

The vastness of the cathedral leaves me breathless. Polished black glass stretches on in all directions endlessly. The temperature is noticeably colder. A white puff of my breath floats in the air.

"Follow me." She turns, several steps ahead of me already, to get my attention.

"Right, sorry." I close my awestruck open mouth and follow her.

The nave is lined with rows of empty black pews facing an altar. Ornately designed and frightening, a faint humming sound radiates from it. A heartbeat, a pulse—it pounds in my ears. I don't like looking at it.

I thought fairies were supposed to be sweet creatures in the forest. There is nothing sweet about this place. The stories are all wrong.

In silence, we walk down a long hallway, up a long flight of stairs, and then down another hallway. I was right about this place; it never ends.

"Here we are," she opens the door. "You will stay here."

"Wait, I can't stay here." The reality of this situation—the truth I've been pretending not to see—is sinking in. This might not be a dream. If

I'm really here, I need to figure out how to get home. "I'm looking for my friend. Is she here? I need to go home."

She looks at me, studying me carefully. "Stay here."

The heavy door closes with a thud that echoes, and then the lock clicks.

FIVE

"Hello?" My raw, bloody fists beat against the door, the pain barely an afterthought. "Hello? Please!"

I'm exhausted mentally, physically, and emotionally. I just don't have any more to give. This place is sucking the life out of me.

The longer I spend here, the more I feel it. My skin and bones are different. I'm lighter and heavier. My hair and teeth are sensitive, each individual strand is sentient. My fucking shadow is bouncing off the walls.

I hear whispers but can't find them. They are just here to torment me.

I've taken to humming between screaming to drown them out. It's the only thing I can do to save my sanity.

Sitting on the cot, my only piece of furniture, the full weight of my body, every single cell, gives in—gives up. I let my head fall onto the pillow, and my eyes flutter closed.

There is still a small flicker of hope in me that believes that when I open my eyes again, I'll be home. I know I won't be. This place, Noctyra, it's real. Accepting it was a hard pill to swallow. How is it real? It just is. I'm done fighting that truth.

Sleep comes slowly, like water filling a tub. I feel it inch by inch, rising until I'm submerged.

My dreams are haunted. My shadow taunts me. With ease, it opens the door I've spent hours pounding, and it walks out. When I try to follow it, I slam, painfully, into a forcefield that holds me trapped here.

Snapping my eyes open, I know immediately that I'm not alone.

Sitting up, I turn to find a man sitting in a chair, watching me.

"What is your name?" His voice is like ice on my skin. Rough and masculine and completely undeniable.

"Kiah ." I have to force my eyes to blink. My brain has lost control of my body. There is something so predatory about him. I think I would feel the same way if I were seated in front of a lion or a wolf.

"I'm going to ask you some very simple questions, Kiah ." His eyes pierce through me, dissecting the layers and stripping me bare. I can't hide anything from him.

He runs a jeweled hand through his dark hair. "Why are you here?"

"I'm looking for my friend. I didn't mean to come here. I was just trying to find her." If I'm forthcoming, maybe he will let me go.

"How did you get here?"

"I was in the forest, and I found this." I pull her barrette from my pocket. "Then I felt like someone pushed me. When I stood up, I was here."

Completely uninterested in the barrette, he stands suddenly, his imposing height forcing me backward. I don't know that I've ever physically cowered in my life.

His presence is heavy, and the weight of his authority is palpable. Even the whispers have stopped, and my shadow is suddenly behaving. A thousand years show in his eyes, like he is somehow old and new.

"Wait! Please let me leave. I just want to find her. I don't want to cause any trouble!" I jump up when I realize he's about to leave.

"Your friend isn't here. I would know if she were." His deep voice is so final that I immediately believe him.

"I'm not saying she's here, but I won't find her locked in this room. She is the sweetest, kindest person alive. She's more than my friend; she's my sister. Please."

He reaches for the door, and I panic.

"She's worth finding! I know a lot of people aren't, but she's so good. Innocent. She would give the shirt off her back to a stranger, then she would use the last of her money to buy them another one!" I don't know why I try to appeal to any kindness in him. It doesn't look like he has any.

His expression changes for the first time, his irritated scowl morphs into an irritated surprise.

For a moment, it looks like he's going to speak, but he storms out instead.

"Hey!" I pound the door. "Wait! You can't just keep me here!" I'm met with silence.

Dejected and frustrated, I drop down into the bed and watch the shadow pace around the floor.

"What are you so stressed about?" I take out my pent-up anger on it. Snapping at the weird little thing that seems as upset by this situation as I am makes me feel guilty instead of better. "Sorry."

It comes to sit beside me, acting like a shadow for once.

"Can't you leave? Just slip under the door or something."

It peels itself off the bed and tries to crawl under the almost nonexistent space between the floor and the door. It can't slip through.

"Are you stuck here because of me?"

It nods and sits beside me.

"Sorry about that." I rest my elbows on my knees. "He left his chair here."

Grabbing the chair, I push it against the wall. If I stand on it, I can look out the window.

"Some view," I grumble. A wall—that's all I have to look at in every direction. "I think I could jump down to the ground from here and only hurt myself minimally." I look at the shadow, hoping for input.

Before it can give me any, the door opens again.

"Kiah, I'm Elion." He comes into the room. His demeanor is completely different from the last man. It's fitting that he looks so opposite the others that I've seen. With white hair and wings, he looks like an angel. "If I bring you back to where the Paladins found you, could you lead me back to where you entered?"

"Yes." Probably. I don't show him my hesitations, though. I'm not going to pass on a chance to escape.

His lip twitches, a smile tugging at the corners. "Don't try anything. I'm not as nice as I look."

But he *does* look nice. Built like the others—broad shoulders, towering height, luminous skin, pointed ears, and sharp fanged teeth— but there is something lighter about him than the others. I can't put my finger on it. There is something youthful about him, carefree and soft.

"Come on," he gestures for me to walk out ahead of him.

First, the hallway, then the stairs, I try to memorize the route. He walks too quickly, I'm jogging behind him to keep up.

He doesn't say a word, the dark halls whisper as we pass, talking about us. I'm almost sure I heard my own name a time or two.

The air outside feels lighter than the stifling atmosphere in the cathedral. I suck in a breath, feeling my lungs fill.

A boat is waiting for us on the silver water. This one is bigger, with roses etched into the glass.

"Sit there." He points. "Don't touch the water."

"Why not?" I can't hold back my curiosity.

With three large steps, he's in front of me. He sits beside me, his eyes narrowed.

"You don't seem appropriately frightened." He studies me.

"No, I am, but..."

"No. Why aren't you afraid?"

"I am. I just want to go home." I pick at my bloody knuckle. "This is a nightmare."

He leans in, his crystal blue eyes staring so intensely that I can feel him in my chest - digging around. "You don't know about us, do you?"

"No?" None of this existed before I stood up in the middle of the forest.

He smiles, his sharp teeth glinting in the low light. "I thought so."

With no explanation, he leaves me alone to replay the conversation over and over again.

"The Ebonstream is a living entity. It calls to you, draws you near. It will pull you under and drown you before you even realize you're in trouble." He answers my question suddenly.

"Oh." I inch away from the edge of the boat. I feel it—the same longing as before—and I want to jump in.

"You feel it, don't you?" He hums, with obvious amusement.

"Yes." I look down at the bench seat, noticing that I'm somehow closer to the edge again, my body moving toward the water on its own.

"So, humans have forgotten us, then?" He smiles, a reminiscent kind of haziness on his features, as if he's remembering an old memory.

"What do you mean?" The guards from yesterday come to mind. They mentioned humans and our short memories.

"All of our doors used to be open wide. Fae and humans lived side by side. That would have been several hundred years before you were born, but I'm surprised the stories don't live on. Cautionary tales." His eyes sparkle.

"Cautioning of what?"

"The dangers that lurk here beyond the Ether." He is obviously enjoying this cat and mouse game where I am the mouse, smaller, out of my depth, and at a disadvantage.

Closing my mouth, I decide to take myself out of the game. I'm desperate for information, but I get the feeling that any answers I get from him come at a cost.

We move through the water, and the sound sloshing against the boat starts to sound like voices. Low and mocking, the water is taunting me.

Elion seems content in the silence. A small, serene smile on his lips as he drives us up the river toward the crater.

"Ah, here we are." He jumps gracefully over the side of the boat and into the water. I watch as it morphs, like hands taking hold of his ankles. He kicks it off, as if it were nothing. "Come on." He holds a hand out to me. "I won't let it get you."

SIX

"Can you please slow down?" I grumble, running to keep up with him.

Unexpectedly, he stops completely, and I run into his back. Stumbling back, he turns to catch me before I hit the ground.

"Wow," he says, setting me on my feet. "You really did a number on this place."

The field full of yellow flowers is very different from the black flowers. It's more cheerful and brighter, and the air is softer and smells sweeter.

"I didn't mean to." In fairness to me, the flowers seemed to be pretty desperate to change. They crawled toward me. Even still, I feel guilty.

We walk down the slope, and all of my questions eat away at me.

"What is the ether? You mentioned it before..." I look at the ground so he can't see my embarrassment. I lost the fight against myself. If I'm going to get home, I need to know what I'm up against here.

"It is the veil that separates us from you—the human realm from Noctyra."

"W-What dangers lurk here?" I try to sound nonchalant, like the words haven't been playing on repeat like a broken record in my head since he said them. It doesn't sound nonchalant. I sound completely terrified. I am completely terrified.

"That's the level of fright I was looking for." His smile looks more sadistic than before. "We lurk here, darling. The Fae."

"And we should be cautious around you?" My voice wobbles. I'm in the middle of nowhere with him, with nowhere to hide. This line of questioning is making my heart rate spike.

"You're perfectly safe now. If you happen across a Shadowrithe in your travels, I would run."

"What is that?" It would be nice if he was more forthcoming with the information. Obviously, I'm going to need additional details after a statement like that.

"Unless you are out in the Fringes, you'll be fine. They don't venture out where we civilized people live." His smirky grin tells me that this game is fun for him. He gives me an answer that scares me and only brings about more questions.

I knew this was a game that I didn't want to play, but now I feel like I can't stop. I never should have started. Now I'm stuck, I have to keep asking.

"And the fringes are what exactly?"

"Not what, where. It's the darkness beyond the borders of the kingdom. The Shadowrithes are banned to rot there." The disgust he has for them reminds me of the way everyone else here looks at me.

"But what are Shadowrithes?" My frustration is showing.

"You've asked so many questions. I think it might be time for me to ask a few."

"I guess that's fair." I prepare myself to be grilled about what I'm really doing here.

"What is your family like? Do you have any siblings?"

"Oh," such a simple question, is not what I was expecting. "I have an older brother. He's in the Air Force, so I haven't seen him in three years. He lives in Florida. I actually wanted to join the military too, travel, leave my tiny hometown, and all that. But I felt bad for my mom. I didn't want to leave her alone. Chey either. She is like a sister. I-" Snapping my mouth shut, I grimace. What am I even talking about? Rambling on and on. He didn't ask for all of this. Does he even know what Florida is? Or the air force? What is wrong with me? "I'm not usually a nervous rambler."

"Don't apologize; that was very informative. You mentioned everyone but your father. Where is he?"

"Pass." I shake my head.

"Pass?" He cranes his neck to look at me.

"Yes. Next question."

"Interesting." He hums. "Do humans no longer remember the fae, really?

"No, not as you are. We have stories about fairies. But they aren't like you. They're small and cute, living in magical gardens and sleeping on flowers and stuff." As the words leave my mouth, I regret them. This could be very offensive to him, and I just casually said it.

A loud, joyous laugh fills the crater. He throws his head back and cackles. His fangs glint in the orange light.

"Maybe it was a self-preservational instinct," he smiles. "Remove us from memory to forget the horrors."

My feet stop, rooting into the ground. "What horrors?"

He rubs his tongue over his teeth. "One thing your stories got right is the magic. Do you feel it?"

"Yes." I wait for him to answer my question.

"Shadowrithes take the lifeforce from humans. They could do it in a way that allowed them to live, but they chose not to. Personally, I think they enjoyed the last bit the most—the last drops of life before the lights went out." He's watching me carefully for a reaction.

"So if I see one, they'll kill me, got it." I force the fear aside. I don't want to give him the satisfaction.

"Not just kill you, darling, drain you." He licks his sharp teeth.

My heart starts to pound. My mind is making up crazy theories to fill in the blanks. God damn him. He's being purposefully withholding. He knows what he's doing.

"Your heart is beating faster. I can tell by the way this vein is pulsating." He runs his finger up my neck, sending an icy chill up my spine. When he asked me to come with him, I was so desperate to get out of that room. I didn't think this through.

"You're not a Shadowrithe, are you?" I gulp.

"How dare you." He laughs, but his eyes flicker and his jaw ticks before he forces it away. "I'm Rimefae. We're from the Frostlinds." He looks down at me over his nose.

"Sorry." My unease is growing by the second.

"Where do we go from here?" He looks around, and I realize that somehow we made it through the basin and have come up the other side.

"Um, I'm not sure." Flop sweat gathers on my back as I frantically look around. "There was a road here yesterday l! I... It was right here!" Spinning around, I look back down at the meadow. "I came from here! I ran out of the woods onto a road and followed it right here!"

"You sure about that?" He gives me a knowing smile.

"I'm positive! It was yesterday. I haven't forgotten already." I plant my hands on my hips. "Did you know this would happen?"

"Why would you think that?" Mischief sparkles in his eyes.

"You're cruel." I bite into my trembling lip.

"Oh, darling." The smirk drops from his face, and he looks genuinely concerned. "I'm just having a go at you. This forest moves around, the road to the fringes is never where you last left it."

"Well, you could have just told me that." I wipe the back of my hand over my eye and spin around, marching back toward the crater.

"How about I make it up to you?" He hums. "Ask me a question. Any question, and I'll give you a straight answer."

So he was doing it on purpose. Bastard.

I consider the best way to word my question to get the most out of my answer. "Do you know where my friend is?"

"Not as of yet, but our king, ever watchful, is looking."

"So you think she's here?"

He wags his finger. "Ah-ah, that's two. I didn't say that. I said the king is searching. If she is here, he will find her." He emphasizes 'if.'

For the first time, I notice a scar on the back of his hand. The silver mark looks like burned skin.

I look away quickly, but he saw me staring.

The silence between us is uncomfortable now, walking back the way we came. This trip was a waste of time, he knew it would be. Why would he bring me out here to have me show him where I came from if he knew the road would be gone?

"I want to go home." I can't stand another second of this quiet.

"That is not up to me."

"The king?"

"The king." He smiles. "I'll put in a good word for you, though."

"Thanks." I kick at the ground as we walk. My little shadow twirls on the ground beside me. I'm still uneasy, something about him, his highhandedness—it makes me feel unsettled. But I don't think he wants to hurt me. Taunt me, yes. But not harm me.

I have some answers, but everything still feels hazy.

With my head down, I catch another glimpse of his hand. Layers of melted skin, gnarled and slightly raised. It's the only blemish on him; he's otherwise perfect. Inhumanly beautiful, with a strange kind of grace. The way he walks and his posture are too perfect.

His wings are different, smaller, and more curved than the others. Similar to the golden pattern on the black wings, they have silver symbols etched into the ivory.

Climbing up the other side of the crater is difficult again. I'm struggling with each step. It's like I'm walking against the wind, being forced backward.

"Come here." He offers his hand to me. "There is a protective force that keeps outsiders away."

Exhausted, I take his hand, letting him pull me up to the top.

The more I learn about this place, the more I dislike it.

Huffing, I look back over the meadows. He is here this time, so the fear isn't at the forefront of my mind, but it still lingers in the background. There is still this feeling—a whisper just behind us—and it's always there. But whenever I turn around, there's nothing.

"What are you looking for?"

"I keep hoping if I can turn around quickly enough, I'll be able to see whatever is behind us."

A low laugh rumbles in his throat. "Everything here is alive. Everything has something to say if you know how to listen to it. What you are hearing now is probably the flowers."

"What are they saying?"

"They're probably warning you." His lips turn upward as he walks toward the river.

SEVEN

I've kept my mouth shut as we move through the water. I'm drained. His taunting has left me anxious and unsettled. The intentional and consistent messing with my mind is like a slow leak; my control is dwindling. I want to hide alone and break down.

Am I safe here? I don't know. Is everything here out to get me, to drain me, to hurt me? Maybe. I think so. I can't trust anything. Having a wall up like that is exhausting. Protecting myself from everything is impossible. This place doesn't play fair. Even the flowers talk?

My shoulders slump as we step off of the boat under the looming monstrosity of a cathedral. I'm struck with deja vu. The woman is waiting for us again.

She ignores me completely. Her flawless skin is etched with worry as she takes Elion by the hand and pulls him away. "I need to talk to you."

I walk behind them inside. I'm not sure if I'm supposed to, but I do. I don't have anywhere else to go, and if I stay outside by the silver river, I'll dive into it headfirst.

"The fringes are empty." She whispers to him. I assume she meant for this to be a private conversation.

"Completely?" He rubs his hands through his hair. His body looks tense, the muscles in his arms tensing against his sleeves.

"Not a single one. And no sign of a human either." She turns, looking over her shoulder at me. "What about her?"

"I believe her, she's telling the truth." He looks back, giving me a quick wink.

She looks at me again, this time, gesturing with her hand for me to follow her.

"I will take you to bathe and eat." She spins around, walking down the hallway without me.

Elion grabs my hand. "Until next time, darling." He presses a kiss to my hand before quickly leaving me alone.

"Follow me," she says, stepping back into view down the long, dark hallway.

"Sorry." I scurry after her.

"I am Calais." She doesn't break her long strides.

"I'm Kiah." I jog behind her.

"I know." She looks over her shoulder, a hint of a smile on her lips.

"Oh, right." I chase her down a flight of stairs. "Of course you do."

"Here we are." She uses both hands to push at two large black doors. Intricate carvings cover both of them, and they creak, like they are incredibly heavy or old, or maybe it's both.

"What is this place?" I force my gaping mouth closed. Heavy darkness, only illuminated by dim purple lights and faint light from gothic-style stained glass windows surrounding the room.

"The bathhouse." She comes back to me, gently pushing me forward. In the center of the room, I can barely make out that the reflective floor is water, not more of the same black glass. "Derobe and climb in." She walks back to the doors and, with some effort, pulls them closed behind her. They thud loudly, punctuating that I am stuck here.

Slowly pulling off my jeans, I can't help but feel like I shouldn't be allowed in a place like this. I'm going to break something or make it dirty.

In the center of the pool, there is a statue, a single stream of water creating a quiet splash, a calming drip that soothes my tension slightly.

With cautious steps, I walk down the slope into the water. By the time I reach the statue, I'm chest-deep. The water is perfect—not hot or cold, precisely in between. At the base of the fountain, there are glass panels with liquid inside.

"This is the fanciest soap dispenser I've ever seen." I study it closely as I put some of the iridescent blue liquid into my hand. It smells like honeysuckle and has a mildly gritty consistency. Spreading it over my arms, I breathe in the scent as it perfumes the air around me.

Moving through the liquids, I test them all. Alone, each one is soft and delicate, with a sweet floral smell that permeates the air. Together, they create a scent I can't place. I know it, like a memory, but I don't know it. It's a smell from a dream.

"As delightful as this is to watch, I'm here to collect you for dinner." Elion's voice makes me scream. The sound echoes and flies around the room. He has an outfit in his hands—the same clothes that they wear. A dark, hard-looking uniform. "Put this on. I'll be right outside the door. If you take too long, I'll come back in." His eyes rake over my naked skin. Even covering my chest with my arms, his gaze touches me. I feel his fingers on me, creeping up my chest and onto my neck, the tips sweeping over my pulsating vein, just like before.

"O-Ok, get out of here." My voice wobbles as I sink down to cover more of myself.

The door closes loudly, and I drop below the surface of the water and let out a scream. Better here than in front of them.

Sighing and groaning, I walk out of the pool. The clothes he left me are strange, militant, and stiff, but still somehow elegant. The slight flare on the sleeves and at the hem of the jacket are an interesting touch. There are two slits in the back, for wings that I don't have.

The door opens as I fasten the button on the pants—six of them.

"Ah!" He pretends to pout. "Too late."

"Shut up." I grumble and push past him into the hallway.

"Tonight you dine with the king."

"Me?"

"Well, and me." He laughs. I know how much he likes my discomfort. I don't want to let him see it.

Mentally preparing myself while we walk, I try to ignore the nervousness I feel. He isn't my king. I don't know anything about him.

Inside a long dining hall, a chandelier flickers, the only source of light in the nearly all black room. Carvings of faces come out of the walls, each in a panel of its own. They're so realistic; for a moment, I swear the eyes were following me.

At the center of the room, a long, white marble table absorbs the light from the chandelier so that it glows. There are at least fifty chairs, stretching on forever, but only four places are set.

The chair at the end of the table moves, sliding out away from the table.

"You!" I gasp. "I mean..." No, that's what I meant.

His dark hair is pulled away from his face tonight, but it's the man from the room.

"Kiah," he says, dipping his chin, but his eyes never leave mine.

Calais is sitting on his right, while Elion takes the seat on his left. It looks like I'll be taking the seat beside him. Fantastic.

"I am Canaan." His voice bounces off the cold, dark walls. "Please, sit." He gestures, the jewels in his rings shimmering unnaturally under the lights.

Clearing my throat, I try to gracefully pull out my chair, but it scrapes loudly on the ground.

Sitting down, I keep my eyes on the plate in front of me. I'm afraid to look up; I'll stare.

Now that they are both in front of me, their differences are striking.

The king towers over Elion. There is a certain elegance to both of them, but the king has a darkness—a coldness—that makes him seem more rugged. Where Elion taunts and teases but is more approachable, the king is not.

Beautiful but dangerous.

From behind me, another plate is set on the table. Everyone gets one at the exact same time, down to the second.

Looking over my shoulder, I make eye contact with the man who gave me mine. A deep, concentrated line sits between his brows, and his lips are pressed together. It's strange, the way they all look at me like that, as if I am some kind of alien. They know about humans. I had no idea about the real existence of Fae, and I think I'm holding it together better.

"Please, eat." The king's voice is low and soft but commanding.

Spinning back around, I'm met with all eyes. They are waiting for me.

"Right, sorry." I tuck my head down.

"Do not apologize. How are you adjusting? The magic is very heavy here." His words are measured, spoken so carefully. I don't think he speaks unless it's absolutely necessary.

"Um, I'm fine." I'm not really fine.

His eyes narrow, but he doesn't say anything; instead, he takes a bite of food. The others follow suit.

"Eat." His voice is slightly harsher.

I know what I am. I know what I'm capable of. He can fly—or at least he has wings—but I have yet to see anyone in the air. I am fully, painfully, and acutely aware that I am no match for them. Yet, for some reason—maybe it's the official-looking uniform—I feel bolder than I should. I'm angry and frustrated, and just below that sit fear and guilt. I need to find my friend. I need to get home to my mother.

My fists slam down on the table, shaking the glasses. "I need to go home. I don't want to eat. While I appreciate it, really, I can't stay and eat."

Calais stares at me with wide eyes. Elion covers his mouth with his hand to hide his smile. The king looks blank, like he didn't hear me.

"You can't leave." He doesn't even look up from his food.

"Why not? I have to find Cheyenne. I have a mother who is undoubtedly losing her mind right now. I have to get back to her." I don't know if the fae have mothers, but I hope to tug at his heartstrings, if he has any.

"The port you entered from is closed. I will not risk opening another one to allow you to leave." His harsh voice makes me flinch.

"Are you positive Cheyenne isn't here?" I take the tiny, incomplete bit of overheard information to continue to be a nuisance. "Are you looking for her with the Shadowrithes?"

His eyes flick to Elion, then back to me. "We are pursuing them."

"And Cheyenne?"

He sucks his teeth, and I notice his fork in his fist, bending slightly.

"I'm not trying to cause trouble here. If you let me, I'll go look for her myself." I try a different approach.

This earns me an angry laugh. "You wouldn't last a day."

"So, I'm a prisoner here?"

"No."

"The room was locked." I fold my arms over my chest.

"For your safety."

"That's bullshit." The volume of my voice rises higher than I mean for it to.

"Bullshit or not, that's the reality we're faced with." His jaw clenches.

This is going nowhere.

The rest of the meal is spent in tense silence. The only sound is the occasional scrape of my fork against the plate.

"Take her back to her room." The king stands abruptly. "Make sure it's locked."

When I look up, he's glowering at me.

"Come along, darling." Elion stands, offering his hand.

EIGHT

As we walk past the carved faces, I can feel their disapproval. Their lips purse as they scrutinize me. Admittedly, that didn't go as well as I wanted it to, but I don't need their judgment. I shouldn't have yelled. If I'm going to get anywhere, I need to hold my temper, but they are so cold with their upper hand.

"Please, don't take me back there," I whisper, pleading with him as we make our way through the halls.

"I have to. I was given an order." He doesn't even attempt to sound contrite.

"You could always ignore it." I pout. I don't actually expect him to disobey an order for me.

"Oh, come on. It's not so bad here."

"Well, you're here by choice. It's a little different for me." I scowl and cross my arms.

Something flashes in his eyes. It's gone in an instant, but I saw it; it was there. Standing in the narrow hallway, looking up at him, I feel suddenly too close.

His chest moves up and down slowly, easy breathes—this isn't flustering him at all. I, on the other hand, am a mess.

When he leans down, I'm completely paralyzed. He presses his face into the crook of my neck, inhaling a long, slow breath. For a fleeting moment, I think he might kiss me. His hand comes up to my neck, gently running the pad of his thumb over my skin.

"Rest well," he gives me a gentle nudge into the room.

I'm so flustered, I just stand there in a daze. What was that?

"Elion, wait!" I spin around as he starts to close the door behind me. "Where are the clothes I was wearing? The ones I left in the bathhouse."

"They've been returned to your room." He points to the neatly folded pile on my bed.

"Oh, thank you. I didn't see them there." My mind races to think of another way to stall. I don't want to be locked into this room.

"Goodnight, Kiah." He smiles as he closes the door before I have a chance to say anything else. The lock clicks, the echo bouncing around in my head.

Falling down into the bed, I force my eyes to close. If I'm going to escape from this place, I will need to rest. The king might have given an order, but I am not one of his people. I refuse to just sit here, waiting until whenever he decides to let me go.

Gasping, I sit straight up in bed. I think I slept, but I can't be sure.

Running my fingers through my hair, I find it. A bobby pin.

It was like a vision—a dream. I forgot about the pin completely. This little piece of metal might be my salvation.

Bending it open slightly, I jam one of the prongs into the lock and start aimlessly moving it around. I've never picked a lock before. After several minutes with no luck and several grumbled expletives, I turn to my shadow. It's just standing there, watching me struggle.

"Can you help with this? You can't leave, right, because I'm stuck in here? Well, can we escape together?"

It moves across the floor, coming up to the lock.

Holding my breath, I watch as the misty form of its hand enters the lock with my pin.

A click.

"Holy shit, you did it." I whisper.

My body freezes, and I rethink the whole thing. Is this monumentally stupid? I didn't think I would actually be able to walk out. Now that I can, the implications of this make me take a pause. I might have my life force drained, whatever that actually means, or I could be consumed by a living river or who knows what else.

I have to try.

Pushing the door open, I peek my head out into the hallway. It's empty.

Creeping with my trusty sidekick beside me, I tiptoe down the hallway to the staircase. The lights flicker, and my heart does too. This place is so ominous. It feels like danger—something evil—is waiting around every corner.

As I walk down the second hallway, a sound from the cathedral stops me. It's footsteps, the click of a heel against the glass floor. They are moving away from me.

Coming to the end of the hallways, I look into the nave, past the pews. The altar is surrounded by black candles that burn red fire. A kaleidoscope of blacks, reds, and grays come together into a stained glass portrait of suffering. I don't know what it is—my mind can't comprehend it—but it's sorrow and agony. I can't look at it for too long; it makes my chest ache.

Hunched over, I stagger away. The doors are wide open, letting the strange orange glow of the moon shine in.

A voice in the distance, followed by a loud cheer stops me again. Dropping to the ground, I panic. On the black sandy bank of the silver river, at least twenty fae are dancing in the moonlight. Their laughter echoes around me.

They're wearing gauzy white dresses and soft trousers. Elion and Calais are in the crowd, with the king seated off to the side, watching them. For the first time, there is a genuine smile on his face. He looks peaceful and soft. It's jarring to see. Usually so cold—there is something kind about his face now—love, maybe. He loves them, and it shows.

The wind blows through the trees, kicking up flower petals that dance in the breeze. They move like feathers through the crowd, spinning and twirling in the air.

"Drink!" The king calls out to them, and everyone cheers again, raising glasses in the air.

The silver goblets shimmer, a mesmerizing glow that I can't take my eyes off of. I watch Elion lift his glass to his full lips, taking a sip of the contents. My throat goes dry. I've never felt so thirsty.

The knot in his throat rises and falls as he gulps. I'm awestruck.

I feel myself starting to stand. I can't stop it.

They look like angels—so perfect and pure. It hurts. So many emotions flood my brain with such intensity that I can barely breathe through it. It's a lucid dream; I know I'm awake, but the sight before me is so far from reality I can hardly believe I'm seeing it.

The glow of the moon, hanging as their backdrop, they move together, a perfect ballet. Tears drip down my cheeks. I feel so utterly small and human. I'm witnessing something forbidden, something too good for my eyes.

When he pulls the goblet away, red liquid runs down the sides of his mouth, dripping onto his bare chest.

Covering my mouth, I hold back a scream.

It's blood. Even from here, I just know it.

Frantically, my eyes move from one to the next, watching as blood runs down their faces, dripping onto their airy white gowns.

Their beauty and the scenery around them don't match up with the gruesomeness of what they're doing. Tears well up in my eyes again. They are chanting and laughing as they gulp down enough blood to fill the river.

Where is it coming from?

I can't imagine how much death would have to happen to produce that amount of blood.

They look like monsters. All of the elegance and grace, the flawless-ness of their features—it's covered in blood.

"You should not be here." The king's voice makes me scream. Jumping up, I turn to find him standing beside me.

"Whose blood is that?"

He looks across the glass steps to where the rest of them are dancing still.

"Is my friend here? Did you eat her?" Bile rises in my throat.

His wings flap once, sending a gust of wind toward me before he lands directly in front of me. I start to fall, but he grabs me, holding my arms too tightly. "Go back to your room. This ceremony is sacred. You don't understand it, so you don't deserve to witness it."

"Don't deserve?" I whimper. "Whose blood is that?" I ask again, more forcefully this time.

"Kiah," his voice is low, completely controlled.

"Canaan." I try to keep mine equally icy.

"Do not test me."

"You're a monster."

From the corner of my eye, a flash of white catches my attention.

"Canaan." A blood-covered Elion steps forward, placing his hand on the king's arm gently.

"Take her back to her room again." His eyes never leave mine. "I suggest you stay there this time." He sets me on my feet.

Elion reaches for me, but I jerk my arm away. "Don't touch me."

"Come on, Kiah." He grabs me anyway, pulling me inside.

"I'll walk." I yank my arm. "You don't have to hold me like that."

"You don't understand what you were seeing. That ceremony-"

"That ceremony was fucking disgusting. I don't have to know or understand anything else about it." My fists clench by my sides.

His mouth snaps closed, and his grip on my arm tightens painfully. He's practically dragging me across the floor, my feet barely touching the ground.

When we reach my door, he opens it and starts to shove me inside.

"Wait! Please! Is Cheyenne here?"

"We didn't drain your friend." His eyes narrow, and he takes a step toward me. "Humans have such a small perception of the world. Your capacity to understand what is going on around you is so limited."

With each step he takes, I take one too, mirroring his actions, backing away.

My back hits the wall, and I'm trapped, his body surrounding mine like a cage.

"There is no world where you would see a ceremony like the one you witnessed tonight and find the beauty in it. We do not have your friend."

"How could I find beauty in that? Where did you get that much

blood?" I'm starting to doubt myself. It seems impossible to miscon-
strue what I just saw, but maybe I am.

"It was a gift."

NINE

"It was a gift?" I repeat for the fiftieth time. What does that mean? I'm going to pace a hole through the floor by the end of the night. Their faces keep playing in my mind. They seemed upset about my judgment, more so than that I saw them or that it scared me.

"What did he mean?" I ask the shadow.

Sitting on the edge of the bed with my head in my hands, I take a deep breath and regroup. My frustration and helplessness are getting the best of me.

"Ok, Shadow. I need a game plan." I tap my toes on the floor. "I called the king by his name. That's probably bad, right? I should apologize and speak calmly and rationally. I can't stay here. I have a family that I need to get home to. That's what I'll do. I'll apologize and fix it."

Leaning back on the bed, I stare at the ceiling.

"Just as soon as someone comes, I'll apologize. Eventually, someone will come. Probably." I turn to the shadow that looks like it's cowering in the corner.

After several minutes, I groan and roll over, thrashing around like a child throwing a tantrum. That moment of release is what I needed. Now, I can compose myself.

Resigned to my fate, I close my eyes and give up for the night.

I can't do anything until they come and get me. There isn't any good that's going to come from sitting awake thinking about it.

I feel myself fading. It's slow at first, then I'm floating.

When I open my eyes, I'm above my body, watching myself. It's a strange perspective, seeing the way others see me.

I'm disconnected from my body as I watch myself stand up from the bed and walk to the door. It opens.

Then, in a dizzying rush, I'm back inside myself, standing in the empty hallway outside of the room.

Last time I did this, it ended badly. My gut is telling me to turn around. I can't turn around. Even if this is a bad idea, I'm compelled to move forward. Walking through the hallways, I continue down the staircase. Instead of continuing through the hallways toward the nave, I open a door that leads to another staircase. It's as if my body already knew it was there.

Lights flicker at the bottom of the stairs, candles on the walls reflecting off of the black glass.

The air is buzzing—humming. As I move down the hallway, the intensity of the sound grows. It's like a heartbeat, a pulsating rhythm that surrounds me. It's soft and inviting. I follow it down past another row of carved faces hanging on the wall.

This time I know they're watching me. The eyes move, following me as I walk past. Disdain is etched into their elegant faces. They aren't even alive, and they don't like me. They aren't trying to hide it.

With light steps, I walk down to the end of the hallway. Another staircase. I'm descending into the depths of hell.

Following it down, the air starts to feel stagnant. Unusual symbols are etched into the walls, thin rays of red light glowing from inside of them.

With each step, it gets colder, goosebumps spread over my skin, and puffs of my breath hang in the air.

A thick, metallic smell wafts around me; it's slightly sweet, and I can't quite place it. I've smelled it before, maybe in my real life, but in this dream—I can't figure it out. The memory is jumbled up in my head.

The humming is louder now, a chorus of voices in harmony. It's haunting and creepy, but hypnotic. It beacons me forward.

At the bottom of the stairs, I come to an open door.

Normally, I would run in the other direction. After what I witnessed earlier, this seems like trouble. Instead, I walk through the door.

A group of Fae, the same ones from before—still dressed in their blood-stained clothing—are gathered around an ornately designed altar. Intricately carved wings are splayed open on either side. I watch them, waiting for them to move - they look real.

Elion and Calais stand at the foot of the altar. Their arms are stretched out in front of them, palms facing the ceiling. And in their hands rest small pieces of bone.

The candlelight flickers as Canaan enters. A gust of wind following him, swirling around everyone like mist. His presence changes the air in the room. It's thicker - heavier.

He's wearing white now—it looks out of place on him—the softness against his inky black wings and hair.

He lifts his head, and his eyes glow like the dying embers of a fire. Intense focus creases his face.

No one notices me as I stand in the shadows, heart pounding in my chest. I feel like I'm intruding on something sacred. I'm a peeping Tom, violating the sanctity of whatever this is. A voice in my head screams at me to leave, to turn and run before I witness something I don't want to see, but my body is paralyzed.

The humming grows louder, a low, resonant sound that vibrates in the floor, sending ripples through my bare feet.

Canaan steps forward, positioning himself between the wings of the altar, and raises his hands into the air. The light in the room dims and floats toward him, like it's being drawn into him. A beam of concentrated light forms in his hands—a dagger, its edges sharp and gleaming.

From the opposite side of the room, a heavy door creaks open, a door I'm not sure existed just a moment ago. Two more Fae, with their eyes rolled back, lead a man—another one of them—into the room. His wings are bound tightly to his back with thick, rough cords, and a blindfold covers his eyes. He doesn't struggle, he willingly steps onto the altar. He kneels, his hands pressed together - like saying a prayer.

This can't be happening. Not again.

The humming swells, louder, more intense, deafening. It's all I can hear, drowning out the frantic pulse of my blood in my ears. I press my hands to my ears, but it doesn't help.

Canaan takes a purposeful step forward. With one hand, his fingers brushed gently against the man's cheek softly.

With his other hand, he raises the dagger of light, the blade glowing brighter. Then, in one swift, fluid motion, he brings it down. The light pierces the Fae's neck, slicing through like a hot knife through butter. There's no scream, no sound at all, just silence. At once, the humming stops completely.

The bound Fae's body slumps forward. The light from the dagger dims, then fades completely, leaving nothing but the flickering candlelight.

I open my mouth to scream, but no sound comes out.

Blood sprays upward, then runs into carved grooves on the table. A basin at the end of the table collects a large pool of it, filling so quickly that it starts to run over the sides onto the floor.

Canaan dips his finger into the blood before bringing it up to his lips. As he licks his finger, tasting it, his eyes flash up to mine. We hold each other's gaze for a moment—just a split second, but it's long enough.

Power radiates from him.

Horrified, I watch him bring his head down to the blood so dark it's almost black. He tips the basin and gulps it down, drinking until it's empty.

The bound fae starts to tremble, his skin paling as the life drains from his body. A deep, raw ache settles into my chest, nestling in behind my heart to hurt with each beat. I can feel him dying.

A rattling, pained breath slips past his lips—his last breath. It's quiet, not desperate or fearful—just calmly slipping away.

Tears roll down my cheeks. I've never watched anything die before. I shouldn't be here. It's intimate and violent.

When Canaan stands upright again, he looks taller. There has been a physical change in his body. The room is smaller, energy pulsing through it as he opens his eyes.

He looks like himself but different—changed. It's as if lightning is running through his veins now. Power, uninhibited and raw, oozes from him.

The longer I stare, the less recognizable he becomes.

I'm horrified and fascinated.

His strength isn't new. I felt it immediately when we met, like it's somehow visible on him, but this is a heavy, oppressive, loud show of power that wasn't there before.

What I'm seeing before my eyes can't be real. It's beyond comprehension. I'm watching it unfold; all of the pieces are here, but the puzzle isn't coming together. I can't see the full picture.

I want to reach out and touch him, to run my fingers through his hair. He's made of magic—everything beautiful and lovely. And somehow also everything dark and frightening.

His eyes are bright, like they've got starlight behind them. I just watched him kill someone, but all I see is an otherworldly glow. He is irresistible.

I shouldn't feel this way.

I shouldn't be drawn to this.

Backing away, I try to find the door I came in through. I don't want to be here anymore. It's gone. There are no doors in any of the places where there had definitely been one before. I'm trapped in here.

Powerless, I stand pressed against the wall, watching as everyone bows.

Everyone has stopped humming, but the room isn't quiet. The walls whisper, crying out in a language that seems so ancient and forgotten, I won't even attempt to identify it. A beam of light shoots out of the ceiling, illuminating his skin.

He glows, from the inside out, igniting like there is fire in him.

My knees wobble, completely awestruck by him. I'm disgusted yet somehow, so drawn to the force. He demands attention—not with words, but his very presence requires it. Our eyes meet again, and my heart beat slows. The slow thump, thump, thump in my ears drowns out the whispers.

He can see right through me. It's like I'm not here at all.

When he starts to walk toward me, I will move my feet to move—to run—to hide. He is like a shadow, descending on me, eating the light.

"You should not be here." His tone is icy and cuts straight to my bones.

"I-I'm sorry."

Snapping my eyes open, I sit up in my bed. I'm covered from head to toe in a layer of sweat, and my heart is racing.

"Oh my god!" I fall back on the pillow. "It was just a dream."

The relief I feel is fleeting. It wasn't a dream. I can feel it somehow. It was real.

"Kiah." Calais knocks at my door. "I am here to collect you."

TEN

I feel small, like a scolded child, as I follow her down the hallways. She's obviously upset with me.

I never got warm, welcoming feelings from her, but she is particularly icy now. I don't think she's actually looked at me once.

If I had a choice, I would have stayed in the room. The thought of seeing Canaan makes my legs turn to jelly.

The images from my dream are at the forefront of my mind. This strange, magical place has blurred the lines of reality. It was a dream; I never left my bed. But it wasn't a dream. I saw something real. Whether it happened last night, a thousand years ago, or it was a premonition of something about to happen—I can't say. But it wasn't made up. I don't know how I saw it—but I did, and he saw me there.

His lips and sharp teeth dripping with red—I see it in slow motion. The tip of his tongue swiping over them, making sure to get every last drop of blood—I can't unsee it.

I don't know how I'm going to be in the same room with him.

When we pass the carved faces, they close their eyes and turn their noses up. Even they are disgusted.

Unlike last time, when I enter the dining room, he doesn't stand. Neither does Elion.

With my hands in my lap, I stare at my plate until someone sets food on it.

"Thank you," I whisper to the man, the only one in the room who doesn't look like he wants to melt me into sludge with his eyes.

My fingers tremble as I move to pick up the fork beside my plate.

In the rational part of my brain, the place where my nervousness and fear aren't clouding my judgment, I know I should just keep my eyes down. Unfortunately, that part of my brain is buried under the stupid, curious part, the part that always seems to get me into trouble. It's like a relentless itch I can't ignore, compelling me to look. I don't want to look at him, but I have to.

Peeking to the side, I catch sight of Canaan, and I drop my fork. It clunks loudly against the delicate plate, the sound echoing in the silent room. The noise makes me flinch, but I can't tear my eyes away from him.

It wasn't a dream.

The changes I saw in him last night have only solidified in the hours since. His features, once familiar, are now sharper and more defined.

I don't understand how someone could be both beautiful and frightening, so completely and utterly two things at once. It's all the way, fully, one hundred percent. Terrifying and alluring. He is power and strength, an unstoppable force wrapped in the facade of something almost human, but not. His presence is overwhelming, like the room isn't big enough to contain him.

"I'm sorry," I fumble with the fork again, my hands shaking so badly I scrape it against my plate. "Sorry."

His eyes flick up to meet mine, cold and irritated. He knows that I know. I can see it in his face, the fury barely contained behind the ice-cold gaze. The sharp line of his jaw clenches, the muscles ticking. His wings flick slightly, a small, almost imperceptible movement, but enough to make my breath hitch in my throat.

He doesn't say a word, and the meal passes in painful silence. I can only force down a few bites, each one sitting heavy in my stomach. My appetite has vanished, replaced by a gnawing knot of anxiety. Being scrutinized while trying to eat quietly is nerve-wracking enough, but with him watching, it's impossible. His gaze feels like a weight pressing down on me, crushing me slowly.

If I thought I was unwanted before, I really didn't know how much worse it could get. They do not want me here, and now, no one is making a show of trying to hide it.

"Your Majesty." Someone rushes into the room. His head is high, and his steps are quick and steady. He looks composed, but the energy that follows him is frantic. "You are needed urgently."

Without a word, he drops his fork and rises from his seat. His movements are graceful, fluid, and calm. He follows the man out of the room.

When he's gone, I can finally take a breath. Calais and Elion are still here, still angry, but it's not nearly as oppressive.

"Ready?" Calais snaps.

"Let me take her," Elion offers, a slight edge in his voice but not as sharp as hers.

"Fine by me," Calais mutters. She stands quickly, her chair scraping against the ground, the sound echoing through the room.

For the first time, I really look at him. He's different, too. The change isn't as noticeable as Canaan's, but it's there, subtle yet undeniable. His eyes, once warm and inviting, now hold a coldness that wasn't there before, a distance that makes me uneasy. His wings look larger, still paper thin and delicate, but bigger.

"You fucked up, precious." The usually playful, teasing tone in his voice is gone. He's cold—not as icy as Canaan, but it's still there.

"I didn't mean to insult you. Your rituals are..." Horrifying. Gruesome. Frightening. Evil. Vile. Any of those will work.

A smile spreads over his lips. "He told me you were there. I didn't believe him." The humor is back at my expense.

"What?" My heart rate skyrockets, sending the rushing sound of blood into my ears.

"Oh, come on. You knew it was real."

I did. But hearing it out loud, confirmed, has me reeling.

"Why?" That's all I can say. No other words will form.

"Because of you." His smile grows.

"Me?"

"Your presence here is a threat to us. Blood is a rare treat now."

He stands, slowly walking around the table toward me. I shrink down in the seat. I feel like a cornered animal. "I suppose thanks are in order. I can't remember the last time I had blood." He spins my chair around so quickly. I scream, clutching the armrests. He places his hands on top of mine, locking them into place and caging me in. When he leans in, running the tip of his nose along my throat, I don't so much as breathe. "The blood we drank in the Lunaris Nocturne was given freely—offered. Our ancestors who have gone beyond the Eternal Veil left it for us. No one died. It wasn't even human. Before you throw around insults—like monster—you should learn first." He growls.

"Someone died." I look into his eyes. I don't feel brave, but I can't show him how rattled I really am. He gets a high from it.

There is that fucking smile again. Dark and slick.

"Ah, yes, but he also gave his life freely. He was a willing sacrifice to give our king the strength he needs for what's coming."

"What's coming?"

Instead of answering, he grabs my hand, pulling me up and out of the chair. Biting into my cheek, I try to sort the information out enough to understand it. I still have so many questions.

"What is the eternal veil?"

"When we decide to move on—into the hereafter—we have to be drained. It's the only way we die." His eyes sparkle. He's really enjoying this.

I attempt to keep my face neutral, giving no reaction; he's eating it up.

"When anyone chooses to move beyond, they give their blood. It's held until we need it."

"And you need it now?"

"That's right. You being here is throwing off the delicate balance. We need strength now." There is a peppiness to his step. He's loving my fear and confusion.

"How did I see the ceremony last night—the one with the king? I was there; I saw everything, but I didn't leave my room. It was a dream." I have to ask, even though I don't want to; I have to know, or it will drive me to insanity.

"The magic of this place can be accessed by all. You brought yourself there. He felt your presence the whole time. I must say, I'm impressed."

"I didn't bring myself there! I was trying to leave the whole time! I didn't want to see that!"

"Did it make you feel things?" He licks his lower lip.

"What? No!"

"Really? The surge of power is so erotic." He hums, a low, rumbly sound in his throat.

Heat creeps up my neck. "N-No. It wasn't erotic. Someone died."

"That kind of power is intoxicating, isn't it? Raw and limitless." He rolls his neck.

"I don't think so." My hoarse whisper sounds uncertain. I don't even know for sure how I'm feeling right now.

"I think you do." He draws in a slow inhale. "I think you fucking love it."

"I-" My throat feels tight.

"You've never felt this kind of strength before. Humans don't have it; you can't possess it. But here in Noctyra, you can feel it—taste it."

"Elion," my voice trembles, weak and pleading. "Please, just for one minute, no games or riddles. Just tell me what's going on."

"The truth is, darling, we don't yet know. We don't know who opened the door to your realm, but we might have an idea why." He tucks a strand of hair behind my ear.

"Why?"

He clicks his tongue, "I've already said too much."

Of course, he has. He's barely said anything, but it's too much. My minute must be up because he's back to touching me, running his fingertips up my arm.

"Elion, leave us." Canaan's voice comes suddenly from over Elion's shoulder.

"What a pity." He pouts playfully. "Until next time, darling."

I reach for him, desperate to grab hold of his hand, silently begging him not to leave me here alone. He slips through my fingers and disappears.

Eleven

He's in front of me, dangerously close, in a single step. His body is trapping me here, not that I could escape even if I did dare to run. His wings move forward, almost wrapping around us, blocking out the already dim light.

"Where did they bite you?" His hand comes up to my neck. "Show me!"

"What?" My brain can't keep up with everything happening at once. My back hits the wall with enough force to knock the air from my lungs.

"Where did they bite you?" He growls. Anger radiates from him, swirling around above us.

"Who?"

"Tell me the truth. How long have you been here? What are they planning?"

The accusation in his trembling voice catches me off guard. I don't know how to answer his questions.

"The guards found me not long after I got here. I don't know of anyone planning anything." I press my back into the wall, trying to create space between us.

"I don't fucking believe you." The hand on my neck tightens, squeezing just enough to scare me.

"Canaan, please!" My eyes widen and fill with tears. "I don't know anything."

"There's absolutely no way that you learned to harness magic by yourself. And in this amount of time? It's not possible. How long have you been here, and who taught you?" His sharp teeth are dangerously close to my face.

"Harness magic?"

Quicker than I can process, he releases my throat and uses his hand to rip my shirt open. Yelping, I try to cover up, but he's too fast. He yanks it down my shoulders and searches my chest before spinning me around. "Where did they feed from? Here?" His hand comes down between my legs.

"Wait! Stop!" I panic, thrashing and bashing my face into the wall. "Please! Whatever you're looking for, I'll help you find it, but you have to explain!"

"You're a liar."

"I'm not." I pull my trembling lip between my teeth.

"How did you dreamweave with reality? I could feel you in the bloodletting ceremony!"

"I don't know how I got there! I promise! I wanted to leave, but my legs wouldn't move. I wasn't there on purpose." I can only hope that he will recognize the truth.

"Impossible."

"I didn't mean to." I stare at the rage in his eyes, head on, watching the flames flicker.

"If I find out you're being dishonest with me, I'll drain you myself." He spins me, slamming my back into the wall again. With narrowed eyes, he watches me, waiting for a moment before releasing me and storming down the hallway. "Get in your room and fucking stay there!" He growls over his shoulder before disappearing.

Sinking to the floor, I cover my face with my shaking hands.

He wanted to kill me. I could feel it, as real and physically threatening as his hand on my throat. I can't explain it, I just know. His hatred for me has changed the air around me—it's colder and thicker. My lungs burn trying to breathe it in.

Tucking my knees up to my chest, I wrap my arms around my legs, holding myself tightly. It's the only comfort I can find.

"Fuck." My voice wobbles as I try to calm myself down. Taking several long, slow breaths doesn't help at all. Pulling myself up off the floor, I use the wall for support as I stumble into the jail cell masquerading as a room. The door isn't locked, but I'm trapped here.

Sitting on the bed, I hold my head in my hands. I feel weak and exhausted. Not just tired from lack of sleep but truly drained of energy and emotion.

His face keeps playing in my mind on a loop. Even now, alone, I cower back, trying to distance myself from his image.

I've never seen rage like his—pure and unfettered—it seeps from him and wafts through the air. I can see it like heat waves leaving his body. The beauty in his face and his eyes, his hair, the structure of his bones—it's turned colder. Instead of any single feature standing out for its pleasing aesthetic, his long, sharp fangs come forward, glinting in the light, making themselves known.

A strange feeling—a heavy but soft pressure wraps around my body, cocooning me in an eerie sense of comfort. I sink into it, letting the sensation pull me deeper. When I open my eyes, I see him—Canaan—sitting on my bed, his presence like a shadow in the dim light. Elion is here too, standing close by, his tall frame looming over me with a quiet intensity. The air between us feels charged, electric. They aren't mad at me now. The tension that usually crackles between us is absent, replaced by something soft.

When he reaches for me, it's gentle, a stark contrast to the roughness I've come to expect. His hand moves up my arm, the slow, deliberate motion sending shivers racing down my spine until he reaches my throat. His fingers linger there, not hurting me, but with an unexpected tenderness that takes my breath away. This time, he doesn't squeeze. His touch is warm, delicate, as if I'm something precious.

He runs his fingers over my thumping pulse. My skin prickles in response, a wave of heat spreading through my body. His touch is intoxicating, confusing—pleasure mixed with danger. I know I should be afraid, but all I can feel is the desire curling within me, urging me closer.

"Bite her," Elion encourages him quietly, his voice low, rumbling. There's a note of hunger in it.

With a slow, deliberate motion, Canaan brushes my hair aside, his fingers trailing lightly across my skin. I tilt my head, baring my neck to him. He leans in, his breath ghosting over my skin. Every inch of me is hyper aware of his closeness, of the way his teeth scrape, raking over the vein just beneath the thin layer of skin. His lips brush against me, and a whimper leaves my throat.

The sound of my rushing blood pounds in my ears, drowning out everything but the raw sensation of his touch. He smells like the woods —earthy and warm, like damp leaves and rich soil after a storm.

"Canaan," I manage to whisper.

My eyes pinch closed. I can't watch them. His arms wrap around me, pulling me closer, holding me. The anticipation coils tightly within me, a knot of desire and fear tangled together.

"Kiah," My name is like honey on his tongue. It's so tender, so unexpectedly gentle. I want to hear it again, to lose myself in the way he says it.

This is wrong. My mind screams at me, urging me to resist, to push him away before it's too late. But my body betrays me. When my treacherous hands move, they don't push him away. Instead, I grab him, my fingers curling into his shirt, holding him tightly in my fists.

And then, just as his teeth sink into my neck, breaking the barrier of my skin. I gasp, the sound a mix of pain and pleasure, and suddenly, I'm jolted upright, my body drenched in sweat, heart racing. My cheeks are still wet with tears as if time stood still for a moment, suspended, and now I'm back.

Frantically, I reach up, searching for the punctures, the tangible proof of what just happened. My skin is smooth, unmarred, but the memory lingers, fresh and real.

"What were you dreaming about, darling?"

Elion is standing in the doorway, leaning against the frame with a bored expression as he watches me.

My scream echoes off the walls. I didn't hear the door open! How long has he been there?

"Why are you here?" I half whine, half beg. "Please, leave me alone!" I ignore his question.

"I come with news." He stands upright. "But if you're not interested..."

"Wait." I wipe my face. "What news?"

"Canaan is sending another patrol to the fringe. If your friend is out there, they will find her. If you are telling the truth and you have not been giving blood to the Shadowrithes, then it only makes sense that your friend is with them." He shrugs, almost disinterested in what he is saying.

"What are they doing to her?" The thought of them harming her makes me physically ill. My stomach knots up as I picture her on an altar being drained. I have to shake the thoughts from my head.

"It still doesn't explain how you were able to watch the bloodletting, though, does it?" A mischievous glint twinkles in his eyes.

"I promise, I had nothing to do with that."

"I believe you, darling."

His words do nothing to calm the storm raging inside me. My heart hammers against my ribs, and my stomach churns, twisted up in knots. Every muscle tensed and ready to snap. The hierarchy here is suffocating. I'm powerless in this world. It's killing me, this feeling of being trapped with no answers, no control. I need answers, or it's going to eat me up inside.

"Can I have another question? I'll give you two." I hope the offer entices him.

A lopsided smile plays on his lips, and something shifts in his gaze. "Oh, you want to play now?" he asks, a hint of amusement in his tone.

"If that's what it takes. Yes, I'll play."

Crossing his arms over his chest, he leans back against the wall, waiting. He's completely at ease.

"If the Shadowrithes have her, what would be the reason? Why hold her there?"

"The three races of Fae used to live together, here, in the Frostlinds and in the Bluffs. When the Shadowrithes were banished, they grew weak, most of them losing the ability to present a human form. All blood makes us stronger, but human blood—there's nothing like it." He shivers, his voice wobbling with a needy, desperate rasp.

Elion is a puzzle I can't seem to solve—playful and taunting one moment, frightening and intense the next. It's like watching someone flip a switch, shifting between personalities, one after the other in rapid succession. There are times I almost feel at ease with him, thinking I can handle the games, and then, I'm terrified he's about to do something unspeakable. The unpredictability of it all leaves me constantly on edge, unsure of where I stand. I'm on the edge of a thin blade, one wrong word and I'll fall.

"Why were they banished?" I blurt out, unable to stop myself from asking another question. I need to understand, to piece together the fragments of this twisted world.

A smile tugs at the corners of his mouth. "You can't help yourself, can you, darling? You ask for one question, I oblige, and then you ask more. It's in your nature, isn't it? Humans are such curious creatures," the teasing lilt that makes me feel small and exposed.

On instinct, I lean back, even though he's across the room, it's too close.

I don't love being called a creature.

"It's my turn to ask you." He smiles, taking a step forward. "What were you dreaming about?"

My face and neck burn, blood rushing to redden my skin. "I..."

I can't answer that. It was so... intimate.

"It seemed a rather good dream."

"It wasn't." I lie. He can't find out. If he knew, he would never let me hear the end of it.

"Really?" He hums. "How interesting."

"I was having a nightmare about Cheyenne. It wasn't good." I can't make eye contact with him while I lie. Staring at the ground, I clear my throat, forcing away the ball of emotion lodged there, threatening to make me cry again. "What's your next question?"

"You know, I think I'll save it." He takes my chin in his hand, forcing my gaze upward. "It might come in handy."

TWELVE

As soon as the door begins to creak open, I'm on my feet. I've spent the entire night on edge, practicing and waiting. My pulse quickens, and I steady my breathing, determined to present myself with the composure I've meticulously practiced instead of sleeping. Today, I will be calm, collected, and respectful, but still firm.

Calais glances at me with a mix of surprise and curiosity. My eagerness to join her for breakfast must seem out of character. I nod, striving to convey the respect I hope will be reciprocated, but her eyes narrow slightly in suspicion.

"Good morning," I keep my voice steady.

"Good morning," her brow furrows as she looks at me suspiciously.

My nerves are all over the place as I follow her to the dining room. Elion stands as we enter. Canaan doesn't, but that doesn't surprise me. He's probably still mad at me. As I step around to my seat, my stomach drops. He isn't here.

Elion's smirk is as sharp as ever as he settles back into his chair. "Something the matter, darling?"

I force a smile, battling the wave of disappointment threatening to break through my barely there calm. "No, nothing."

I'll ask him when I see him. I won't lose my nerve. This is fine.

"So," I nervously scoop food onto my spoon, my hands trembling slightly. "How are the searches in the fringes going ? Have they found anything?"

Calais shoots a look at Elion that would kill him if looks could. "Is there anything you haven't told her?"

Elion's gaze shifts toward me, a hint of mischief in his eyes despite the tension. "Many things," he says with a half-smile.

"This isn't a game, Elion." Her voice hardens. "Some things are serious."

"I am well aware," His tone is cool and dismissive, though a flicker of annoyance shows itself in the way his jaw clenches.

"Then perhaps you should act like it."

Elion folds his arms over his chest, matching her irritation. "Point out the ways I've diminished the seriousness of our current situation, Calais." He tilts his head, his eyes challenging hers.

I feel like I'm missing something here. There is a history—an old argument—something I'm not privy to that's part of this.

Calais' lips thin into a line, but she doesn't say anything else.

His eyes are dark, swirling with anger as he stabs at his food.

I shouldn't have asked. I didn't realize that I wasn't supposed to know. We sit in silence, my question unanswered, and the mood spoiled.

The rest of the meal passes uncomfortably. They're annoyed at each other, no one speaks, and my resolve is starting to crumble. I didn't account for him being absent in any of my practiced speeches. Staring at his empty chair, my confidence is dwindling by the second.

"I'll take her to the bathhouse," Calais announces as soon as she finishes her plate, never mind that I'm not done.

I half expect a cheeky comment or look from Elion, but he only grumbles something curtly and stands, letting his chair scrape against the ground loudly. Without so much as a glance, he storms out of the room. I think he's mad at me. Him too? I'll just add him to this list, it seems ever growing.

Something about Calais makes me feel like a child. Following her down the hallways has the same feeling of looming trouble—like she's leading me to the principal's office.

"I will return to make sure you get back to your room." She pushes the heavy door open.

"Um, actually." I clear my throat. "Would it be possible to speak with Canaan? If he has time, I just need a minute."

Her eyes narrow. "I'll let him know."

"Thanks," I call after her as she turns on her heels, leaving me alone in the dim purple glow of the bathhouse windows.

Mumbling my speeches quietly to myself, I strip down and step into the water.

The warmth of the water seeps into my muscles, easing the tension I feel everywhere. Lathering up the floral soap, I absentmindedly move my hands over my skin. I'm lost in my head. This world is overwhelming. In the quiet moments when I'm alone, it hits me, and the weight of it all sinks in.

Suddenly, a shadow flits across the windows, swallowing the room in darkness. The dim purple light from the stained glass windows is gone. The flickering candles are out, the slight smell of smoke lingering in the air.

Sliding down, I submerge myself up to my chin, taking slow steps backward.

The distinct feeling of not being alone makes the hairs on the back of my neck stand up and my skin prick.

With my back against the far wall of the pool, I squint in the dark, searching. The water ripples on the surface. I try to tell myself that it's just the fountain, but I know it's not. The fountain doesn't make the water move that way. There is someone else in the water with me. Someone I can't see or hear.

A cold grip wraps around my wrist, and a terror-filled scream scratches up my throat. It's muffled, muted like something swallowed it up before it could be heard.

"Kiah!" Canaan's voice booms over the water.

For a moment, a split second, I'm relieved, but before I can call to him, I'm pulled below the surface. Inky black water moves and shifts around me. A pair of golden eyes pierce through the darkness, staring right at me.

I know instantly that those eyes will haunt me forever. I'll never forget them as long as I live—which might only be a few more seconds. Panic surges through me, and I inhale a mouthful of water. It sears my lungs as I choke and flail, my limbs clawing desperately at the hand, but I can't get free.

"Kiah." My name drifts through the water in a soft and eerie whisper, like the shadow of a voice. The sound paralyzes me. "Kiah." He coaxes, drawing all of my fear to the surface.

I try to turn, but the darkness surrounds me. I'm inside the shadow, enveloped in it. The voice whispers my name like a song, long and slow, louder and louder until I feel it against my ear as if his mouth is just there.

A face emerges from the swirling black. Some features are still obscured by shadow, some forming slowly as if they're being sculpted. The golden eyes glint, piercing through my chest. I can't escape him. He has entered my soul—he owns a piece of it now.

A smile slowly spreads across his lips, razor-sharp teeth made of obsidian glass.

He leans in, ready to tear me to shreds.

The sharp sting of a scratch opens the tender skin of my throat. It's not a bite - not yet.

Another hand grabs me, pulling me upward. With a jarring thrust, I'm pushed from the water and dropped onto the edge of the pool. Coughing and gagging, I spit out water as I watch Canaan fighting against nothing. Forcing myself up, I keep my eyes on him, trying to understand what I'm seeing. A shadow comes out of the water and grabs him by the throat.

From the pool's depths, the shadow comes up into the air with wings that are just a shape in the dark. I can hear myself screaming, but it's muffled in my ears.

"You should have waited until you were stronger, Thaloein," Canaan snarls. With almost graceful ease, he clasps his hands around the shadow's neck and snaps it.

All at once, the shadow disintegrates into a red liquid, spilling into the pool and spreading like ink. It runs down Canaan's body, covering him.

"Calais mentioned you wanted to speak with me," he offers me his hand. His voice is disturbingly calm after the violence I just witnessed him so effortlessly rain down.

"W-What was that?" I stammer, struggling to stay upright on shaking legs.

He tilts my head upward, holding it in his hands as he looks at my neck. "He didn't bite you." I can see myself reflected in his eyes, blood dripping from my neck.

My breath catches, stuck in my throat. Just as I think he might nestle his face there, like he did in my dream, he takes a step back.

"That was a Shadowrithe," he swipes his hand over his chest, moving the blood around.

"Um," I stare at his red-stained chest. "I wanted to ask you..."

All of my practicing didn't take into account the possibility of a shadow monster attacking me and then being murdered in front of me. I don't remember what I wanted to ask.

He sighs, "Come with me."

I feel myself swaying as we walk. I'm not going to pass out. I simply won't allow myself to do it. Taking in long, slow breaths, I focus on the way my chest expands and not the nausea in my stomach or the way my head feels light. Wrapping a towel around my shoulders, covering my trembling body.

"Shadowrithes need human blood in order to have the strength to have a physical form. Without access to humans, they are-"

"Shadows." I whisper as the pieces come together in my mind. It seems simple, but it doesn't seem possible at the same time. "Do they have Cheyenne?"

"I believe so. I have no evidence of this other than their sudden departure from the fringes. But it's too much of a coincidence. And now they attack? Not once in three hundred years, but all of a sudden?" For the first time, he shows something—I can see the exhaustion on his face.

"Can I help?"

He stops walking, turning to face me fully. I think he's about to say no, but he sighs instead, running his hand through his hair.

"Shadowrithes are not just darkness. They are cunning, and in physical form, they are strong. If they found a way to open a port to the human realm, we're all in danger. We can't let them get you, they would use you to gain power. You're helping by staying here."

"I mean, I don't want them to get me. But if I can do something—anything at all—to help find Cheyenne and stop them, I want to try." I resolve myself to really mean that. Anything they need, I'll do it. Even if the thing they need is the one thing that scares me the most.

"I would send you home if I could, but we can't risk opening another port." For the first time, there is something soft in his voice. He's vulnerable. He doesn't hate me—at least not right now. "If I can find a way for you to be useful, I will let you know." The unexpected gentleness in his voice wraps around me.

Nodding sharply, I grip the towel tightly. I open my mouth to speak, I feel like I should thank him for saving me. But Elion storms around the corner, ruining the quiet moment.

"Are you alright?" He looks at me for a moment, studying me, before turning toward Canaan. "We had a breach?"

"Thaloein." He growls his name in a way that makes me shiver.

"He was here? In physical form?" The usually easy-going nature is gone. He looks deadly serious.

"Not fully, but I know it was him."

"Did he bite you?" He turns back to me, his eyes dropping down to my neck.

"No." I shake the thought out of my head to get the image out of my mind. "He didn't."

THIRTEEN

Every noise, every creak, and every whisper in the dark makes my blood run cold. The silence of the night amplifies everything— each sound is another Shadowrithe coming to drag me away.

My mind is playing tricks on me, seeing and hearing things that aren't there. But then, maybe they aren't tricks. Maybe it's not my mind. This place is cruel. The whispers and bumps in the dark are real.

Nighttime is the worst. It stretches endlessly. I can barely sleep. When exhaustion finally overwhelms me, forcing my eyes shut, nightmares take over.

He's always there—Thaloein.

His cold, golden eyes. His raspy whisper calling my name and his teeth on my skin haunt my waking and sleeping thoughts. I can feel his shadowy hands wrapped around me, his grip tightening each second.

His teeth on my skin are so vivid, so real, that I wake up gasping, clutching at my throat. There are never marks, though, none that I can physically find anyway.

Fear gnaws at me constantly, but it's not the only thing. The intense boredom of being trapped in this room, with nothing but my thoughts and my dread, is slowly driving me mad.

The four walls of this room seem to close in on me, inch by inch. It's crushing me, slowly. I can feel it—I'm sure of it.

I'm not locked in any more, but I don't dare leave. I've seen enough horrors outside of this room to last a lifetime. I won't risk it.

Sighing, I stare up at the ceiling. Waiting for something—breakfast, an attack, my slow but inevitable death by malaise. The shadow sits up from its spot beside me. Straight-spined and alert, I'm immediately nervous.

The door bursts open with such force that it slams into the wall behind it, sending cracks through the plaster. The sound echoes through the halls. My heart lurches in my chest as Canaan storms in. His eyes dart around the room like he's expecting someone else to be here with me.

He looks exhausted, his eyes bloodshot and sunken in with large hollowed circles below them.

"What the fuck are you doing?" His voice is a low growl, raw and angry. "They trained you!"

"What?" I instinctively scoot back in the bed until I'm pressed into the corner, my back against the wall.

Not this again.

"Thaloein didn't bite you because you're working with them!" His words tumble out in a frenzied rush. He's accusing me of something again. He doesn't even seem sure this time. The conviction isn't there. He seems confused and desperate. "How are you dreamweaving? It's not possible! Are you lying to me?" His pacing is frantic, his movements jerky and erratic as he stalks back and forth across the room.

"Canaan." I keep my voice low, like I'm talking to a frightened animal. "What are you talking about? Explain it to me."

But beneath my calm exterior, panic is clawing at my insides. I don't know what's happening—how we ended up back here in this loop of accusations. It's like we're trapped in a vicious cycle, and I can't see a way out. He thinks I'm working with them again. The fear in his eyes, the raw, unfiltered anger—it's all directed at me, and I don't know how to get out from under it.

"Dreamweaving!" The word explodes from him like a curse, laced with venom.

"What does that mean?" I inch forward on the bed, every movement slow and careful. I don't want to startle him or push him further over the edge.

His gaze snaps to mine, and for a moment, I see a flicker of something else—confusion, vulnerability, pure exhaustion. "You really don't know?" His voice is softer now.

"I swear to you, I do not." My voice is firm, steady, even though my hands are trembling.

"You should not have been able to pass beyond the ether." His fingers slide into his hair, raking through the strands. "You don't belong here."

He doesn't sound angry anymore—just thoroughly defeated. Two steps forward, three steps back.

"I understand that you don't want to open another port in case someone else slips through, but..." My voice falters, guilt gnawing at me for approaching him in this low moment of vulnerability. But I don't have a choice. "Is there any way?" I have to get out of here.

"No." His reply is flat—final. His eyes meet mine, and the anger is back—simmering. "I won't risk it. You have disrupted the power balance enough. If another human slips through, it would give them too much strength." There isn't any room for discussion in his tone, but I'm going to make some.

"I haven't done anything intentionally." I feel the need to defend myself here. I'm not here because I want to be, and anything that has happened because of my presence is not my fault. Things are happening to me, not by my choice.

As his irritation becomes more apparent, so does mine. Here we are again. We can't seem to escape this.

"I just want to find my friend. I never meant to come here, but I'm here now. Instead of fighting, we could work together to figure this out! I'll do whatever I need to help find her!" Despite my anger, I feel myself wanting to reach out and touch his arm.

Offering him comfort or friendship seems like a kindness that would be thrown back in my face with a quickness. I'm the intruder here, the one who doesn't belong.

"Tomorrow." He backs away from me, like the thought of my hand touching him disgusted him.

"Tomorrow, what?"

Instead of answering, he leaves. Just like that, no explanation or reasoning.

"Tomorrow, what?" I run to the door, poking my head out into the empty hallway to yell after him.

As per usual, I'm left with more questions than answers after an interaction with him.

I think I might hate him. But there is something there, something that I can't put my finger on that makes me not give into that feeling fully.

Sulking and annoyed, I sit at the end of my bed. I wonder if I can go look for Elion. He might answer some of my questions. There will obviously not be a straightforward answer, and it will come with frustration and strings attached, but it's better than nothing.

"Hello?" I call out into the silence. "I'm leaving the room."

I feel like a damn fool calling out into the emptiness, asking for permission, but I'm afraid not to.

When no one appears and tells me to sit down and shut up, I creep out into the hallway.

"Kiah?"

"Elion?"

He strolls around the corner just a moment after my escape. "I come bearing breakfast. Where are you headed?" He shifts the tray in his hands to gesture back toward my room.

"I was coming to find you, actually." The words taste bitter on my tongue. I hate admitting that.

"What for?" The amused, teasing tone is notably missing from his voice.

"I have questions."

"Don't you always?" He smiles, but this time it doesn't feel like it's at my expense. There's a softness there. "Go ahead and ask." He sits down on my bed, opening the lid to the tray.

"What's it going to cost me?" I pick a piece of warm, fluffy bread from the selection of pastries and fruits.

"I'm feeling generous today." He grins, the expression reaching his eyes in a way that catches me off guard.

"You?" I arch a brow, trying to hide my surprise with skepticism.

"Ask your questions before I change my mind." He leans back, resting his back on the wall.

The mood between us feels lighter. He's not taunting me, and I don't feel as fragile and vulnerable. The emotional charge that is usually there is gone. I actually feel comfortable.

This is probably a bad thing.

"What is a dreamweave?" I decide not to hesitate.

His brows furrow, and ease is momentarily overshadowed by surprise. "Where did you hear that?"

"Canaan accused me of doing it. I'd like to know what it is. It's hard to defend yourself against something you've never even heard of." I watch him closely, waiting for the smirk, the mocking glint in his eyes, but it doesn't come.

"Dreamweaving is the ability to change or alter dreams. It takes a lot of practice and a real grasp of how to wield magic. Canaan thinks you're doing that? To who? Him?" He sounds genuinely baffled as he answers my question directly.

"He didn't say. But I can promise you, I am not doing that!"

"That explains so much." He shakes his head, his lips tugging downward. "He's in a terrible mood today."

"He stormed in here and yelled at me. I think he hates me. After he saved me from the Shadowrithe, I thought maybe he didn't, but..."

"He doesn't." His voice is firm, leaving no room for doubt, but there's something in his eyes—there's more to the story—something he's not saying.

"Do you know what is happening tomorrow?"

Again, he looks taken by surprise. "How do you know about tomorrow?"

"I don't." I chuckle. "I asked him if I could help, and all he said was 'tomorrow' before leaving."

He hums and looks down at his hands. He knows what's happening tomorrow. I can see it in the way he's avoiding making eye contact with me.

"What's happening, Elion?"

"Tomorrow we're going to attempt to draw the Shadowrithes out of wherever they're hiding." He mumbles.

"How?"

"What do you do in the human realm? Do you have a job? A relationship?" He ignores my questions.

"I'm finishing school. I'm getting a degree in civil engineering. I work at an ice cream parlor, an old-timey diner-type place where I had to wear roller skates." I shake my head. "And no relationship. What about you? Do you have jobs here?" I quickly move past my answers.

"We do. I am the court liaison for the Rimefae. I am the representative in court, and I seek out our best interests." He holds his head high.

"That sounds important."

"It is."

When he looks at me, his piercing eyes meeting mine and holding my gaze, he smiles.

"Aren't you going to ask about me?"

"Ask what about you?" I feign innocence.

"I'm not in a relationship either. Other things have seemed more pressing recently." He answers the question that I didn't ask.

I have to force myself to look away from his face. When he's not making me feel self-conscious with his teasing, I can focus on how attractive he is. I shouldn't focus on that.

"Sometimes," he continues, "someone comes along, and they are inescapable, though. It makes it difficult to focus on other things."

"Really?" I bite my cheek to keep from smiling.

He hums, raking his eyes over my body in a way that feels physical, as if it were his fingertips exploring me.

"Do you want to come somewhere with me? I want to show you something."

FOURTEEN

As he expertly navigates the boat through the bends and turns of the river, my mind drifts back to the last time I went out with him. It turned out to be a trick. He was just trying to feel me out.

It's not like I trusted him only to have him betray me with ulterior motives, but I can't help but hope that's not what this is. I'm oppressively lonely here. I can feel myself seeking connection, warmth from anyone.

No one seems to want to give me that—no one but the water.

The pull is particularly strong today; its call is almost hypnotic. It tugs at something deep inside me, a force that feels much stronger than I am. It's as if it knows my heart and is offering me the things I want most.

I keep my gaze fixed on the sky, pale orange and cloudless. I have to try to ignore the way it calls to me. The sound of it lapping against the front of the boat as we glide through it is unbearable.

"You alright up there?" Elion's voice cuts through my thoughts. He sounds casual—unaffected.

"I'm fine," I lie.

"Really?" He hums softly, his eyes flicking toward the restless water surrounding us. "The water's a bit moody today. It's not calling to you?"

I spin around to face him, narrowing my eyes in a glare. "You know, you're kind of a dick."

A bright smile spreads across his lips, and he laughs—really laughs. It's not the cold, taunting laugh I've come to expect from someone like him, but something genuine, warm even. It's the kind of laugh that catches you off guard, the kind that makes it hard to stay mad. And I want to stay mad. It's safer that way. If I let my guard down, even for a second, I know he'll take the opportunity.

But his laugh is disarming; it feels like a trap. I force myself to look away, to focus on the sky. The air is thick with the tension of everything I'm trying to ignore. The water—him—I'm not sure which is more dangerous.

"Tell me about your friend." He steers the boat toward a small, weathered dock surrounded by jagged black rocks on both sides.

"What about her?" My voice tightens as I search his expression, looking for any hint of mockery, any sign that he's about to twist the knife. I can't take it where she's involved. He can taunt me, but not about her.

"Anything," he shrugs.

"She's..." I pause, searching for words that won't make my voice wobble. The knot forming in my throat aches, but I ignore it. "She's an angel. The sweetest person I've ever met." My voice softens as memories flood my mind—images of her laughter, her kindness, the way she could make anyone feel loved. "And the most talented artist."

I force myself to think of things that won't make me cry, things that won't remind me of how much I miss her, or the fear that gnaws at me whenever I think about what might be happening to her if she's even alive.

"She used to paint these incredible landscapes." I clear my throat. "She made all of the paints herself. She had a way with light. All of her work seemed alive somehow. Like you weren't looking at a canvas but at the real thing. I've known her forever. She's more like my sister than a friend."

I can feel his eyes on me, boring into the side of my face, but I don't look at him. I can't. I'm afraid that he'll be able to see the vulnerability. I feel it all over me, crashing down on my head.

"She sounds special," he says after a moment, his voice lacking the usual edge.

"She is," I whisper, more to myself than to him.

He ties the boat to the dock and steps out, offering me his hand. I hesitate for a moment, then take it. For a brief second, our hands touch, and I'm struck by the warmth of his skin and the gentleness of his grip. It's unexpected, almost comforting, and it catches me off guard.

As I step onto the dock, I instinctively pull my hand back, severing the brief spark that I felt when we touched. I don't like that one bit. That's weird.

I think I prefer his taunting. Gentleness from him feels like a trick. After the slightly flirty tone in our conversation in my room, I can't fall for this. We need to keep our distance.

"What is this place?" My voice comes out in a rush, my words tumbling over each other in my rush to break the silence.

"The Colonnade," He points out beyond the rocky shoreline to the strangest forest I've ever seen. Row after row of trees, all perfectly symmetrical—identical even—growing one after the other in straight lines.

"Oh my god." My legs move, carrying me toward it involuntarily. Between each tree, there is a measured space, about the length of my outstretched arm. "I've never seen anything like this. How are all of the trees the same? Who did this?" The consistency and meticulousness are almost unnerving.

"No one did it," he says softly. "It just grows like this."

"How?" My mind struggles to grasp the idea—the sheer impossibility of such symmetry occurring without anyone doing it. "It seems too exact and measured to be natural."

"It's magic." That Cheshire grin is stretching across his face again.

"Magic," of course.

"This place is very special to me." He follows me as I walk through the first row into this strange and enchanting kind of forest.

"Why?" I ask, my curiosity piqued by the sudden change in his demeanor. He's too soft. Too thoughtful. I don't trust it, but I want to know any information he's willing to tell me about anything.

"As kids, we played here. It was our favorite place." He touches the trunk of the closest tree gently. There is a faraway sadness in his eyes, and his lips tug downward.

"By 'we,' you mean you and Canaan?" I take a guess, trying to picture the two of them as children, running and laughing in this forest. It's impossible. I can't even imagine it. They don't seem like they were ever children.

"And Calais." He smiles, but it doesn't look happy; it doesn't reach his eyes. "We were inseparable."

"Really?" I don't mean to sound so surprised, but I am. They don't seem inseparable now. They eat together, but it's nothing like when I eat a meal with Chey. We can't stop talking and laughing, anyone who sees us would know we're best friends. They seem so cold and formal.

"Before he became king, things were different," He looks sad. Genuinely and truly sad.

I never thought I would find myself feeling bad for Elion.

"We used to spend hours here. We would come at sunrise and stay well past dark. These trees have seen everything,"

I feel his words in my chest. I can relate to a painful degree. We did the same thing. Our parents used to have to force Chey and me inside during the summer. Young and innocent, playing in the forest without a care in the world. We didn't know any better. And now everything is different.

It feels like there is no innocence, not anymore. It's been stripped away—lost. Everything is dark and frightening. Shadows are waiting around every corner to drag us away.

"We used to pretend to be dream weavers," he continues, his voice breaking through the silence that had settled between us. His eyes meet mine, and there's something there, a spark of something. What it is, I can't tell.

But it makes sense why he brought me here.

"It's an ancient form of magic manipulation," he offers me the explanation freely. "It's difficult for fae, but for a human... it would be nearly impossible. Twisting someone's subconscious takes precision and power, a mastery over the mind that few can achieve. Harnessing magic like that takes a lot of practice. It's almost forgotten now, it's more of a myth than an actual practice." He looks up at the leaves hanging over his head.

"Then why would he think that I could do it?" I don't understand.

"He must be dreaming of you." A lopsided smile tugs at the corner of his lips. T

I choked, and my mind immediately filled with images of the dream I had about him. My face instantly flushes, and I'm out of breath. On instinct, my hand wants to move up to touch my neck—to check the place where his teeth would have sunken into my skin.

"Are you alright, darling?" His voice is laced with a playful laugh. There isn't an ounce of genuine concern there. He's onto me.

Clearing my throat and looking at the ground, I nod. "Yeah, great." My voice comes out squeaky and definitely not great.

That dream is the last thing I want to be thinking about right now. It makes me feel dirty and embarrassed in equal measure.

My mind is racing. The thought of Canaan dreaming about me makes me feel jittery, like I've had too many cups of coffee. My insides are buzzing. Was it like my dream? Oh, god! I'm trying to act normal so he can't tell that I'm completely melting down inside. I hope it wasn't like my dream.

But that only raises more questions.

If it was the same as the dream I had, why was he so angry?

I'm spiraling.

The thought of biting me, drinking from me, makes him violently angry. Got it. I should be pleased by this. I don't want him to drink my blood. But for some reason, I'm also offended.

"Anyway, how big is this place?" I change the subject. "It looks like it goes on forever."

"It does." He grins. "Want to explore?"

"Yes!" I haven't been out of that room in so long, I hardly know what to do with myself. Plus, the idea of exploring more and talking less sounds appealing right now. No more dream talk, please.

Shadows dance along the ground, moving together like they're playing a secret game that only they know. Along the ground, little clusters of yellow and white flowers grow together in the sunshine breaking through the canopy above. They move, like a breeze is blowing through them, but it's not.

It almost looks like they're bowing.

"Everything here is so strange." I whisper, bending down to look at them more closely. They look alive, swaying back and forth.

"Come here, I want to show you one more thing." He walks through the trees.

We walk for so long. The path stretches endlessly before us, a straight line cutting through the heart of the trees. Row after row, the trees stand tall and perfectly identical. The air is thick, and the smell of forest is getting stronger. We're so far away from anything else, there isn't anything to dilute it now.

The trees blur together, each one indistinguishable from the last, their sameness gnawing at me. I try to focus, to find something—anything—that might break the eternal repetition, but the forest is playing tricks on me. The more we walk, the more disoriented I am.

"Almost there." He looks over his shoulder.

Our definitions of almost must be very different.

"There," he points, stretching his arm out.

Squinting, I look in that direction. In the sea of trees, there is a large black rock, shiny like a crystal, in the distance.

"What is that?" I feel suddenly nervous to approach it. We've come all this way, but there is something frightening about it.

"Come see." He smiles.

FIFTEEN

S till feeling unsteady on my feet, I follow him toward the rock. The closer we get, the larger it grows. It towers over us, a huge, polished oval stone.

All around it, there are symbols carved into it.

"What is it?" I ask, circling around it, my fingers brushing against the cool stone. It's the same on all sides.

It's alluring—magnetic. Big and powerful, there is something captivating about it—I'm drawn to it. I can't read the engraved print, but it feels ancient and sacred. It's as if we've entered hallowed ground—a place with purpose and meaning. I get the same sensation as standing before the ocean, looking out over the vastness of it—the enormity and weight of something much bigger than you, something with strength far beyond my own.

"A crypt." His voice a low murmur, almost reverent. There is no humor or teasing in him now.

"I'm sorry?" I choke. "A what?" I take a large step back.

"My father is entombed here." He runs his fingers over the carvings.

Why would he bring me here? Of all places, his father's tomb?

"My father was Esren, King of the Rimfae. He ruled the Frostlinds for centuries." His voice hardens as he speaks, his crisp blue eyes darkening. A deep frown tugs at his lips, and I can see the storm brewing behind his gaze.

"Your dad was the king?" The question slips out, my curiosity getting the better of me.

"Until the Great Wars."

"And then what happened?" I hesitate, not wanting to ask the obvious question that hangs in the air. If his father was the king, wouldn't that make him a prince? Why is Canaan the king?

"He gave his life for the cause." His voice is cold - the words heavy with the bitterness of defeat. He stares at the stone for a moment before turning and looking up at the sky.

I have a million questions. Little pieces come together, but not enough for a clear picture.

"Go ahead," he grins. A smirk that tugs at the corner of his lips as he leisurely turns and begins walking back in the direction we came from, his stride unhurried, calm—very different from the anger that was there just a second ago.

"Go ahead?" I quickly follow after him. I don't want to be left behind in this place.

"Ask your questions," he clarifies, glancing over his shoulder. "I wouldn't have brought you here and shown you this if I couldn't handle a few questions about it."

"Are you a prince?"

His response is immediate, and a fierce pride swells in his voice, like he's reciting this answer countless times. "The Prince of the Frostlinds, first and only heir to the throne. The would-be king of the north. The sovereign son of the Rimfae." He lifts his chin—powerful, unyielding, and proud.

"But-" I stop, hesitating. I don't know how to ask this without rubbing salt in the wound.

"But, now I'm just a liaison at court." He finishes my sentence.

I search him, watching his face but it doesn't change. I don't find any anger or frustration in his eyes.

"Why was there a war?" He told me I could ask, but I keep expecting him to change suddenly - to be irritated.

"Differences in opinion. A tale as old as time." He shrugs, almost carelessly, but I catch the brief flash of something in his eyes. He can try to play it off, but he has a tell. His crystal eyes flicker, I've noticed, whenever he truly feels something deeply.

"What was the opinion?" This feels dangerous.

"The Shadowrithes wanted to keep the human realm borders open."

"Oh." I think I understand without needing to pour salt on that wound.

"Don't you want to know why I'm not the king?" His brow quirks upward.

"I didn't want to ask an insensitive question like that."

"But you do want to know." He laughs.

"Yes."

"Canaan's father betrayed mine, stole our land from us after we helped him win the war."

"But you're still close to him?" I don't even pretend to hide my shock.

"Our fathers were close too, until they weren't. We don't let their disagreements affect our friendship." He hums.

"That's very mature of you."

A surprised laugh comes from his nose. "Mature?"

"Yeah, you know. Your dad's fighting a whole war would probably end a lot of friendships."

"Our 'dads' were kings. They weren't just men squabbling over meaningless nonsense."

"Maybe that's true, but it doesn't change the fact that people choose to hate each other over less."

We walk in silence past several trees. When he stops suddenly, I almost run into his back.

"Tell me something about yourself that no one knows." He spins around to face me. We're too close. His chest is right up against mine.

"Like what?" I stutter, fumbling over the words.

"Anything. Just tell me something." He spreads his palm out in the middle of my back, pressing me forward.

He hasn't said it, but the look in his eyes makes me think he wants to know a secret of the sexual variety.

I feel the blood rushing to my cheeks. "I like to read fantasy books."

His eyes narrow. "And that is a secret?"

"It's a secret because of the kinds of books I read. They're explicit." I push past the fear of his judgment.

"Explicit fantasies?" He hums, almost purring. Our chests are so close together I feel it vibrate against my ribs.

"Yeah."

"What kind?"

"You know, werewolves and vampires." I immediately regret telling him.

His eyes, usually bright and blue, are dark and hooded. "What about fae? Are they ever featured in your preferred reading?" It's like a switch has been flipped. If he was teasing before, he's not now. There isn't anything taunting in his expression—no smirk.

Oh god. Embarrassment radiates through me. What is wrong with me?

"Y-Yes." I cringe. Why does my voice sound so breathy and soft?

"And in your fantasy books, what are we doing?" His large hand wraps around the back of my neck, holding my head still. The depth of his voice sends a shiver down my spine.

"Um," I panic, words stuck in my throat, my pulse racing. I can't say it. I can't tell him what I've imagined as I read the words.

"What are we doing, Kiah?" He steps forward, forcing my body back until I'm against the trunk of a tree.

Just as I start to tell myself that he's going to pull away at any moment—he's going to leave me hanging here on the edge—he doesn't. It happens so fast I hardly register it.

He's kissing me. I'm returning the gesture. We're kissing.

It's sudden. His lips on mine—claiming them with an intensity that shocks my system. His mouth is hot, demanding, a perfect blend of roughness and raw need. No one has ever kissed me with this kind of urgency before.

Trapped between a tree and his body, I only have one movement available to me, so I seize the opportunity. Reaching up, I wrap my arms around his neck, clasping my hands together to hold him close.

A tingling buzz courses through me, like a current of electricity. It starts in my chest, a tight knot of desperate desire that quickly unravels, spreading until it radiates through every inch of me. My heart pounds in my ears, drowning out everything except him—the feeling of his body, the taste of him, the way he devours me like he's been starving for this— for me.

Time blurs, the world around us fading into nothing as we lose ourselves to the kiss. Every nerve ending is alive, every sense heightened.

He smells amazing and tastes even better.

"Kiah," he groans, his voice tight and desperate. "We have to stop, darling. I can't lose control with you."

"Sure you can." I come up on my toes and kiss him again, sliding my tongue between his lips.

He moans, and I swallow it down. My chest swells with pride as he melts against me.

"Stop, Kiah." He pulls away, but this time his face is resolute. This is the end. "We need to get back."

The walk back to the dock feels like we're moving in fast-forward. I can't think of anything but his mouth. My mind is lost in a hazy fog that I can't find my way out of. The forest chirps and rustles - the shadows dance and play - none of it matters. He kissed me.

And even more shocking was how desperately I wanted it.

He holds his hand out to me—an offer of help into the boat. When I hesitate to take it, he throws his head back and laughs.

"A little late for that, love. Don't you think?" The wide smile on his face is endearing.

Dropping my hand into his, I ignore the way his touch makes me feel warm and shaky.

As he brings us back up the river, the call of the water is almost completely silent. If it's trying to lure me in, I can't hear it.

"Listen, we need to be careful about this. If Canaan found out, he would probably have my head."

Ordinarily, my cynical mind would immediately go into a spiral of overthinking—maybe that he was embarrassed about kissing me and trying to think of a cover to keep it under wraps. I don't see that on his face. He looks genuine. For better or worse, I believe him.

"I won't say anything," I promise.

"How did it compare to your filthy reading fantasies?" The smirk is back in full force.

"I'll never tell." I fold my arms over my chest.

"Ah, come on! I have to know how I measure up." His laugh is free, more joyful, and real than before. I like it.

Stepping off of the boat at the cathedral, I ignore the ache in my chest. I don't want to be back here—my prison.

"Tomorrow is a big day." He walks with me through the dark hallways. "Get some rest."

"You know, no one has told me what's happening tomorrow."

"It's probably best that you don't know until right before it's time." His forehead creases.

"That's not going to keep me up all night." I don't try to hide my rolling eyes.

We reach my door in record time. I don't want to go inside.

"I'll see you tomorrow, darling." He presses a soft, unexpected kiss to my forehead before disappearing. There is no lingering, no hesitation. He's gone.

All alone, there isn't anything to do but crawl into my bed and let the thoughts come. I'm going to think of that kiss until sunrise, I just know it.

Sixteen

Sleep hits me so fast it's like I fall all at once. One second, I was awake, then I wasn't. It was almost forceful the way it dragged me under. I can feel it, though. I know I'm asleep.

Panic grips me, like a vice around my chest, tightening around my ribs. I know instantly what is happening. I recognize the feeling.

"Please, no!" I beg out loud for anything willing to listen. But it doesn't work. My body rises out of the bed, and I move down the hallway. My feet don't even touch the ground. I float, an invisible string pulling me through the cathedral.

I'm not in control. Closing my eyes, I try to fight. The only thing I can think to do is wake myself up.

"Wake up, Kiah!" I scream, but there is no sound. I can't get the words out.

My body isn't moving anymore, I've stopped, but I keep my eyes pinched shut. Whatever magical force is holding me here can't make me look.

Or maybe it can.

A sharp pain, like the bitter sting of ice, touches my cheeks, moving up to my eyes. A phantom hand, a gust of cold air, pressure. Something is pushing against me, forcing my eyes open.

"No!" I shake my head violently, fighting against it, but it's stronger than I am.

My eyes peel open, burning with tears.

Canaan is in front of me, even from behind, I know it's him. His shoulders, his tension, the way the air feels heavier when he's around.

We're in the oldest library in existence. The vaulted ceilings, shelves of leather-bound books, and wrought iron chandelier are straight out of a gothic-era cliche.

Cupping my hand over my mouth, I hold back the sniffling whimpers and stuttered breaths I can't help but make as I cry.

Why does this keep happening to me? He's going to blame me for this. He'll storm into my room and yell at me. More than anyone, I hate this. I would never, ever, do this.

My body lurches forward, and I'm directly behind him, so close that I can see over his shoulder.

On the table in front of him, there are stacks of books. He's flipping through the pages almost manically, obviously looking for something specific.

He growls and slams a book down on the table. His hands come up, gripping at his hair, tugging at it.

Suddenly, with a swift motion, he knocks one of the stacks of books onto the ground. I've seen him angry before, angry at me, but this seems worse somehow.

"The answers are here somewhere." His voice is low and full of rage. I assume he's talking to himself until I look up and our eyes meet. He's staring right at me.

"Canaan," I panic. "I'm sorry! I'm not doing this on purpose! I don't-"

"I know you're not doing this on purpose. Even if you were somehow powerful enough to enter my mind, I doubt you would be stupid enough to continue doing it after I caught you." His eyes pin me down. Even if I could move right now, I wouldn't be able to. The way he's looking at me is paralyzing.

"I have to find the Shadowrithes. There must be something documented here—a place where they might go." He starts to pace around the room. "We have to stop them before they get too strong. I just have to fucking find them."

It's only now that I notice the map spread out across the table. It looks old—ancient. The frayed paper shimmers slightly, catching my attention.

As I stare at it, it moves. The waterways ripple and flow, frost spreads over the mountains, and the forest and grassland sway in the breeze.

At the edge of the page, an inky black mist swirls, moving as if it were alive. It sends a chill down my spine. That place is dark and frightening on paper. I can't imagine being there. It looks like death, like a place where only shadows survive.

"The fringes." He answers my unspoken question. "They should be there. They were banished in shadow form. They should be too weak to change forms or break through the barrier around our realm. Your friend is with them. She has to be."

"How are we going to get to her?" A desperate helplessness takes root in my chest. It feels like a sinkhole, pulling everything down with it as it grows by the second. Forgetting who I am, where I am, and who he is, I reach out, grabbing his arm as I plead. "We have to help her, Canaan! We can't let them kill her!" Then it hits me. She might already be gone.

"She's alive. There is no way they grew that strong from one drink. They have to keep her alive and healthy. You don't slaughter the cow after one glass of milk." He shakes me off of his arm. "She will be fine as long as she's useful."

The thought of her being held hostage while they drink from her makes my stomach roll.

"Okay, so what are we going to do?" I cross my arms.

"*We* are working on it." He grabs a book from the pile and opens it. I hit a nerve there.

"Why were the Shadowrithes banished?"

He's not as open or friendly as Elion, but he might give me some answers without strings attached. My lips tingle when I think of Elion. I shouldn't think about him right now.

"There was a war, and they lost."

"Right, but-"

He turns the book in his hands toward me, holding it open to show a detailed illustration of a dark fairy holding a lifeless woman—his fangs buried in her neck. Behind them, a pile of broken bodies reaches the sky. Hundreds, maybe more, thrown together like garbage, drained of their blood, then discarded.

Gasping, I clutch my chest. This sudden cruelty from him is unexpected. Why would he show that to me? What good can come from it?

"I want to leave." I turn toward the door, my voice cracking. "Let me go!" I yell out to whoever is holding me in this room. Covering my face with my hands, I let my emotions erupt. I don't care that he's here. The tears come, and I can't stop them.

I expect ridicule or anger from him. Instead, his heavy hand comes down on my shoulder. It's not a warm embrace, but the gesture feels supportive enough to calm me down.

"Take a breath." His voice isn't warm, but it does make the panic in my chest feel looser.

Taking a long, slow breath, I ignore the way it trembles.

"When you were under the water with Thaloein," he says, his voice a little quieter now, as if weighing his words, "did he take anything from you?" He steps even closer, his presence unnervingly calm, looming. "I know he didn't bite you, but did he take a lock of hair? Was he able to take your breath?"

I don't think he realizes how intense and intimidating he is. His voice and the heaviness of his authority are terrifying, even if his demeanor is calm.

"What do you mean, 'steal my breath?' What does that mean?" Panic starts to creep up my spine.

"It would seem like a kiss to you, taking the air from your lungs."

"No, he didn't do that."

He sits down, frustration etched into his face. "Well, that's a good thing, but it doesn't explain how he was able to establish a connection to you."

"He's dead, right? Wouldn't the connection have severed then?" My voice sounds small—weak.

"No. Not with Shadowrithes. They are connected by darkness, like a web. If he established a connection, all of them will have it." Canaan's voice is so unnervingly calm, and the words are delivered with a steady ease that doesn't match the gravity of what he's saying.

My stomach lurches. "Fuck." My legs wobble, and I collapse into the chair beside him before I fall to the floor. "He didn't do anything like that, though," I reassure myself. My pulse thumps in my ears, and my vision is blurry.

He sighs, and I can't help but watch him. He looks exhausted. It's etched into his face.

"Can you explain something to me?" I'm cautious even asking, but having one less question makes it worth it.

He doesn't speak, just looks up at me, waiting.

"Why can't you come to my room and wake me up? Pull me out of this?"

"Your spirit isn't inside of your body. Whoever is controlling the dream has pulled your consciousness. I can go to your body and try to wake you, but I can't unless they release you."

"So, my body isn't actually here?" My hand presses flat against my chest—I can feel it. I'm right here.

"No."

I have one more question then. One more awful question.

"What if they never release me?" I can hardly push the words past the lump forming in my throat.

"Then you would be trapped inside of whatever dream state you were put into." The weight of his words and the strain in his voice are like scissors that cut into me, severing the line I'm gripping to stay calm.

"Oh god!" Full-fledged panic takes over, and I feel myself sway. Luckily, I'm already seated, or I wouldn't be upright much longer. My stomach twists into a knot, and I feel like I can't take a breath. My lungs burn, and tears sting my eyes. Pinching them closed tight, I cover my face with my hands.

"Kiah." His voice feels distant, like it's being pulled away from me. I blink rapidly, trying to focus, but when I open my eyes, I'm no longer in the room. I'm in my bed, curled up, drenched in sweat. The sheets cling to my skin like a suffocating second layer, my soaked shirt glued to my body.

There's no sense of relief. No smooth transition back to reality. It feels like I've been yanked violently from a nightmare. Disoriented and afraid, I sit up. His name is still in my mouth, I can feel it on the tip of my tongue. I was about to call out to him.

Jumping up, I run out of the room. I'm not sure exactly where I'm going, but I'll find it eventually. Through the cathedral, I search every door. I don't have time to care about rules or privacy right now.

"Canaan!" My voice echoes off the walls, and for a moment, all I hear is the empty, hollow sound of my own desperation.

Then, a reply. "Kiah?" He's close by.

I break into a run, racing toward the sound of his voice, rounding the corner just as he steps into view. We collide, my momentum sending us both stumbling. His hands steady me, keeping me upright.

"Hopefully, we will find answers today." He nods curtly. "Are you ready?"

"Yes!" I still don't know what we're doing. No one will tell me the specifics, but I'm all in. I don't have to know the specifics to know that I want to help. Anything to end this.

"You're going with Calais."

SEVENTEEN

J ogging quickly behind Calais, I try to keep up with her. She definitely doesn't want to be stuck with me. The human. The liability. She keeps looking at me like she wants to say something, but instead of just saying it, she huffs and turns away.

She's done it at least ten times since we walked from the cathedral, across the bridge, through the city, and into the field beyond it.

I'm not going to provoke her, so I keep my mouth shut. No one will tell me what we're doing today, but I know it's bad because everyone is tense.

"Listen," she groans. "My brother is trusting you. Don't let him down." She stops walking to look at me.

"I won't." I promise. I don't think they understand how helpful I want to be. Being a nuisance is not my goal here.

We walk until we reach the crest of a hill, the city behind us, and a valley stretching out in front.

"Now what?"

"Now," she steps out of my way. "You go down there."

"Down where?" Surely she doesn't mean down into the valley alone, right?

"Down into the valley," she points.

"By myself?" I don't want to go down there alone. Truthfully, I don't want to go at all. There is something uneasy about it. The hairs on my neck are standing on end.

"I thought you wanted to help." She throws her hands in the air, and her wings twitch.

"I do." I blurt out. I've been asking them to help for days. Borderline pestering. Now I don't want to do what they need. "I just want to know what I'm supposed to be doing."

"Go down there and wait." Her already thin patience is getting smaller by the second.

"For what?"

"A Shadowrithe, hopefully."

"Wait. Am I the bait?" As I speak, my shadow runs away. Little traitor!

"Yes. They aren't stupid, they won't likely come. But you might distract them. Even a moment of distraction might be enough for us to find them."

Pausing, I take in what she's saying. No wonder they wouldn't tell me the plan beforehand! This is the worst idea.

"Ok, I'll go." I square my shoulders. I said I wanted to help. I offered to do whatever they needed. This is what they need. I've pestered and bothered them, now they are sending me to my likely death. This should teach me to keep my mouth shut.

She looks shocked but doesn't stop me.

Taking a deep breath, I straighten my posture and start to walk down the long hill alone. My pride is going to get me killed. I can't back down.

My feet feel heavy as I force them forward. I won't crumble. I won't fold.

If this is what I have to do to help get Cheyenne back, this is what I have to do.

The valley is calm and quiet. There's a softness to it. Long grass blows gently in the breeze. There's a slightly floral scent in the air. There's peace here.

But there's a sharp, insistent fear creeping up the base of my neck. This place feels too serene, as if it's designed to lull me into a false sense of safety. It's drawing me in, tugging at the edges of my hypervigilance, the quiet is so deliberate it becomes unnerving. I can sense it—this isn't peace, it's a trap.

I take another step forward, and my gaze catches on something just off the road, hidden by the tall, swaying grass. A pool, its water, so still, it seems unnatural. Something shimmers inside, catching the light and twinkling.

The surface is impossibly clear, like glass, revealing flowers I've never seen before, floating just beneath. Their colors are mesmerizing—vivid yellows, soft pinks, deep blues—each petal gleaming as if encrusted with tiny diamonds. The way the sunlight dances off them, casting their colors onto the white pebble floor of the lake, is utterly hypnotic.

There's something otherworldly—enchanting—about them.

The flowers sway beneath the water in a rhythm, as if an invisible current is guiding them, though the surface is perfectly still.

The air feels thick, the scent of something sweet pulling me closer.

It's not floral, it's sugary.

I crouch down without thinking, drawn in. They seem close enough to touch now, the delicate petals almost within reach. The thin, translucent stems twist gracefully in the water, rooted to the bottom.

My mom's face flashes in my mind, her pain sends a pang through my heart. The ache in my chest is sharp, a familiar kind of sorrow. She would love these flowers. One of these flowers would fix everything. She would be happy again, and all would be forgiven.

Without fully realizing it, I'm on my stomach now, the cool dirt pressing against my skin, my hand outstretched. Sweat trickles down the back of my neck as I inch closer, my heart pounding in my chest.

I have to get one. It's the only thing in the world that matters.

Everything outside this pool fades into the background. All that matters is the shimmer of the flowers. If I can just reach one... maybe two. Cheyenne's mom could use one, too. When we go home, I'm sure she will want something for her mom.

As my fingers graze the surface of the water, a strange chill runs up my arm, like ice sinking into my bones. But before I can react, the realization hits me.

This is all wrong.

But it's too late.

Before I can pull my arm back or get up, I'm in the water. A leafy, translucent vine is wrapping around my wrist and pulling me below the surface.

The water looked shallow, no more than knee high. But I'm being dragged so far down that the temperature is changing. The deeper I go, the colder the water becomes, biting into my skin, and the light above me fades. The once-shimmering surface is now a distant glimmer, growing dimmer by the second, swallowed by shadows.

An inky black shadow wraps around me like blood in the water. It creeps up my legs, taking hold of me.

The more I struggle, the tighter the grip becomes. I'm painfully aware of how urgently my next breath is needed. My body is fighting against inhaling a big gulp of this water.

"Kiah."

My name echoes through the water, a soft, calming voice that sounds familiar and unknown all at once.

I feel myself going limp. The tension in my muscles loosens, and I feel tired, like the moment before slipping away to sleep.

With a smile on my face, I close my eyes.

Everything is going to be fine somehow. I just know it.

A warm hand grips my arm, and I'm yanked away from the serenity all around me.

"Kiah!"

The voice is different now—no longer calm and steady, but harsh and loud, cutting through the panic fogging my mind.

Coughing violently, my eyes jerk open. Water spills from my mouth as I blink, disoriented, against the harsh sunlight.

"Couldn't you hear me calling you?" Calais shouts, her voice tight with fear, yet laced with anger. "I was screaming at the top of my lungs!"

"I'm sorry." I whimper, looking around at the concerned faces kneeling on the dirty shoreline of the lake.

Canaan's hands are on me before I can process what's happening, his strong fingers gripping my face, tilting my head as he inspects my neck. His gaze is intense, but when he finally pulls back, there's a flicker of relief in his eyes.

"No bites," he mumbles, more to himself than to me.

"What was that?" I tremble.

"A shadowrithe was lying in wait. How could they have known that you were going to be here alone?" His gaze drops from studying me, a faraway look in his eyes. He looks like he's about to say something—like it's right there on the tip of his tongue. Instead, he turns his attention toward his sister. "I'm bringing her back. Elion was right. This was a mistake."

"I'll meet the others on patrol." She quickly volunteers. The man who's with them, a new face, leaves with her.

"I'm sorry, Canaan." Shame wraps around my chest like a vice. I had one job. I couldn't even be alone for one minute without letting that damn water entice me.

"It's not your fault. Humans can't resist. I should have known better. I do know better." He grits his teeth.

"I didn't really give you a choice." I shrug.

"You are persistent." He narrows his eyes, but his tone is unusually lacking in irritation.

He lifts me up, taking me from the dirt into his arms. He's warmer than I was expecting. His warm chest against my wet clothes feels like snuggling up to a fire.

It happens so gracefully that I hardly notice that he's lifting us off the ground.

"Oh my god." I grip him tightly, clinging to his shirt as he soars up the hill in seconds flat. His wings are strong, powerful and steady, cutting through the air with ease. Within seconds, the lake is far behind, the cathedral rising before us like a distant beacon.

For a moment, all I can hear is the rhythmic beat of his wings and feel the warmth of his body wrapped around mine. Despite everything, there's something oddly reassuring about being in his arms, suspended between the earth and sky.

"Go inside to your room. I'll send someone to guard you." He must notice that my eyes have tripled in size and my grip on his shirt tightened. As he gently sets me down on my feet, he places his hand on my shoulder, reassuring and firm. "Just as a precaution."

"Oh, right." I feel shaky on my feet.

"I shouldn't have let you anywhere near that. I apologize. I thought you could distract them enough for them to make a mistake. Instead, I put you in danger." His mouth flattens into a thin line. "I won't allow you to be in that position again."

"No!" I turn too quickly and collide with his chest. "I meant it when I said I wanted to help! If there is any way, I still want to!"

His eyes narrow as he studies my face. My cheeks heat as I realize that he's holding me by the arms, steadying me from when I rammed into his chest.

"Sorry." I clear my throat and step back.

"You are very interesting to me." He tilts his head before turning to walk away. "Someone will be here to sit with you."

"Ok." I nod, feeling breathless as he walks away.

EIGHTEEN

"Kiah?" Elion's voice is like a soothing balm; my body instantly feels it. As soon as I hear him, the tension in my neck starts to ease. He'll probably tease me for being such a weak human. But I think, deep down, he actually cares.

The door flies open, slamming loudly into the wall.

His chest is heaving as he stops in the doorway, his wings spread wide.

"I'm alright," I whisper, my heart pounding in my ears.

He doesn't look like himself. The teasing, easygoing nature I'm used to isn't in the man before me now. Maybe he doesn't just care deep down, maybe it's right on the surface.

"I told him not to let you go out there. When the idea of using you as bait was brought up, I told him not to!" He runs his hand over his face and into his hair. "This should never have happened." His voice is raw fury.

"I could have said no." I step off of the bed cautiously. "It was my choice."

"Kiah! You have been asking to help since the day you arrived. Of course, you weren't going to turn away from the opportunity to help find your friend. They knew that!" His voice cracks, thick with frustration as he paces the cramped room, each step filled with barely-contained anger. "They put you in that situation! Anything could have happened to you!"

"But nothing did." I reach for him, stopping his quick, pacing steps around my small room. "Something almost happened. But I'm fine."

He stops, eyes searching mine, as if he can see the cracks beneath my surface. "Are you?" His hand cups my chin, gently but firmly, tilting my head so I'm forced to meet his gaze. The concern etched in his features makes my chest ache.

"Yes," I whisper, nodding, but the word feels hollow. I don't even believe them.

Because something else had complete control of my body. Of my thoughts, my actions. The memory creeps in, sharp and invasive—it wasn't me. The worst part of it, even more frightening than the fact that I had no autonomy, is that I didn't even realize. Not at first. My body was moving, my thoughts coherent, feelings still flickered—everything seemed fine until it wasn't. Until it was too late.

Something crawled inside me and took over without my realizing it. A puppeteer, guiding every motion, every thought.

I feel disgusting, like there's filth in places no water can reach. I don't know how to move forward or how to trust myself. What if I'm not in control of my body right now?

My body reacts before I can think—flinching as I pull away from him.

"Kiah." His voice is so soft, so gentle and caring that it breaks something inside of me. Like a rubber band snapping under too much tension, my name, spoken so sweetly, brings a monsoon down on my head.

Covering my face with trembling hands, I try to muffle the sob that's clawing its way up my throat. I don't want him to see me like this —weak and broken.

His arms wrap around me, holding me against his chest. "You're safe."

He lifts me, moving to sit on my bed. Then he just lets me cry. Holding me on his lap, with my face tucked into his neck, I let everything out.

I feel safe in his arms.

The darkness I've been dragging behind me, the shadows lurking at the edge of every corner, waiting to swallow me whole—it feels distant now. Like it can't touch me while I'm here, in his arms.

The soft, steady thump of his heartbeat against my ear is like an anchor, holding me here and telling me it's real.

I let go of all the things I keep shoving down. My fear, the guilt, the worry, the pain I know I have caused my mom. I imagine each day as stealing away a day of her life. Even when I get home, somehow, she won't ever get those days back. The burden on her soul has taken them, they don't belong to her anymore.

I did that.

She asked me not to go, and I did it anyway.

Now I'm trapped here. And what's worse, I haven't even rescued Chey.

He never speaks. The taunting I was so sure was coming never does. His silence wraps around me, soft and steady. It feels strangely familiar, as though we've shared this quiet a thousand times before.

There's no tension, no undercurrent of the heat from the kiss. This is just comfort when I need it most.

My eyelids grow heavy, each blink lasts a little longer, the world around me blurring, softening at the edges. I drift, floating into a space where nothing follows—no pain, no fear, just warmth and safety. I know I'm slipping into sleep, and for a fleeting second, panic flares. I expect to be dragged away, pulled into some nightmarish vision. But this time, it doesn't come. This time, it's just sleep.

When my eyes blink open again, the room is dark. The soft quiet of night lingering around us. He's still here. Leaning back against the headboard, his body solid and unmoving. My cheek rests against his chest, and the slow rise and fall of his breathing is slow and steady. He's asleep, too.

Minutes trickle by in silence, but I'm hyper-aware of every second that passes.

His arm is draped over my waist, heavy and warm, his body completely at ease beneath mine.

The thought of him asleep beside me stirs something deep in my chest. My curiosity blooms, drawing my gaze up to his face, though I can't quite see him. I want to. I want to know what he looks like when the walls are down. There's something about him—something powerful, despite his lean frame, the tension always simmering just below the surface. I wonder if sleep makes him softer, gentler, maybe.

My fingers twitch against his thigh, and before I can stop myself, I'm moving. Slowly, very slowly, I let my hand drift upward. The top few buttons of his shirt are undone, and I catch a glimpse of skin, smooth, warm, almost taunting. My fingertips graze his chest.

When he doesn't move, I grow bolder, tracing the planes of his muscle and letting the pads of my fingers explore his skin.

He's so smooth.

"What are you doing?" His voice startles me.

I freeze, guilt and embarrassment flooding me. I'm caught. "Oh, sorry." I start to pull my hand away, but he grabs it, keeping me in place.

"I didn't mean to fall asleep," he mumbles, his voice soft. "You're so warm."

Leaning back to look up at him, I meet his watchful eyes. "What happened today? Where were you?"

"While you were down in the valley, we hoped that your presence would distract them. They're too smart to fall for it, but the scent of your blood would at least make them more careless. I was on patrol near the fringes, watching for signs." He holds me tightly to him, as if I might float away.

"Did you see anything?" I don't want to get my hopes up.

"No, not while I was out, but there was a shift in the current when you went into the water." His lips meet my temple, pressing a quick kiss. It's not the first time we've kissed, but it still takes me by surprise. There was so much sweetness in it.

The air in the room changes, a chill crawls up my bare skin, the temperature drops suddenly.

"What does that mean?" Deep down, I already know the answer.

"They're in the water. That's how they left the fringes; that's how they're traveling. We'll find them." His voice is so sure, even and steady.

I search his face, looking for cracks in that certainty, but his gaze is unwavering, cold like the air around us.

"What if you don't?" The question escapes before I can stop it. I don't want to know the answer, but I have to. "What do they want?"

"The throne."

We sit in silence. The cold air is heavy, stinging my lungs with each breath.

"When I was being dragged down, I felt empty. Hollow. Do you think that's what death feels like?" He's probably not the person to ask, but I have to get this out. The feeling—dark and lonely—won't leave me alone. Even here in his arms, I still feel it.

It's like it got inside of me, coiled tight around my organs, and lives there now. I feel it pressing on my lungs with every breath.

He's silent for a long time, his hand stroking gently through my hair. When he finally speaks, his voice is soft. "I don't think that's what death feels like at all."

His fingers weave through my hair. "I think when you die, you'll feel warm. Content. Like you're being held by everyone who's ever loved you. And in that moment, you will only feel peace."

"I hope so."

He shifts beneath me, moving me so that my face is in front of his. I'd be lying if I said that in between the moments of chaos, his lips haven't crept into my mind.

With my breath caught in my throat, I watch his eyes move down to my lips.

A rush of excitement courses through me.

He lets out a low, huffed laugh. "Your heart is racing, darling." His thumb runs up the length of my neck. "What's got you so excited?"

At the risk of embarrassing myself completely, I lean in just enough to open the door. He'll know I'm interested. Unless he's a complete idiot or he doesn't feel the same way, he'll make a move.

He hums in the back of his throat, his thumb still on my pulse.

There is a darkness in his eyes that isn't normally there. The longer we sit here in silence, the more I wonder if I misread everything.

My spine stiffens, preparing to run, to leave my own room behind, but he grabs me.

"You're tempting me into something that will have dire consequences." The sudden low rasp in his voice calms every doubt.

"What consequences?" I lean in again, more obviously this time.

"This is strictly forbidden."

"What is?"

"All of the things I want to do to you right now." He moves his hand up, roughly kneading my lower lip with his thumb.

"Oh." My insides flip-flop.

"Fuck it." He moves so suddenly that I hardly have time to understand what's happening when he kisses me. My back meets the mattress, and he is hovering over my body. The kiss is all fire and lust. I can feel how much he wants it—it's in his lips, his tongue, the way his hand roams my body.

All of my desperation bubbles up to the surface, simmering beneath my skin. I want to rip his clothes off. I want him to rip my clothes off.

I can only imagine, but he must have very capable hands. I need him to use them on me.

I crave affection, touch, and pleasure. He has been here for hours, holding me and comforting me—I need more. I want him to erase the lonely ache that I've felt since arriving here. I want him to remind me of what it feels like to take a full breath.

The fact that this is apparently forbidden only makes me want it more.

"I've been dying to taste you, darling." His mouth suctions around my neck, and I freeze. He moves downward, leaving a trail of warm kisses down over my collarbone. "I'm starving."

Again, with the potential double meanings.

He smirks, taking my shirt by the collar. He knows exactly what he's doing. His taunting, teasing nature is back in full force. The double meaning behind his words is intentional.

"Go ahead and have a taste." I won't back down. If he wants to tease, I hope he can take what he so happily gives out.

"Oh, darling. That was a mistake." Grips my shirt right down the middle. The fabric frays, obeying his hands. Immediately, his mouth is on my skin, nipping and kissing my chest and down over my stomach. "I'm going to leave nothing left."

His fingers slip beneath the waistband of my pants, and in one swift tug, I'm naked.

"Now, isn't this a sight to see?" He never takes his eyes off of me. "Soaking, just for me." His tongue slides across his lower lip as he stares. He sweeps his fingers through my wet pussy and brings his fingers up to my mouth. "Tell me how good you taste."

As I suck his fingers into my mouth, tasting myself on my tongue, he suctions his mouth around my slit.

The shock of pleasure that runs through me takes me by surprise, and I bite down on him, hard.

He moans and continues his assault.

When I release his fingers, he moves his hands down, cupping my breasts and kneading them in both hands.

"Oh, god! Elion!" I know I'm being too loud, but he has a very talented mouth, and I can't control it. I should have known for all of his cocky shit talking, he would be able to do amazing things with that tongue.

He brings me right to the edge, licking, sucking, and flicking his tongue. I'm barely hanging onto reality. I'm floating somewhere in between.

"Come all over my tongue!" He growls as he coaxes it out of me. "I want to drink it."

My back arches up off the bed, and all sense of time and space fades away. I don't know who I am, where I am, or what I am. There is nothing but my body and his tongue.

"I'm so hard." He groans. And that's all it takes.

My body contorts, all of my muscles going rigid at once. Lightning shoots through me, a feeling that starts low in my belly and radiates outward.

And true to his word, he doesn't waste a drop.

"Holy shit," I heave, desperate for air.

"You have no idea how badly I want you." He kisses the tips of my fingers.

"Have me then." I don't care that I sound desperate.

"I can't, darling. This was already highly inappropriate. You're alone and afraid here. Canaan would assume I'm taking advantage of that. Before we go further, I have to be sure that it's because you really want to." He stands, and I realize he really is about to leave.

"Wait!" I grab his hand. "You aren't taking advantage! I mean that."

"Don't make this more difficult for me than it already is." He rubs his palm over the prominent bulge in his pants. "Get some sleep. I'll come get you for breakfast in a few hours." He tucks a strand of hair behind my ears.

"But what about you?" I feel defeated. He looks like he's about to burst through the fabric any second.

"I'll go take care of this." He smiles. "I'll be thinking of the sounds you make when you come and how delicious you taste."

NINETEEN

My body is relaxed. He sucked all of the tension out.

My mind is a different story. I'm reeling.

He left?

I understand why, deep down, I really do. But that doesn't soothe the sting of rejection.

Somewhere in this unholy cathedral, he might be rubbing one out. In real time. While thinking about me.

I wish he would have done it here. I didn't even get to see it.

Just thinking about it makes me warm. Is he doing it right now? God, I hope so.

Closing my eyes, I try to imagine it. For once, I wouldn't mind the dream weaving. If I were actually controlling it, I would be out looking for him right now.

My body starts to drift, weightless, my mind floating from reality. It's like I'm slipping beneath dark water, suspended somewhere between waking and dreaming.

"Kiah." My name ripples in the air. A whisper from the shadows. It's low and rumbling, coiling around my hand and pulling me forward.

"Why are you doing this to me?" I ask it. This time, I don't fight. I'm too tired.

"It's all lies, Kiah. Open your eyes, see the truth."

"My eyes are open."

The voice laughs, a sound like thunder—deep and primal-that—vibrates down to my bones.

I blink, and I'm standing outside the doors to the bathhouse.

"Go ahead. Go inside." The voice urges me forward.

"Last time I was in here, a shadowrithe tried to kill me. How stupid do you think I am?" I reach for the door anyway, tugging it open. I am very aware of my lack of options here.

Inside, steam billows through the air, creating a thick fog that makes it harder to see than usual. The dim purple lights glow beneath it. It's eerie.

"Well, hello, darling." Elion is standing in the center of the bath. "I was wondering when you would come visit me in a dream. I was starting to feel very left out."

"You know I don't have a choice." I fold my arms over my chest.

For a moment, the silence stretches on in every direction.

"Come in." He holds his hand out to me, stepping closer.

Tugging my clothes down my shoulders, I let them pool at my feet before stepping into the water. It's warm and smells like soft florals.

I pause in the ankle-deep water.

"I'm lonely over here." His smile is almost enough to coax me forward.

"Is the person controlling this watching everything? If we were to do something, would they be watching?"

"Do something?" He runs his tongue over his lip.

"Elion, you know what I mean." I huff. Calais is right about him, nothing is ever serious.

"Truthfully, I don't know how it works." He takes a step forward, beads of water running down his chest. "It's thrilling, isn't it? The thought of being watched."

"I'm not usually an exhibitionist."

"That's a shame."

Chewing the inside of my cheek, I consider my options.

"Why would he bring me here?" I take another step into the water.

"He usually brings me somewhere to show me something. The dreams might be unpleasant, but they're always informative."

"How do you know it's a 'he?' It could be a woman." He quirks his brow.

"I've heard his voice."

This seems to pique his interest. "Maybe he sent you here to see how we react—to watch what we do. Maybe he suspects us."

"Then perhaps you should stay on that side of the bath." I point to the far end as I wade into the water.

"Perhaps not." He steps closer, just an arm's length away.

I don't like this game. I have no control over anything. Whoever is controlling this, the puppet master with the strings might yank me away at any moment.

"You have no idea the things I dream of." His hand dips down into the water, and I know exactly what he's doing.

"Tell me." The distinct thump of my heartbeat between my legs is making it impossible to think of anything else.

His arm moves, the motion making me clench. He lets out a shaky breath. "I want to spread you open. To watch you writhe and shake around me. I want to taste your blood."

The deep rasp in his voice sends a shiver down my spine.

"Come here, darling. Touch me." He takes another step forward, the water settling around his hips. The head of his swollen cock comes up above the water as he strokes it. "End my misery, wrap your hand around it."

Stepping forward, I reach out desperately. I'll do anything he wants.

As soon as we touch, I'm jolted awake. It's not soft or pleasant. I'm completely disoriented and dizzy. Light is streaming in through my window, and somehow that short encounter lasted all night. I don't feel rested at all. My neck aches, my shoulders are stiff, and a tired, achy feeling has settled behind my eyes.

I'm so worked up. I have no idea what time it is or how long I was there, but my body is still in the same state. I'm achy and fluttering, my heart hammering in my chest.

A patterned knock at the door pulls me out of my spinning state. "Yes?"

Elion, with a big, stupid smirk on his face, peeks his head inside. "Breakfast?"

"What the hell was that? That was worse than any of them. I feel like he jumbled my brain that time." I hold my head in my hands. I feel hungover.

"Food will help." He holds his hand out. "I'm not dizzy, but I was definitely left wanting." He adjusts his pants.

I bite my tongue, forcing back the urge to say something snarky. He left of his own accord, at least the first time. That's on him.

The mood in the dining room is somber. Calais looks like she wants to punch something or someone, and Cannan hasn't moved. His eyes are dark, unreadable. He's sitting, slouching, or at least as close as he can come to slouching. One hand on his chin with a deep frown etched into his features.

Elion is the only one acting normal, but that seems out of place, too. He should be solemn and stoic.

"Yesterday was a mistake." Canaan's voice is low. "We are going to The Falls tomorrow. We will be able to keep you safe there." He looks at me, a stern authority in his eyes.

"Wh–" Whatever I was about to say turns into a squeak in my throat as Elion runs his hand up my thigh, stopping just short of actually being inside of me.

I try to cover it with a cough.

"You'll love The Falls." Elion strokes my skin with his pinky.

"W-What is it?" I stutter. Damn him.

Shifting in my seat, I start to move to adjust and cross my legs, but he grips my thigh hard, pinning it down and stopping me.

"It's a stronghold fortress in the mountains." Canaan narrows his eyes slightly, and I wonder if he knows what's happening beneath the table.

As subtly as I can manage, I reach down, grabbing his hand to keep it still. Pressing my thighs together, I hope to at least make it harder for him, but it's more like I've trapped his hand there.

"I wanted to say..." He clears his throat, his eyes meeting mine. "I want to apologize. I know you want to help find your friend, but I

should never have allowed you to be in that position. I take full responsibility."

"No." I feel small in front of him—vulnerable and weak. "I wanted
to help! I still want to help! Don't blame yourself. I could—"

"I am the king." His voice is soft but steady. The weighty authority
makes me shut my mouth. "The fault lies with me alone."

"If you think of some way that I can help, please don't hesitate. I'll
do it, no questions asked."

"I believe that." His lips tug, and for a split second, he actually looks
like he might smile. "We will leave..."

He's still talking, telling me the plans, including me, but I can't
fucking hear him. My heart thumping in my chest and panic coursing
through me are drowning out the sound of his voice. His fingers are as
close to being inside of me without actually entering my body. I can
barely breathe. This is information that I want to know.

Reaching over, I rub my hand up his thigh softly before pinching him
as hard as I possibly can. He's going to make me moan. I'm so frustrated,
but it feels amazing. In any other setting, I would be putty in his hands.

He withdraws his fingers, but only enough for me to be able to turn
my attention back to Canaan.

"I'll send for you." He smiles.

Great, I missed the whole thing.

"Thank you." I try to smile, but I feel his hand move, and it makes
me look like I'm malfunctioning. I wish I could turn and punch him in
the face right now, but that would definitely draw too much attention.

"Let's go get you ready to go, shall we, darling?" He stands, finally
releasing me.

My legs wobble as I rush after him. As soon as we're in the hallway, I
open my mouth to send a few expletives his way. He takes the opportunity to kiss me.

He grabs me so fast, my head spins.

"You are such an asshole," I moan into his mouth. "What is wrong
with you?"

"I couldn't help myself." He grins. "My cock is aching." He grinds it
against me before lifting me up. "I've been holding myself back. Once

we cross that line, we can't undo it. I'll be insatiable for you. I'll crave you. I'll be consumed by the thought of you." His voice gets lower and raspier with each word.

"Elion." Wrapping my legs around his waist, I just give in, letting him do what he wants. I'm so hot, and the thump between my legs is unbearable now. "No more teasing!"

A gust of wind blows around us, and I open my eyes.

We're in the air, moving quickly through the hallways.

"I'm taking you back to the bathhouse, and this time, we won't be leaving until I've felt you come on my cock."

TWENTY

We crash through the doors of the bathhouse, and he rips my clothes off.

"I can't bear it for another second." His hands roam my body. "Say yes. Please. I'll beg on my knees if I have to."

"Funny, I was thinking the same thing." I run my hands through his hair.

He groans deep in his throat before rubbing himself against my stomach. "I need you."

Hearing those words in his raspy, desperate voice makes my already frenzied movements all the more frantic.

"Have me then, Elion. I'm not the one who keeps walking away." I'm playing my hand here, but I can't take it anymore.

Something about him makes me feel like a storm—powerful and all-consuming; it's the primal drive for sex bumped up to levels I've never experienced before.

Each passing second is like a slow, gnawing suffocation. I hold onto him, desperate to make him stay this time. I don't understand these moments, how they come on so quickly.

"I'm trying to do the right thing here." He groans. "You're making it so hard for me."

Guilt courses through me. I don't know this world. I'm not used to their balance of power and how they do things. It feels very strange. We're adults, and we both want this.

"Will you be in trouble if someone finds out?" I pull back enough to look at his face.

"Not enough trouble to stop." His mischievous smile makes my knees wobble. His devil-may-care attitude irritates me sometimes, but then... in moments like this... I'm so drawn to it.

Deep in my chest, in a part of me that I'm trying desperately to ignore, I'm afraid. I've had casual sex—the odd one-night stand or friends-with-benefits situation. This doesn't feel like that. Letting Elion inside of me feels like something serious.

I don't want to think right now. I want to shut off my brain and enjoy myself, to revel in the feeling of his skin. But I have to go into this with my eyes wide open. This isn't a low-stakes game.

"Kiah," he kisses the corner of my lips. "What's going on in that head of yours?"

"I don't know. I'm kind of freaking out."

"Why?" He kisses my temple this time, letting his lips graze my skin.

"I don't want to seem crazy."

"That ship has sailed, love. You volunteered to be used as bait for Shadowrithes. You're crazy." His voice is gentle and teasing. He's obviously not feeling any of the pressure that I am.

"If we do this, I'm worried about what happens after, that's all." I can't believe I just spoke those words. If we stop again, I'm going to combust. My heart will stop. I'll lose the last brain cell clinging on for dear life in my head. But I have to say it. I can't go through with this while holding my breath about the future. "I know I sound like—"

"You don't sound like anything. It's reasonable to wonder. If we do this, we have to understand that while I care for you, we can't have more than this. A beautiful night together, allowing ourselves to find comfort and pleasure together. I'm not allowed more than that with you, even if I want it. The choice is yours, darling. We can stop right now, and there will be nothing lost between us. I will understand. But if we continue, I will give you everything, just for tonight."

The spark that ignited between us is just an ember now. The energy is still there, swirling around us, but we're levelheaded. It eases my mind to know that we're making this decision responsibly and not in a lust-fueled haze.

Carefully, I unbutton his shirt, taking every opportunity to let my fingers touch his chest. Holding eye contact, I undo his pants and drop them at his ankles.

He doesn't move, perfectly still and waiting, he lets me lead the way.

Taking his hand, I wade into the water.

How the fuck am I supposed to walk away from that? He'll give me everything for tonight? In sixty years, when this is all a distant memory, and I'm sitting on my porch in a creaking rocking chair with Cheyenne knitting beside me, I'll look back on this. I'm seizing the moment. This is an opportunity of a lifetime.

"If it's my choice, I think I'll grab it with both hands, just for tonight."

His lips twitch as he lifts me up, wrapping my legs around his waist. Our wet, naked bodies pressing together in all of the right places.

All of the doubts melt away.

"I'm desperate for you." He whimpers, and I almost lose my mind. If he does that again, I'll be reduced to nothing but a ball of melted goo. Big and powerful, I never knew how sexy it could be to hear him plead.

Reaching down between us, I grip him in my hand. He's solid. Thick and long, perfect. "I'm impressed." I give it a squeeze, and his chest tenses.

"Thanks," he chuckles, but I don't miss the way it falters slightly.

"So, I'm thinking maybe we skip the foreplay. I don't know about you, but I'm ready." I slide my hand down and back up.

Really, I'm afraid that if we don't get to it, we'll be interrupted or he will decide it's not worth pursuing. I don't care if I come across as completely desperate.

"Eager, love?" He slams his mouth to mine. "Me too. I just can't decide how I want you. Do I want to watch your face as I fill you or the way you bend over?"

"Oh god." A shiver runs up my spine. "I don't care how you do it."

He hums, rolling his neck when I pump my fist again. "I think I want to see that pretty face." He slips his arms under my thighs, hooking his elbow beneath my knees so I'm forced to release my grip on him. "Ready, darling?"

"Yes." I barely get the word out before he's lifting me up just enough to press himself inside of me. With my legs spread wide, I'm defenseless against his movements. I can't do anything but let him press in.

With a slow but deliberate stroke, he's in to the hilt.

It's a shock to the system. I'm completely overwhelmed.

The purple light in the room, the warm water, and the soft smell in the air make everything too stimulating. Pinching my eyes closed, I try to focus on remembering to take a breath.

"Look at me, Kiah." His voice wavers as he slides out, then back in.

Forcing my eyes open, the rest of the world fades when I look at him. Insignificance. There isn't anything else.

"There she is," he growls, his voice a deep, primal rumble. His pace quickens, each movement of his hips deliberate and steady. "I forgot how small—how fragile—humans are."

His eyes are endless pools of deep blue, piercing and wild. There's a flicker of something unspoken there—hunger, possession... both—making it impossible to look away. My heart pounds against my ribs.

The water sloshes around us as he moves in a perfectly timed rhythm. Each drag of his hips pushes me toward a rapidly approaching cliff. I know I'll soar, free-falling into the unknown. It will be everything.

Each deliberate drive of his hips sends a shudder rippling through me, like the surface of the pool around us. The world blurs, and all that exists is him—his strength, his heat, the way his body seems perfectly attuned to mine.

My breath hitches as he presses deeper, his movements both tender and relentless, coaxing my body to heights I hadn't known existed. It's more than pleasure—it's a claiming, a pulling apart of all the careful walls I've built around myself.

And god, it feels good. Too good.

Even as it's happening, right in the thick of the moment, I know that this is the kind of sex a girl could easily get addicted to.

Is it him, or do all Fae do it like this?

It's raw and primal. The sounds he makes have my head drowning in lust. My whole body is reaching for him.

I know I'm on the edge, teetering on the brink of something I can't control. The way his body moves against mine—hard, focused, like I'm the only thing that matters—makes me feel like I'm weightless and untethered, yet somehow more grounded than I've ever been.

I've never felt like this before. With anyone. My high school boyfriends, the college frat guys—they were clumsy—all eager hands and half-hearted efforts. Nothing like this. Nothing like him. He isn't some fumbling jock that doesn't know what he's doing.

This isn't just sex. He isn't just chasing some pleasure, using me to fulfill a need.

"Elion!" I choke, hardly able to speak over the emotions in my throat.

"I've got you," he locks eyes with me, the intensity in them leaving me breathless.

I can only nod.

"It's so good, love. So good." He scrapes his teeth against my cheek before leaving a trail of sloppy kisses down to my neck. "I want to bite you. Just a taste. One drop would be enough."

I almost tell him to do it. Instead, I bite the inside of my cheek. I can't cross that line.

My head falls back, the pressure pushing a moan up my throat as I tighten around him, crashing.

"That's it." He coaxes, moving me through the single best experience of my life. It's not just my body—he's fucking my soul—on another plane of existence, our consciences are wound together.

Digging my nails into his shoulders, I hold on for dear life.

When he whimpers my name, I jerk my eyes open and watch him, pleasure etched into his features, his mouth slack—he's beautiful.

His muscles go rigid beneath his skin, and his wings flex, the water lapping at our skin as he quietly finds release. I was expecting something loud, profane, something dirty, but it wasn't at all.

His eyes open, and he looks almost shy. His expression mirrors what I'm feeling inside, a timid nervousness. What happens now?

"Maybe we can make this a two-time deal." He smiles, his arrogance coming back as his breath evens out.

A stupid smile spread across my cheeks, the kind you can't stop. "Maybe." Definitely.

TWENTY-ONE

I had sex with a winged fairy prince last night. My mind is scattered in a thousand different directions.

On one hand, I'm fucking fantastic. I'm a goddess of reckless decision-making. But on the other hand, I'm spiraling into utter chaos. I swear, everyone knows. It's like I've been branded, the glow of some ethereal scarlet letter pulsing beneath my skin, visible to anyone who looks too closely.

And right now, the person doing the looking is Canaan.

This is the strangest, most awkward situation I've ever been in. I keep starting to ask him how long it takes to get to The Falls. Not knowing makes it seem so much longer. I wish Elion were here. He would be unserious and cut through the tension.

We're alone in his boat, the black glass frame cutting through the cold water. Behind us, Calais floats in her own boat, blissfully unaware —or at least that's what I'm telling myself. She probably knows too.

I have glowing neon arrows pointing down at me from the sky— big, loud, shiny, sex arrows.

He hasn't said a single word since he told me to get in his boat. He didn't ask. He didn't explain. He just... ordered. His voice low, curt, a command. He's never been the chatty type—not one to joke to break the tension. But this feels particularly bad.

He knows.

I try to play it cool, keeping my hands in my lap, my expression neutral, and my breathing steady. I'm going for calm and collected, like nothing in the world could possibly be bothering me. I'm failing.

And then it happens. Again.

Elion's body flashes in my mind in a vivid and pornographic flood of images. His broad chest, his wings, his hands—his hands. My cheeks burn, and I'm sure I'm bright red. I squeeze my eyes shut for a moment, desperate to wrestle the memory back into the shadows where it belongs.

I can't shake the idea that he will know what I'm thinking about just by looking at me.

Can the Shadowrithes control my mind when I'm awake? Why can't I stop thinking about it?

I should be able to control this.

I take a deep breath, willing myself to focus on the ripples in the water, the quiet rustle of leaves as the breeze blows through the tree-lined shores—anything but the memory of Elion or the crushing weight of Canaan's silence.

But it doesn't help.

Because when I close my eyes again, Elion's naked body is still there. And I don't know if I'll ever be able to make it leave.

"We're splitting up."

"Huh?" I jerk around to look at him.

"There is a fork in the river up ahead. They reconnect, but we're splitting up." His voice is harsh and angry.

He definitely knows.

Looking back over my shoulder, I watch as Calais maneuvers her boat to follow the other path.

"We are taking the more difficult path." He stares straight ahead. "The Shadowrithes have been a step ahead of us, they will likely know that we are there, but it will be harder to attack."

"Will Calais be alright alone?"

"She will." He sounds absolutely sure. She disappears behind a wall of trees, and that's the end of that.

The water starts to move faster. It's a palpable shift in the current—choppy and rough. In the distance, mountains rise up against the horizon.

"Oh my god." I look forward to what we're approaching. On either side of a narrow waterway carved through a stone canyon are two fairy statues. 'Statue' feels wrong; they're monuments. They're impossibly tall—at least as tall as the tallest buildings I've ever seen.

The wings are so realistic, open wide and proud. I half expect them to fly away.

It's eerily otherworldly. Sometimes I forget, despite everything, that I'm not at home. Places like this zap me back to reality quickly. It's like we're at the bottom of the Grand Canyon. Dark gray slabs of rock wall us in on either side. Looking up, the fortress of stone goes up for so long it melts into the sky.

"How much longer?" I feel like a child whining, 'Are we there yet?' from the backseat. Jagged rocks surround us on all sides, and the once pleasant breeze is now much colder. He is standing up now, his eyes constantly moving over the water, almost like he's expecting something.

He turns, like he's about to answer me. But his jaw clenches shut instead. I don't have time to process what's happening when he lunges forward, grabbing me.

I gasp, but the sound is smothered by his hand clamping down over my mouth. Before I can thrash, he spins me, pinning my back against his chest. His breath is hot against my ear, a sharp whisper slicing through my panic.

"Quiet. Look." His other hand points toward the water.

Every instinct in me screams to struggle, but then I see it. My breath hitches in my throat, and I freeze.

What the fuck is that?

It glides just beneath the surface, long and serpentine, but not—its movements like water itself. Longer than my body and thick as a tree trunk, it weaves through the current with predatory grace, leaving behind a murky red trail. Is that blood?

The faint ripple of its motion reveals tendrils, dozens of them, slithering like the arms of an octopus in all directions. They twist and flex, brushing against rocks and reeds with eerie precision.

I press back into him without thinking, desperate to put even a sliver more space between me and that thing.

"Shh, it's a marrow serpent. Stay still," he whispers before releasing my face from his closed grip. "They can bite clean through bone. They don't have eyes, but they can hear."

I nod, closing my mouth tightly.

His arm tightens, the weight of his warning heavy. "Steady. Don't move."

As if hearing its name, one of the creature's tendrils comes up out of the water, the end opening up like a blooming flower. Inside, there are at least twenty long, thick barbs. The movement sends a fresh wave of crimson through the water, and I swear it shifts, tilting its head toward us.

Every nerve in my body screams to flee, but his whispered command roots me in place.

"Don't even blink." He whispers so quietly, I barely catch the words.

Pinching my eyes closed, I pretend I didn't hear the name of it. Marrow? Why would they call it that unless it eats bone?

He moves slowly, leaving me here alone. My eyes fly open to find him.

The boat jerks, fighting against him as he tries to keep up from crashing into the rocks. Turning as slowly as I can, I watch the monster tracking us. It's far enough away that I think we might be able to get away.

And then, out of nowhere and for absolutely no reason, one of the long arms shoots out of the water like a whip. The boat jerks, and I feel Canaan's arm around me, yanking me up. He throws me forward, pushing me out of the way.

I stay low, ducking under the side of the boat, hoping that's enough cover.

When I look up, there is blood everywhere. One of the long tendrils is wrapped around Canaan's arm several times. He pulls upward, relying on his wings to lift him up to create enough slack that he can slice through the tendril in one clean cut.

I didn't even know he had a knife.

Blood sprays everywhere, into the water, the boat, all over me. He unwraps the tendril, revealing torn skin beneath. He doesn't even flinch as he yanks the barbs out of his arm.

He grabs me and lifts me out of the boat to a thin cliff on the wall face. I have to stand with my back pressed to the rock. It's thinner than the length of my feet, even with my heels pressed to the wall, my toes hang off the end.

"Stay here." He gives me a stern look.

It's not like I can actually go anywhere.

His arm is mangled and bloody, and I can't help but look at the torn flesh. That was coming for me, and he saved me from it.

With nothing but a knife, he cuts through a few more barbed tendrils before grabbing me. He shoots through the sky, bringing me up so high we actually break into the open sky, above the canyon. It looks like it's covered in a white blanket. It's a layer of fog above the rocks.

He grunts and drops onto the edge of the cliff. "I'll be able to bring you part of the way, but my wings can't carry both of us all the way to the Falls." He looks ashamed.

"Hey, it's ok." I instinctively step toward him. He looks very human suddenly.

"No, I should be able to do that." He snaps, an angry edge in his voice. "Let's walk until we need to fly. I really hoped we could make it all the way by water."

Following him as quickly and quietly as I can, I keep my questions in.

A trail of blood follows behind him, dripping from his arm onto the gray slab beneath us.

We're surrounded by thick fog on all sides. I can barely see my own hand if I stretch my arm out.

After at least an hour, he stops, turning around to face me. "It might not have seemed like it, but the water was safer."

The timing of this seems suspicious. The hairs on the back of my neck stand up, and I step closer to him.

"Stay behind me." His sharp eyes hold mine.

"I will."

"Listen, Kiah," he sighs. "You're going to hear things that aren't real. Do you understand? Don't move from behind me. Promise me."

I open my mouth to answer him, but there is a screech from somewhere in the fog.

Reaching out, I grab the back of his shirt, steadying myself behind him.

Something moves out of the haze. It walks like a zombie, slow and unnatural. A long, black cloak is covering its body with a hood over its head.

"Canaan." It taunts. "Give me the human."

As the words hang above us, a pained cry echoes around us. "Canaan! Help me!" Calais screams. The shrill sound makes my stomach heave.

He doesn't move, not even a twitch.

"We won't be banished again, this time, we're stronger!" The man yells before pulling a jagged-looking knife from his cloak. It's dripping blood, and my heart leaps up to my throat. His face is something out of a nightmare. There is no skin on his face, just bone and muscle.

He lifts the knife up and licks a long strip down the black blade. He's part shadow, not fully formed into a person yet.

"Canaan! Help me!" Calais' voice rings out again, rushed and desperate.

Canaan's muscles flex. I watch his spine stiffen and his posture change. Apparently, this is getting to him.

"Aren't you going to help your sister, your majesty? Or do you only care about your seat on the throne?" His words drip with venom, each syllable a calculated strike. He barks out a laugh, cruel and hollow, the kind that echoes in nightmares.

Just as Canaan takes a step forward, another voice calls out of the misty fog. A soft voice that brings me to my knees.

"Kiah! Kiah! Help me!"

It's Cheyenne.

The sound of her scream drives a spike through my chest, and my knees buckle beneath me. Her voice is raw and full of pain.

Every muscle in my body locks, my instincts screaming to move, to run toward her—to help her. But I promised.

He warned me this would happen. He said I'd hear things that weren't real.

Still, doubt slithers in. What if he's wrong? What if it is her?

I clap my hands over my ears, squeezing my eyes shut to force the sound out. "I can't," I whisper to myself, rocking slightly, my voice shaking. "I can't."

It feels eternal, but I won't look up, I won't let myself be pulled away. He said I would hear things that aren't real. I have to believe that it's not her. If it is, I won't ever forgive myself for not helping her—for not at least trying.

A wet hand grabs my arm, and I scream, trying to yank it away.

"Kiah, it's me." Canaan lifts me effortlessly from the ground.

I yelp and stumble back at the sight of him. He's bathed in blood. His hair is matted with it. It's streaked across his face and soaked into his clothes.

"Most of it isn't mine. Let's go." He grabs me and bolts up into the sky. "I can't risk it; we have to get to The Falls." His massive wings cut through the air with graceful ease, but I can't help but think about what he said earlier.

He flies over the canyon until it abruptly ends. Two rivers flow out toward a thick forest where they become one.

The view is incredible, but I can't stop looking at his face. The pain etched between his brow and in each breath he takes frightens me. I imagine us falling out of the sky.

"Canaan," I start, my voice trembling, but he doesn't look at me. I don't even know what to say, but I have to try.

"There." He grunts, pointing with one blood-covered hand.

I follow his gaze to a mountain rising in the distance.

"Up at the top."

His voice is raw, each word full of urgency and pain. And for the first time, I notice the slight tremor in his hands.

TWENTY-TWO

Halfway up the mountain, he is forced to drop down onto a road that splits through the trees. Pain is etched into his face, and I can feel it in his chest when he takes a breath.

"Here," I shuffle beside him, lifting his arm so that he can put it around my shoulder and use me for support. He's going to crush me, but I have to try.

"What are you doing?" His expression is a mixture of shock and... disgust?

"I'm trying to help you. Lean on me. You carried me for such a long way, and you're still losing blood." I look at the shredded skin on his arm, trying not to grimace.

It looks bad. Gnarly. Hamburger meat.

"I can manage." He rolls his shoulders back.

"Don't be prideful!" I blurt out before I have time to think better of it.

"Prideful?" His brow lifts. "I am the king of this realm. I don't need to lean on a human woman to make it up the mountain."

"Fine." I step away from him and cross my arms over my chest.

"Canaan?" Calais yells from behind us, her wings picking her up over the trail as I turn around. She slams into him, hugging him tightly. "You're injured! What happened? I waited at the merge!" She's showing more emotion now than I've ever seen. Her love for him pours from her; it's in everything: the tremble in her voice, her hands that roam over his face and arms looking for injuries, her glossy eyes. "A Marrow Serpent?" She looks over his ripped-open skin.

"We had the pleasure of meeting a Marrow Serpent and a Shadowrithe." His lips spread into a thin, tight smile.

"Where?" Her eyes dart back, searching the path behind us for enemies.

"On the ridge. He was almost fully formed." He shakes his head.

"We're almost there." She stands taller, gesturing to me with an authoritative edge in her voice. "Hurry."

I'm as physically exhausted as I am mentally, but I keep running, each step an act of sheer will. My legs ache, my lungs burn, and my mind races with doubts that threaten to drown me. The Falls—they're supposed to be safe. But how can anywhere be safe in a world that feels like it's unraveling? I don't have the luxury of hesitation. Trusting them feels like stepping off a ledge into darkness, but what choice do I have?

A few steps behind Canaan, I watch the blood steadily drip from his arm into the gravelly dirt.

Each droplet makes my tension grow. I can't shake the feeling that I should do something. I just don't know what.

He hasn't spoken in so long. I wonder if he's saving his energy.

I focus on his movements, searching for signs of struggle, but the sound of my own ragged breathing drowns out everything else.

"There," he says abruptly, his voice hoarse but steady. His hand lifts to point at a bridge in the distance.

My gaze follows, and my breath catches. The mountain opens up before us, a jagged cliff cutting through it. A wide canyon stretches out, waterfalls slipping over the sides and falling forever, endlessly, to the unseen ground below. In the heart of it all, a massive rock formation rises from the misty fog with a castle built on it.

For a moment, the sight is almost beautiful—otherworldly. But the longer I stare, the more frightening it becomes. There's only one bridge, narrow and precarious, spanning the distance from each point of solid ground. One way in, one way out.

I don't want to cross that.

Canaan doesn't hesitate, his focus locked on the bridge as if it's the only thing tethering him to the world. I hesitate, my feet faltering. "Are you sure it's safe?"

He glances back at me, his expression unreadable, but his eyes burn with a quiet determination. "No," he says simply, turning back to the path ahead.

The unspoken weight of his answer settles over me. Safe or not, this is where we're going. There's no turning back now.

But what did he mean by 'no?' Not, no, as in, no, it's not safe. Surely, he meant it some other way.

Shiny black glass and a shimmering metal hang in the air, waiting.

Canaan steps first, then me, with Calais falling in behind us.

"It feels sturdy." I whisper, and Canaan lets out a huff of air.

"The construction of the bridge is not where my concerns lie." He looks back over his shoulder.

"Great. Wonderful." I grip the thin metal rods that someone thought were enough to make a handrail.

With each step I find myself wishing more and more for Elion. I just know he would fix this somehow. He would put me at ease.

But he's not here.

One foot in front of the other, I stare at Canaan's back. Don't look down. Don't look outward. Just stare at the wings. One step, then another until we make it to the other side.

"Mordious!" Canaan calls out, his voice suddenly stronger.

"Canaan." A man's voice cuts through the air.

Peeking around his body, I see a large, blond fairy with huge black wings waiting at the end of the bridge.

"It appears you had a rough journey, brother!" The blond one claps his hands around Canaan.

"You could say that." He groans. "Bring her up to her room." He gestures to me.

He looks surprised, like he didn't notice I was even here. "Pardon my rudeness, miss." He offers me his hand. "I forgot how small humans are!"

Taking his hand, I watch as Canaan and Calais leave without looking back.

"I'm Mordious. The keeper of The Falls. Welcome." He smiles and gently tugs me in the opposite direction from the entrance they used.

"Is this still Noctyra?"

"No." He smiles but doesn't offer any other details.

Just like everything else here, the castle is incredible. It looks older, more ancient, the modern touches from the city are notably missing here. There is the same signature black glass, but there is also wood.

"I've been briefed on your situation. You're safe here. I can assure you that no one has breached the perimeter, and if they tried, I would know." He looks both proud and certain.

"Thank you." He isn't as mischievous or outwardly flirty, but he reminds me of Elion. There is a kindness below the surface.

"I'll bring you to your guest room, you can change and rest, then I'll come get you for dinner. There are robes on the bed for you, but they might not fit." His voice is calm as he steps away from me and begins walking down a long, dimly lit hallway. The flickering light of the sconces casts distorted shadows on the walls, making the narrow corridor feel longer and more oppressive than it probably is.

I can't help but notice how isolated I feel here. The stone walls seem to swallow every sound, and my footsteps are silent against the cold, smooth floor. This place feels like a tomb. I hope he's right about no one being able to sneak in here. If they did, I'm a goner. There's no way anyone would hear me screaming for help down here. I'm a million miles away, in the dark and around a corner.

"Canaan is sleeping in the room across the hall from yours. If you need anything at all, he is there." He reaches for the brass handle of a large metal door, pushing it open with an effortless motion.

Ask Canaan? I don't think so. I'll take my chances with the shadow demons.

When I'm finally alone, I let out a heavy breath and lean against the door. The room is beautiful. The bed looks like something out of a medieval fairytale. It's enormous, a dark wooden four-poster with intricately carved posts that seem to stretch toward the ceiling sits in the center of the room, covered in thick, soft-looking blankets. There is one window with thick, dark curtains that face directly into the waterfalls.

"Wow." I lean against the cool glass, looking down at the rushing stream falling into the abyss. The sound is muffled through the glass, but the roar of rushing water is soothing. Well, it would be if all of my experiences with water in this place hadn't been so negative.

There is also a bathroom here. Not a communal bathhouse but a private bathroom.

I'm both scared and excited.

What if a Shadowrithe comes out of the ornate stone faucets? But then again—a private bathroom. That is a luxury.

Pushing the thought away, I strip out of my blood- and sweat-soaked clothes.

The water feels like magic, which is slightly off-putting. Everything feels like a trick here. When I get home, if I ever do, I'm going to have some major trust issues.

The water feels too good. Too warm. That probably means that something is inside of my mind making me feel this way.

Paranoia ruins the experience. I can't shake it, so I finish quickly without enjoying it at all.

Mordious was right about the robes. They are too big. But they're soft and clean. Securing the center with a braided leather belt, I find myself torn between two equally disruptive thoughts.

How did they mimic Cheyenne's voice so perfectly? The thought makes my stomach roll.

Then, Elion. Always back to Elion.

I wonder where he is and what he's doing. I shouldn't, but I can't help it.

Standing at the window, I search the streaming water for things that seem out of place. From the corner of my eye, there is a flash of movement.

Jerking toward it, I find my little shadow friend. "Hey! I thought you abandoned me! Well, technically, you did." I feel slightly ridiculous.

It approaches slowly, with its shadowy head dropped down and its little shoulders slumped.

"It's alright. Bygones." I shrug. "I probably would have done the same."

It perks up a bit, coming to stand beside me.

"What are you doing here?"

Obviously, it doesn't answer.

"What do you think of this place? Are we safe here?" I'm asking myself more than the shadow.

Twenty-Three

No one speaks.

I should be used to this by now. But the silence is impossible to get used to.

The flickering light from the fireplace casts shadows on the floor. All shadows feel like bad news now.

Tapestries hang from the high ceilings, long-woven histories that don't brighten the place up at all.

The smell of roasted meats and bread fills the air, but it's doing nothing to ease the tension gnawing at my stomach. Bowls of fruit, big, bright, shiny pieces of fruit that smell sweet even from a distance, fill the table, but I don't want any.

This place feels oppressive.

A beautiful gilded prison.

Sitting at the long, oak table, my fingers tracing the rim of my glass absently.

Canaan was across from me, his sharp eyes scanning the shadows of the room, his posture stiff. He hasn't said a single word. His eyes look far away, like his mind is elsewhere.

Calais is picking at her food with an almost mechanical precision. I've been watching her, she hasn't taken a bite yet.

And then there was Mordious. He isn't talking, but he is the polar opposite of the others. His attitude is light as he shovels food onto his plate, then into his mouth.

He's on his third plate.

"Is the food to your liking?" He finally breaks the silence, his voice soft.

Canaan doesn't answer immediately. Instead, he took a long, slow sip from his glass, eyes drifting over the table like he was trying to see through each of us.

Calais clears her throat and nods, even though she still hasn't eaten anything.

I shifted uncomfortably in my seat. "It's great."

I'm trying to stare at Canaan inconspicuously, but I'm too nervous.

The blood is gone—the bandage on his hand is the only evidence that he was injured at all.

He looks up, catching me staring. His gaze is direct, unflinching. I meet it, but only for a second before looking away.

"Our departure was done in secret." He's still looking at me, I can feel it. "Elion is watching the borders for activity. The rithe we met yesterday may have just been standing watch there, or there is a leak among my ranks."

"What?" I jerk my eyes to look at him.

"There must be." Calais finally speaks. Her voice bites with rage. "You really believe that there was a Shadowrithe just standing watch there?"

"It is possible. They would know that it is the only road leading here. They could be watching for our retreat. If there is a leak, I would expect more than just one." He takes another sip from his glass. Notably, he's not eating either, just drinking.

Calais lets out an angry laugh before gulping down the contents of her glass. "Is it you?" Her eyes shoot daggers in my direction.

I choke, cupping my hand over my mouth to muffle the sound.

"Calais." He growls.

"Think about it! As soon as she arrived, everything fell apart. She is sent here as a distraction. We're focused on the enemy at the gates, meanwhile, we've let them in to eat at our table!" She slams her fist down on the table.

"I'm not a Trojan horse, I promise! I'm—"

"Silence!" Canaan booms. He stands, his wings flexing as his chair scrapes loudly against the ground. "I don't want to hear one more word."

"Exactly! You won't hear it! When we're all—"

Whatever she was about to say is cut off by him shooting across the table. He grabs her by the arms and drops to the ground, his footsteps pounding against the stone as he drags her out of the hall.

"Well, then." Mordious laughs.

"I appreciate the meal, but I think I'm going to head back to my room, if you don't mind." I can't eat.

"Of course!" He smiles as he loads his plate full a fourth time. "Do you remember the way back?"

"Yes." I'm almost sure I do. "I'll find it."

Slipping into the hallway, I pause to listen for the sounds of a fight, but there are none.

The hallway stretches endlessly before me, a masterpiece of shadow and light. The walls, made of black glass, shimmer slightly, and enchanted lanterns hang from intricate iron sconces. Their pale, flickering light casts distorted patterns that dance like restless spirits—maybe they are. Between the glass panels, dark wooden beams like ribs support the building, their surfaces carved with twisting vines and strange runes.

A cold draft blows through the hallway, carrying with it the faint, sweet smell of night-blooming flowers from the gardens. The high, vaulted ceiling above me disappears into shadows, and somewhere in the distance, the soft creak of settling wood breaks the quiet, making my heart jolt.

The walk feels much longer now. Alone, each step I take seems to amplify the eerie stillness around me. My fingertips trail along the cool, glassy surface of the walls, tracing the grooves and etchings. A low archway leads to an adjoining corridor, its black wood frame adorned with delicate carvings of faerie wings and thorny roses. I glance over my shoulder, half-expecting to see someone—or something—following. But there's nothing.

A massive stained-glass window looms ahead, depicting a battle between shadowy figures and faerie warriors. I tried to stop and look before, but Mordious was hungry, so I didn't dawdle.

The scene is beautiful and haunting. The moonlight seeps through, painting the floor in hues of indigo and red.

By the time I reach my room, I'm weighed down with the dull ache of loneliness. Stopping at my door, I listen, waiting for something.

Canaan's door is closed, and the silence around me is so heavy, it makes me think he's not inside.

My shoulders slump. I know he wouldn't have wanted to sit and chat, but I would probably try anyway.

Calais absolutely hates me. I never thought we were about to be best friends, but now I'm sure she would squash me like a bug if she could.

Sighing, I step into my room, and a gasp escapes before I can stop it.

"What took you so long?" Elion grabs me, pushing me against the door. "How is it possible that I arrived, spoke to Mordious, and made it to your room before you were able to get here?"

"I'm a slow walker." I wrap my arms around his waist and press my face into his shirt. He feels like something I can anchor myself to right now.

"I don't have long." He lifts me so that our faces are level. "I'm supposed to be meeting with Canaan."

"How long?" After the day I've had, I'm desperate to spend a few minutes wrapped in his arms while he uses that tongue to make me forget everything.

"I'll make each second count." He grins as he carries me to the bed. "I've been thinking about this all day."

"Me too." I'm already panting as he yanks the bottom of my robe open.

"What have you been thinking about, specifically?" He dips down, the warmth of his breath hitting my thighs.

I'm flustered.

"You. I've been thinking about your body. Your hands..."

"My hands?" He nibbles my inner thigh.

"Yes." I arch toward him. I've gone from zero to one hundred in two seconds flat. He only has a few minutes, I intend to put them to good use. "And your wings."

He hums, "What about my wings?"

"Elion!" I fist the sheets in my hands as he nips the other thigh.

"Tell me." He presses a kiss to my clit.

"I like them, the way they look while you fuck me!" I gasp as he finally licks me, a long, firm strip all the way through.

He chuckles and moves his mouth to where he can inflict the most damage. With the tip of his tongue, he paints a masterpiece between my legs. Long strokes, short and fast, slow and steady. I'm helpless against it. I can only hold on for dear life and let him do what he wants with me.

"Quite," the low rasp in his turned-on voice makes everything more intense. "Roll over, up onto your knees. Put your face in the mattress, you're much too loud, love." He licks his lips as he helps me into position quickly.

With my face buried in the blankets, I let the moans I was trying to hold back free.

He presses his face against me, holding me open with his hands.

"You taste so good." He groans. "I can only imagine what the rest of you tastes like."

I moan incomprehensible words into the bed as I come. It bursts through me, and I'm completely powerless against it. He laps it all up, leaving me a trembling, spasming mess by the time he rolls me over.

"This is going to be a problem." He chuckles again, this time with a painful groan tacked onto the end. His palm presses into the bulge in his pants. "Maybe I can sneak back in before I go."

"Do you have to go? Can't you make an excuse to stay here tonight?" I bite into my lip, hoping he doesn't see the sudden emotions that are hitting me.

"Hey, what's the matter?" He climbs into bed, lying beside me.

"I don't know." My voice wobbles. "I didn't feel at home in Noctyra, but this is worse."

"Did something happen?" The tenderness in his voice does nothing for my chaotic emotions.

"Calais thinks I'm a spy." I laugh, but tears drip down my cheeks.

"What?" He sits up, shock in his expression.

"Canaan thinks there might be a leak." I sit up too, wiping my tears away. "She suggested that it might be me. I'm working with the Shadowrithes to distract you while they make their moves."

"That's ridiculous!" He seems genuinely angry.

"I don't think Canaan shares her opinion, but still. I hate feeling like a burden. I hate being useless, and I really hate that we still haven't been able to find her. I want to help, but I feel like I'm always in the way. And if I'm being completely honest, I understand where Calais is coming from. I might think the same thing. I mean, it is suspicious, isn't it? That they've had opportunities to bite me, but they haven't. It's weird, right?" I rush through the thoughts that have been circling my brain.

"They're taunting us. And clearly, it's working. You're in a panic, and Calais is throwing around accusations." He runs his fingers through my hair. "Don't worry about her. I know you're not helping them, and so does Canaan."

I already feel his goodbye before he starts to say it.

"I have to go, love. We can't have him coming to look for me. I might have to pluck his eyeballs out if he saw you like this." His hand runs up my thigh, stopping to knead my ass roughly.

"Will you be able to come back?"

"I'll find a reason to." He presses a soft, short kiss to my lips. "Rest, you look exhausted. You're safe here, Kiah."

Twenty-Four

I braced myself for an awkward breakfast, but I'm the only one here. So now instead of sitting in quite discomfort with the group, I'm going it alone.

This is probably for the best.

At least Calais isn't here to accuse me of more treachery.

"Kiah." Canaan strolls into the room, a completely different man than the one who sat across this same table from me last night.

He is confusing.

I never know where I stand or what he's thinking. He's angry and then inexplicably not. He hates me and doesn't trust me, and then he stands up for me when I'm accused of being a spy.

"Elion is coming to spend the day with you." He informs me casually as he takes his seat.

I have to act nonchalant here. If I'm too excited, I'll give us away. "Oh, ok."

"I'm going to be away for a few days. Calais and Mordious will be here. You can go to them. Calais will be on her best behavior." He doesn't even look convinced as he says it.

"How's your hand?" I change the subject. If I need anything, Calais will be the last person I turn to.

"It will be fine." He looks uncomfortable, and I feel like I shouldn't have asked.

"Canaan," my voice trembles with nerves. I don't know why I feel compelled to do this. "I wanted to thank you. For yesterday, I mean. For everything."

His sharp gaze flicks toward me, his eyes narrowing slightly as if I just said something incomprehensible. He doesn't respond, and the silence feels like it's swallowing me whole.

Trying to ignore the way my cheeks burned under his scrutiny, I smooth my robe over my legs. "I just wanted you to know that I don't take that for granted." My voice cracks on the last word, and I immediately want to smack myself. Smooth.

He sits there like a statue, his expression unreadable.

"It's not a big deal," he finally speaks, his voice low and clipped.

"It is to me," I sit up, crossing my arms to shield myself from the discomfort. "You moved me out of harm's way, and you were injured."

Something flickers in his eyes, too quick for me to catch. "I'm fine."

"Look, I just wanted to thank you. I owe you." Geez. He's making this difficult.

His lips twitch, almost like he wants to smile but doesn't quite remember how. "You don't owe me anything, human."

The way he said 'human' wasn't cruel, necessarily. I am human. But this is the second time in as many days that he's felt the need to point out my humanness. I feel myself bristle.

"Maybe I don't," I stand quickly. "But gratitude isn't about owing anything. It's about not being an asshole when someone helps you out." God, he's insufferable!

The doors open loudly, conveniently cutting off our conversation. "Well!" Elion walks in leisurely, like he's on vacation. "Good morning!"

Quickly walking around the table, I head for the door and hope that he follows. "Good luck, wherever you're going." I look Canaan in the eye, holding my head high before marching out into the hallway.

"What did I just walk in on?" Elion rushes out after me.

"Nothing." I roll my neck and push the whole conversation out of my mind. "I don't want to talk about it."

"Can I show you something?" He stops suddenly, turning to me.

"Yes." My irritation starts to disintegrate.

"This way." He takes my hand and spins me around, leading the opposite way from where we were headed.

The sound of the waterfalls starts to grow louder as we walk down a long, open-ended hallway. Bright white light shines in, illuminating the whole hall.

The air smells familiar, like the forest after a hard rain—soft and woodsy. We're in a small garden, just a few well-maintained trees and bushes. Beyond it, the stone path leads to a staircase carved into the cliffside.

It's breathtaking in the best and worst way imaginable; one misstep and I would fall over the edge into the canyon. The waterfall cascades over the side of the mountain. The misty air clings to my skin.

"Hold onto me." He looks over his shoulder. "I won't let you fall."

Placing my hands on his wings, I try not to hold on too tightly.

His white-blond hair is longer than when we first met. I hadn't noticed until now.

The sun is low, dipping just below the horizon, casting an orange and pink glow that makes the jagged rocks look softer. The steps are steep, but Elion moves as if he's weightless.

We finally reach the bottom of the stairs, and my breath catches in my throat. The cliff drops away sharply in front of us, revealing a sprawling view of the water. It sparkles in the sunlight, a thick mist all around us.

"This is why it's called The Falls," his deep voice cuts through the sound of the crashing water. He steps closer to the edge, sitting on the low stone barrier as if he's done this a thousand times.

"It's stunning," I breathe, unable to look away.

"It's more than that," he replies, his tone quieter now, almost reverent. "It's a monument."

"A monument?" I turn to him, but he doesn't look at me.

"To the dead kings of the past," he explains. "Every ruler—save one —of our courts is buried here. Their bodies rest beneath the falls, entombed in the mountain. The roar of the water carries their voices, their wisdom."

I blink, suddenly aware of the weight of the moment. His father isn't here.

"It must be... sacred," I hesitate, searching his face. I don't know what to say. Does he want me to be angry? Should I show reverence? I don't want to upset him with the wrong reaction.

"It is." His expression softens, and for the first time, I think I see something in him I didn't expect—sorrow. "They come here to mourn, to remember. Every king, every life lost for the good of our people, is tied to this place. They gave everything for the crown."

There's a bitterness in his words, a sharp edge that makes me want to ask, but I stop myself.

Standing at the edge, the wind whips through my hair.

"Ask." His lips tug upward.

Taking a shaky breath, I sit beside him. "Why isn't your dad here?"

"I didn't want him here." The rushing water reflects in his eyes. "He was too good for this place."

The roar of the cascading water surrounds us as we sit in silence. I feel like he wants to say more, to vent all of the frustrations that are festering below the surface. He sits beside me, his sharp profile studying the water.

"I'd have done everything differently." His voice is low but clear above the rush of the falls. "If I were king, the Frostlinds would never have bowed so low. Never bent to the whims of the Shadowrithes. We'd have stood on our own. Proud. Unyielding. We wouldn't be here hiding." He scoffs, shaking his head.

I stare at him, unsure if he is waiting for me to respond. His tone didn't invite conversation—it rolled out heavy.

"Canaan means well." His lips curving into something resembling both a smile and a sneer. "He always does. Always the noble one. The self-sacrificing hero. That's his problem, really. Too much heart. Too much fucking heart for a king."

I stay quiet, biting the inside of my lip, letting him vent. Even if I wanted to help—to give advice—what do I know about any of this? I was dropped here, in the middle of a shitstorm. I don't know any of the history, the nuance.

"He sees the good in everyone," he lets out a bitter laugh that makes the hair on the back of my neck stand straight. "A king can't be afraid to get his hands dirty. I would have burned the fringes to ash. I would have stormed the waterways. He's being too patient. He doesn't want to risk lives, but sometimes you have to."

I'm so far out of my depth, I can't tell up from down. This is too much. I can't deal with life and death, the weight of a crown, or the political intricacies of a faery kingdom.

He stops, his expression softening. "I love him. He is my brother. My king. I will follow him to the grave." The mischievous smile that is usually on his face makes an appearance, easing the knot in my chest. "I would just rather not die for a long time yet."

"Same." I huff a nervous laugh. I can't add anything meaningful to this conversation.

The air changes, a sudden and dramatic shift. As always seems to be the case with Elion, his mood has changed.

"You know, you still owe me a question." His hand rests on my thigh, an innocent gesture that has anything but innocent intentions.

"Go ahead and ask." I keep my voice even.

"When I'm inside of you, and you're unraveling around me, have you considered letting me bite you?" The low rasp in his voice makes goosebumps spread over my skin. "Just a little taste."

Before I can answer, he grabs me, pulling me to sit on the ledge between his legs. The tip of his nose runs over my neck, right on the vein.

"Y-Yes." I choke on the word.

He hums, pressing a kiss to the pulsing artery. "I knew it."

Letting my head fall back onto this shoulder, I give him room to lick and suck my skin.

"One day, love." He squeezes his arms around me. "I'm dying for a taste." There is a hard resolution in his voice. The teasing is over. He's not going to try anything right now.

That's probably for the best. I would have let him.

I add that to the list of shit that is absolutely terrifying me right now.

TWENTY-FIVE

L ying in the suffocating darkness of my room, Elion's words play on an endless loop in my mind, as if carved into the back of my eyelids. Even in my dreams, they haunt me, pulling me back to that conversation, to the tension in his voice. Does Canaan know that he is holding onto so much bitterness?

I can't say that I blame him.

He was just venting, I tell myself for the hundredth time. I'm probably one of the few people he can speak to so freely without fear of judgment. I'm an outsider here—a convenient confidant because there's no loyalty or love tethering me to Canaan. Still, the whole thing felt... wrong. Not the kind of wrong you can name outright, but a subtle, creeping unease.

The whole thing felt off. I just can't put my finger on why.

I hardly slept. Every time I start to drift, it floats back into my mind, and I wake in a cold sweat.

Even worse than his subdued rage toward Canaan is the question. *The question.*

If he had been truly asking, I think I would have let him bite me. The thought makes me feel queasy.

A soft sound shatters the stillness. A scrape, just faint enough to be mistaken for my imagination. But I know better. My body goes rigid, every muscle coiling with tension. Shadowrithe. The word clawed its way into my mind.

I shoot upright. My heart is about to pound out of my chest. What's it waiting for?

Squinting in the dark, my eyes move around the room.

I'm sure now. I'm not alone.

My mouth opens—to scream for help, to call out—but no sound comes out.

My breath catches as I imagine fangs in the shadows, curling and waiting. Images of a hand—only muscle and bone—stretching out to grab me. Strangling the life out of me. Drinking my blood. Swallowing me whole.

Another sound. Closer this time.

A faint flicker of light illuminates the room. A steady pale blue.

My body twitches, muscles ready to react, but I freeze.

Canaan.

He's sitting by the window, staring out at the water. His usually sharp features look softer, full of weariness. The commanding presence that usually radiates from him seems less... royal. Less poised and powerful.

Even knowing that it's him and not a Shadowrithe does nothing to quiet the pounding in my chest. If anything, it's worse.

"What is wrong with you? What are you doing here?" I snap, my voice trembling. I hate how afraid my voice sounds.

His gaze snaps to me, hard and angry, but so tired.

"You know," His voice is low and gravelly. "It's been bothering me. Something is happening right under my nose. I can feel it." He stops, narrowing his eyes as he stares at me so intensely that it makes me shrink back.

I can't speak.

"I had to come back." He stands slowly, his wings open wide. There is something different about him tonight—something heavier. It isn't just the stress etched into the lines around his mouth or the tightness in his shoulders. It's in the way he's moving, as if his body is being pressed down by an invisible weight. "Any idea what I'm talking about, Kiah?" His head tilts to one side.

"No."

He hums, his mouth twitching into a deep frown.

As he turns away from me, staring out the window again, I notice the way he shakes his head.

"Canaan," my voice is barely above a whisper. "What are you doing here?"

For a moment, he doesn't answer. Then, without turning back, he sighs. "Thinking."

I blink, caught off guard by the honesty in his tone. "Thinking?"

He looks over his shoulder. "I thought I'd see if I could get some answers."

"Ok. Do you have questions?" I'm not about to just blurt out anything freely.

"I came here because I wanted to understand something," he says quietly, his eyes boring into mine. "But now I'm not so sure I want the answer."

I wait, my body tingling with pins and needles. Does he think I'm a spy now, too?

The anticipation is making me fidgety. His presence here makes the room feel small and warm.

"Is there something happening between you and Elion?" He finally speaks, his voice low and dangerous. Not loud, but it thrums with enough tension to set me on edge.

Oh, shit. This is not what I was expecting.

I cross my arms, leaning back against the headboard for some semblance of casualness I definitely don't feel. "There's nothing going on between me and Elion." My voice is steady, but I can't tell if he believes me.

He steps closer, his broad shoulders seeming even larger in the dim light. My breath hitches despite myself. It's impossible not to notice how beautiful he is—like a storm captured in human form. The sharp line of his jaw, the inky black of his hair that gleams faintly in the light, and those damned wings. They make him look like something out of a dream... or a nightmare, maybe.

Everything about him is elegance, grace, and power.

He narrows his eyes, tilting his head just enough to unsettle me. "You expect me to believe that? The way he looks at you—the way you don't look at him? And I swear I could smell you on him last night when he came to speak to me."

I swallow hard, straightening. "Elion looks at everyone like that." I clear my throat.

Lying to him feels like sandpaper in my mouth; it scratches and irritates. I want to be truthful. But I can't do that to Elion.

"I don't believe you."

"I don't know what to tell you." I hope he can't hear my heart. It will give me away.

He steps closer, standing right at the edge of the bed. "Kiah, it's important. I need to know."

"I already told you. My answer isn't going to change."

"So be it." He yanks the door open but stops short of walking through it. He stares at me in a way that makes me feel naked and exposed. His gaze drops to my mouth. "You mumble in your sleep."

And then he's gone.

My little shadow friend creeps out of the bathroom like a skittish cat.

"Was I mumbling? What did I say?" I ask it, battling a wave of nausea that just crashed down on me.

Was he asking, hoping that I would tell the truth? Did he already know the answer?

Jumping out of bed, I stumble around, looking for a robe. I'm suffocating in this room.

The castle feels alive at night, humming softly. My bare feet are light and quiet on the cool black glass floors. The walls shimmer in the faint moonlight filtering through the stained glass windows, each one a story frozen in time.

I've been walking aimlessly for what feels like hours, searching for the door that leads outside. The air feels heavy, charged with the same tension that's been coiling in my chest since our conversation. His words play on a loop in my mind. Each time I replay it, it's more distorted than the last.

His voice and tone change. Suspicious, angry, knowing. I can't remember the truth anymore.

"You mumble in your sleep."

Was he bluffing? I hardly slept, surely I wasn't speaking.

The way he said it—like a threat.

A soft creak draws my attention. I pause, glancing at the towering beams of ancient wood that stretch to the ceiling. Everything in this place is so beautifully ominous.

I run my fingers along the edge of a wooden railing, the grain smooth and worn from centuries of use. My hand trembles slightly. I'm on edge.

Ambling down the hallway, I pass an open archway. Ducking inside, I am met with a small library.

Curling up in one of the chairs, I look at the leather spines, worn and withering. I can't seem to escape thoughts of Canaan. Being here brings me back to our dreamweave experience in a library much larger than this one.

All of the books are black but one. Reaching back, I pull the red leather book from the shelf. It feels like it's drawing me toward it. If I listen closely, I'll hear it whispering my name.

Opening the cover, I gasp and let the book fall to the floor.

Twenty-Six

"Elion?" I stare down at the open book. The illustration on the first page is of him, in full-color glory with blood dripping from his mouth.

My fingers tremble as I reach down, picking it up from the floor and laying it open in my lap.

Turning the pages, I stop again. An illustration spreads across both sides of the book, vivid and masterfully detailed. It's a battlefield, chaotic and brutal. The sky swirls with gray clouds and bright-red streaks like blood in the air. In the center is Elion again.

I feel my breath hitch. He's clad in shimmering silver armor, the plates catching the dim light in the room, making the image feel alive. A massive sword is gripped in his hand, its blade almost too large to be real. His wings—brilliant and white—are spread wide, splashed with red.

My chest tightens.

The Elion I know is calm, measured, even kind. Sure, he can be kind of an arrogant bastard, and he jokes around too much. He can be high-handed. But this Elion? His face is fierce, twisted with an intensity I've never seen. His eyes burn with something primal.

I turn the page, my heart racing.

Another illustration, even more vivid. He's fighting—slashing through his enemies, their bodies crumpling in heaps around him. They have no faces, no features. They're just bodies. It's chaos, but he stands in the center, like a beacon of unrelenting power. I can't tear my eyes away.

But then I flip to the next page and freeze.

This one is different. The battlefield is still there, but Elion isn't fighting faceless enemies now. His sword plunges straight into the chest of what looks like a human woman. Her face is contorted in pain as her hands grip the blade. Blood spills from the wound, staining the dirt below. Her eyes are wide and full of fear.

"No." My shaking hand comes up to cup my mouth, physically holding my panic inside.

This doesn't make sense.

I flip back through the pages, searching for something, anything, to prove what I just saw isn't real. But the illustrations are all the same— each one more vivid, more violent. Each one shows him as a warrior, a destroyer.

The little shadow comes to sit beside me, my only true friend in this place.

"I feel sick," I whisper.

There is no way to tell how long ago this was. It might be from a century ago, but it feels like I'm watching it in real time.

The desperation on her face—the hurt...the betrayal—I feel it in my own chest.

In a moment of self-preservation, I try to explain it away. I don't know her or what she did. Maybe he was the victim, and she was some kind of evil.

The man I know, the one who looks at me like I matter, the one who cares about me—how could he be this, too? How could he do this?

Taking a breath, I turn the pages, searching for answers, for some explanation for those illustrations.

After several pages of text, written in an ancient language I don't understand, I come to the last page, another picture. They saved the worst for last.

Elion—wings wide, sword drawn—at the crest of a snowy hill. Behind him, an army of shadows, poised to spill over the edge and attack. They're following him—he's leading them. There is no alternative way to spin it in my mind, no excuse or exclamation.

Slamming the book closed, I run my fingers over the spine. The leather is imprinted with the name, whatever it is.

Pushing it back into its place on the shelf, I sit in the dark, unmoving, and stare at nothing. I don't have anywhere to go—nowhere to be—nothing to do.

I feel disgusting. Dirty.

I understand war. I know that there are winners and losers in battle. But the look on his face is burned into my brain. The joy. He was happy to kill them.

"Kiah?" Calais' voice slices through the dark, sharp and demanding.

"I'm here." My voice shakes despite my best efforts.

She steps into the doorway, her eyes narrowed and suspicious. "What are you doing here?"

"I couldn't sleep."

She hums, low and unimpressed, stepping further inside. Her gaze sweeps the shelves like she's searching for something. "Read anything good?"

"No." I shake my head, sorrow filling me to the brim. I'm not going to open up to her about what I found.

She doesn't respond immediately. Instead, she floats upward, her movements eerily fluid as she reaches for a very old, very large book from the top shelf. "This one might be of particular interest to you."

When she hands it to me, my body lurches, and I almost drop it. "It's heavier than I was expecting." I cringe.

Her lips twitch in a faint smirk, though her eyes remain cool and disinterested. "You'll find it worth the effort."

I flip open the cover, the pages crackling softly under my fingers. "What is it?"

"A book about dreamweaving. A lost art, really."

I glance up at her, struggling to read her expression. "I know you don't like me, and you don't believe me, but I'm not working with them. I hate them." My chest tightens, heat rising under my skin.

"It's not that I don't like you." She looks at me like a bug she's ready to step on. "You're just so human. In all these years, you haven't changed. Naive and malleable. My brother is risking his neck to find your friend and keep you safe, and you don't even realize it."

"I might be those things." I feel my temper starting to flare up. "But when I slipped into the portal, I tipped you off! The Shadowrithes lost the element of surprise that could have cost you! I'm grateful to your brother for trying to find my friend. I'll admit, in the beginning I doubted how much he was actually trying, but I know that it wasn't a lack of effort, I just wasn't informed." I sit up straighter. She can insult me as long as she's factual about it.

The way she's scrutinizing me makes me want to shrink back but I don't. She's looking for weakness, and I'm not going to give her one on a silver platter.

Her stare hardens, and for a moment, I think she might tear into me again. But then her jaw tightens, and her eyes narrow as though seeing me in a new light. "My brother cares very deeply for humans." Her voice is quiet but weighted. "More than he should. He's doing everything he can. He might be one of the last to truly believe in the human cause. We all say we do, but most wouldn't fight for it. He would."

"I believe you." I can't believe she just gave me any information freely.

She nods, curt, but the usual daggers in her eyes aren't there. "Mordious is looking for you."

Standing on my wobbly legs, I follow her in silence down the hallway. My head is heavy from all of the things I can't stop thinking about.

"In there," she points to another arched doorway as she glides past it without pausing.

"Thanks," I call after her, the word awkward in my mouth. She doesn't stop or look back before disappearing around the corner.

I stand there for a moment, the book still heavy in my hands. "Good morning." I come into the room. He's hunched over a table, his burly back and wings directly in front of me.

"Ah! I've been looking for you. I hope you don't mind but I have a favor to ask." He spins around, blocking the table from my view.

"Um, sure." I'm not thrilled about accepting before he tells me what the favor consists of.

"I make miniature things, and I need your help." He grabs something off the table and holds it out to me. "There is a small button here that I can't manage. You have small human hands, do you think you could sew it?"

The tiny shirt in his hand looks like it would fit a doll.

"You made this?" I start to work the little needle through the button.

"This is my first time trying buttons. It will be my last." He looks at the jar of buttons on the table.

"I can help you with them." I don't have anything better to do. This will distract me from thinking about Elion. And Canaan.

"Really?" He looks like a giant, fang-toothed, winged teddy bear.

"Sure." I sit down at the table, tucking in for the long haul.

"I'm going to make a miniature of you." He nods thoughtfully before clapping his hands together.

"Me?"

"Why not? I've made everyone else. Here's Canaan." He slides a small, wood and clay doll across the table.

Gasping, I grab it, looking at all of the little details. The wings and hair are perfect. The eyes aren't quite as piercing but that's probably difficult to translate into a doll. "Look! You even added his rings! He's so cute!"

"That's one I've not heard before," Canaan growls from behind me.

"I..." Dropping the doll, I spin around. "I meant the doll!"

"I thought I told you to stop making those, Mordious." His eyes flick toward him.

Mordious mumbles something unintelligible but continues to mold the clay into a head for my doll.

"Elion is going to spend the day with you again. He will." His facial expression and voice are stone cold. Without another word, he turns on his heels and leaves just as suddenly as he arrived.

"I'll be right back to finish these," I promise Mordious as I jump up to follow him down the hallway. "Canaan! Wait!"

He stops but doesn't turn, waiting for me to catch up.

"If you're not comfortable with us spending the day together, we won't. I offered my assistance with something." I hope he tells Elion not to come. I'm not ready to see him yet and this is the most effective way to keep him at arm's length.

His lips twitch into a frown, and he stares at me. "He can come. It's fine."

TWENTY-SEVEN

I thread the needle carefully, my hands steady as I sew the tiny button onto Mordious's miniature figurines. It's ridiculous how much I am enjoying doing this. The tiny buttonholes, the absurdly delicate stitching—it's all so charming.

Mordious watches me with a quiet excitement. He's not giddy like I know Chey would be to see these, but he's pleased, I can tell. He has a figurine for each of them: himself, Calais, Canaan...and Elion.

I deliberately avoid looking at his figurine. Just the sight of it makes my stomach twist into knots. Every time I think about what I saw, my chest feels too tight to breathe.

It's an adorably perfect likeness. His little white wings and white hair.

The faint sound of footsteps echoes in the hallway, and my heart sinks. He's coming.

He enters the room, his presence commanding but light as always. I stiffen, forcing my focus back on the miniature Mordious in my hand. He hasn't said a word yet, but I can feel his eyes on me.

"Mordious," They exchange quick pleasantries. I'm sure he's wondering why I haven't looked up or said anything. "Kiah?" His tone is slightly sharper. "Come with me. I need your help with something."

I don't even look up. "I can't. I'm busy." I hold up the needle and thread for emphasis.

Now they're both looking at me, I can feel it.

My face feels hot under their scrutiny.

Mordious sits forward in his seat. "You can go if you want. It's not that urgent."

"No," I answer more quickly than I meant to, with my voice firmer than I intended. "I said I'd do this for you, and I'm going to finish it."

"I'll have you back here working in fifteen minutes!" Elion tries to sound upbeat, but I can hear that he's concerned.

"I can't just leave, Elion! I promised I would finish this!" I jerk my head up to look at him.

The air thickens with the weight of unspoken tension. Elion steps closer, and I feel the heat of his gaze like a physical thing. He knows something is wrong; I can see it in the slight tightening of his jaw, the way his hand flexes at his side.

But he doesn't press. Not in front of an audience. I'm grateful for that at least.

"Fine," he says after a momentary pause, his tone careful and neutral. "We'll talk later."

I nod but don't trust myself to speak. He lingers for a second longer, and then he's gone, his footsteps receding down the hall.

I exhale slowly, my hands shaking slightly as I push the needle through the fabric again.

"You could have gone, you know that, right?" Mordious asks slowly. "I'm not holding you prisoner here."

"Yeah," I lie with a tight, fake smile. "I just want to finish this for you."

But my mind isn't on the tiny stitches anymore. It's on Elion, and the way he always seems to see right through me.

I wish I had more time to figure this out before I had to see him again.

Mordious works silently beside me, molding my miniature figures' heads. He's so focused, putting so much effort into making sure everything is done right.

My chest aches as I sneak glances at him between buttons. Chey would love this. She would want to ask about every detail and technique. I'm sure she would notice so many more of the small things—the things that artists put effort into.

I wish I could talk to her.

Wherever she is, I hope she's warm and fed and being treated well. It eases my mind to imagine her in the same situation as me in whatever place she is.

I need advice and guidance. I need to confess my sins.

I slept with him. All of it feels gross now.

Everything feels heavy—my chest, my lungs, my brain. I want to shut it off and ignore it all.

On top of everything, I feel guilty. I'm over here, having sex, worrying about a man, and my best friend's whereabouts are unknown. I have to believe they are treating her well and keeping her healthy to get more blood, but I can't know with any degree of certainty. I'm selfish and self-centered.

By late afternoon, my fingertips ache and my back hurts from hunching over for several hours.

"I will fire the clay tonight while I finish carving your body. Your hair will take some time." Mordious looks at the tiny clay head in his hand. "Thank you for your assistance today. I appreciate your willingness to lend me your small hands."

"Anytime." I hesitate for a moment. I know it's time to go back to my room. I've taken up most of his relaxation time for my own selfish purposes. But I don't want to go. Being all alone with my thoughts seems like a bad idea right now.

It seems like he can sense my hesitation.

"You can come tomorrow, I may have use for your small hands again." He clears his throat awkwardly. Great, I've made him uncomfortable.

"I'll be here!" I nod and force my feet to move. I've taken enough of his time.

Walking down the hallway, I walk quickly past the library like something is going to jump out from inside and attack me.

Maybe something is. Or someone. .

In my bedroom, I feel so lonely.

I can't stop thinking about it. The image is burned into the back of my mind, searing and unrelenting. Elion's expression of cold, calculated cruelty as he stood over the woman. The pain in her eyes, the way her body twisted in agony. Why would anyone want to illustrate that? Why preserve those horrifying images for all time?

My chest aches, tight with a sadness so profound it swallows me whole.

This feels personal in a way I can't explain. It's like a weight pressing down on my soul, one I can't shake. The room feels smaller with each passing second, the air too thin. I need to escape my own thoughts.

I kick off my shoes, letting them land wherever they fall, and hurry to my bed. I just want to forget this day—push it behind me and move into the next. Tomorrow, I'll figure it out. Tomorrow, I'll be brave enough to confront him, to demand answers. I'll be honest and straightforward.

But for now, I just need sleep.

I close my eyes and let exhaustion drag me under, but peace doesn't come. Nightmares find me instead.

The woman is here with me.

She's begging him for mercy. She's begging for her life.

The cruel sneer on his face as he looks down on her is so full of hatred that I hardly recognize him.

"Elion!" I scream his name, but he either doesn't hear me or doesn't care.

She screams as the blade presses into her, slicing her open. Her hands grip the sharp sword, a useless attempt at stopping him.

"Elion! Please stop! Don't do this!"

I want to run to them, to push him away and save her, but I can't. My feet are stuck to the ground.

"No! Stop!" I scream, my voice weak and powerless. My body thrashes against invisible binds, but it's useless. She's slipping away, and I'm helpless to stop it.

Then, everything shifts.

A force yanks me backward, sharp and sudden. I'm pulled so forcefully it hurts, my body feels shaken.

The scene dissolves around me, the woman's screams fading away. It's not relief—it's disorientation, a terrifying free fall into nothingness.

I'm not in control. It shifted from a real dream to something else. A dreamweave.

Surrendering to it, I don't try to fight against it.

"Kiah?" Canaan looks up as I'm dragged into the dining hall. He's sitting alone at the table, a plate of untouched food in front of him.

With a heavy sigh, I plop into the seat beside him. "Hey, Canaan."

TWENTY-EIGHT

For a moment, neither of us says anything.

"Can I ask you something?" I decide to just go for it. He might not be a completely unbiased, objective third party, but he's removed enough to be honest with me. Or at least I hope he is.

"Yes." His voice is calm, but his eyes flicker with something—curiosity? Wariness? I can't tell.

"I was in the small library and I saw something." For a moment, I worry that I'm tattling on myself for being out, looking around, but it's too late now.

He looks up, this seems to catch his interest.

"There is a red book, the only red book." I force down the fear. "Inside there are illustrations—"

"Esren, King of the Rimfae." He's quiet, almost reverent as he speaks his name.

"Esren?" I gasp. "Not Elion?"

His mouth twitches, just the ghost of a smile tugging at his lips. As if he can read my thoughts. "No. Not Elion."

Oh my god. I shouldn't have assumed. A rush of guilt and shame hits me. I didn't even give him a chance to explain it.

"At one time, a long time ago, before the Great Wars, the Frostlind

Fae and Shadowrithes were allies, friends even." His brow arches up, watching for my reaction to this information.

"I didn't know that." I feel sick. Swallowing hard, I force myself to meet his eyes. "What is that book? Why would anyone want to keep those drawings?"

He doesn't answer right away. Instead, he runs his thumb over his lower lip, his movements slow and deliberate. His eyes are looking far away, at something I can't see.

"It is important to remember our past, Kiah. If we pretend the atrocities didn't exist, we would forget what led us to them—and repeat them."

My heart rate speeds up, but not from his words alone. It's the way he looks at me, his eyes holding mine with a quiet intensity that makes my stomach flip.

Has he always looked at me like this?

Like he sees the parts of me I've tried to hide, the scars, the doubts, the fear. It's unnerving. Disarming.

"Yeah, we have a saying about that." I clear my throat.

It wasn't him.

I wonder if he'll understand. The position I'm in feels so precarious. I'm alone here.

"They were very similar." He cuts through my thoughts. "In every way."

"Were they?"

But he doesn't have time to answer. Our time is up. I'm being pulled away.

Everything is soft. It's not jarring or frightening. I'm just floating back to my body. I feel it when my consciousness and body reconnect. It's like easing into a perfectly temperature bath.

But the peace doesn't last long.

I wake with a start, my senses immediately on high alert. There's someone in my room. It's morning, and the light from outside is streaming in through the open curtains.

"Elion?" I whisper harshly, squinting against the brightness. His silhouette is standing at the window. "What are you doing here?"

He turns to face me, his usual smug confidence replaced by something softer, almost uncertain. "I know you're mad at me." His voice is careful. "But I don't understand why."

His confusion takes me off guard. For a moment, I just sit there, trying to piece together the words I need to say. I thought he'd know—that Canaan would have told him about my questions. But the look on his face says otherwise.

I swallow hard, forcing myself to meet his gaze. "It's about the book," I say slowly. "The pictures in it. You look just like him, and I thought it was you."

His brows draw together, his confusion only deepening. "Like who?"

I hesitate, the weight of the words pressing down on me. "Your father."

Elion stares at me, his expression unreadable for a moment. Then, something flickers in his eyes—a mix of shock and curiosity. "Where did you see a picture of my father?"

"In the library, there's a book." Now I'm confused. He doesn't seem to be connecting the dots here.

"A book about my father?"

"Yes. It was from before when the Shadowwraiths and Frostlind Fae were allies. You—" I pause, gathering my thoughts. "You look exactly like him."

He tilts his head, his eyes narrowing. "Show me."

I slip out of bed, grabbing my robe. He's seen me naked but I feel too exposed and vulnerable right now. The halls are quiet as we make our way to the library. He follows me, even as I make a wrong turn and get lost. It's still early, I don't think anyone else is awake yet.

"Sorry." I'm embarrassed. "I found it by mistake. I thought I could get myself back."

"I actually don't know my way around The Falls." He reassures me.

Once we finally find the small room, I grab the book. My hands tremble as I hand it to him. "Here."

He takes the book, his fingers brushing against the edge of the page. He sits down beside me, opening the cover slowly. He stares at the illustrations, his expression tightening. For a long time, je just sits and doesn't say anything.

Finally, he speaks, his voice low and almost... vulnerable. "I've never seen this before."

"You haven't?" I hate myself for being the one to show it to him. He probably could have gone his whole life without seeing his dad like this. Even if he knew that he did it, it doesn't change the fact that seeing it must be painful. There must be a reason no one ever showed it to him.

"No." He shakes his head, his eyes never leave the illustrations. "I didn't even know this existed."

Guilt twists in my chest. "I'm sorry," I say quietly. "For jumping to conclusions. For not giving you the chance to explain." I bite my lip, forcing myself to continue. "It was immature of me. I should've just talked to you about it. But it freaked me out. I thought it was you."

His eyes lift to meet mine, and slowly, the confusion fades, replaced by his usual mischievous warmth. A small, understanding smile tugs at his lips. "I get it. Those pictures are upsetting. I can see why you'd panic."

Relief washes over me, and I let out a shaky breath. "I thought you would be mad at me."

His grin widens, boyish and teasing now. "No. I'm not mad at you. But we should probably get out of here before Canaan finds us.

Despite myself, I let out a soft laugh. "You know, he asked me about you. Actually," I laugh. "It was more like he accosted me in my room."

"He what?"

It suddenly dawns on me that I shouldn't tell him all of the details about this. Not because I don't trust him, but because now is not the time for them to be at odds. There is too much going on.

"He just asked about us, that's all."

The look on his face makes my heart beat faster and not in a good way.

"What did you say?"

"I told him that nothing is happening between us."

"Did he believe you?"

"I think so. He didn't ask about it again."

He looks frazzled. It's strange to see him like this—tense and uptight.

"Are you alright?"

He doesn't answer.

"Elion? He didn't seem angry." I'm outright lying now. Something about the look on his face is making me nervous. I shouldn't have said anything.

"I'm going to bring you back to your room. I'll come back and see you as soon as I can." He puts his hands on my shoulders, leaning in to leave a soft kiss on my cheek, then my lips. There is a sense of urgency in his movements. He's rushing off.

One second he is here with me, and in the next he's gone.

Alone in my room, I sit on the bed, everything that happened today swirling around in my head.

It occurs to me only now that he never actually said whether seeing his dad like that—murdering a woman— was a surprise or if he was just surprised that the book exists.

"Well, shit."

TWENTY-NINE

T hings feel weird. It's been four days since I've seen anyone but Mordious.

Elion has vanished. Canaan has been gone. I think Calais might be hiding so she doesn't have to be around me.

I've sewn all of the buttons, and there are no jobs left for me to do.

All I can do is think. Sitting in my room, alone with my thoughts, I run through the conversation again and again. I can't sleep or eat. Nighttime is full of strange dreams that are unsettling and confusing, but when I wake up, I can't remember them. They just leave behind a nagging feeling in my chest –the memory of fear. Food tastes bland. Eating alone day after day.

I shouldn't have told him. Canaan never told me not to mention it, but I should have known better.

If he talks to Canaan about it, it will seem like I was badmouthing him. Or he won't care. Maybe I'm making a bigger deal out of this than what it is. Or, he will freak out the way Elion did. That was unexpected.

Then there is the weird dreamweave. Canaan's face was so...

I shake my head. That needs to be forgotten immediately–wiped from my memory. I'm going to act like it never happened.

Elion's reaction to seeing the book won't leave me alone either. Why wasn't he shocked by the content of the images rather than just the existence of them? Did he know that his dad did those horrible things? He was an ally to Shadowrithes.

Maybe they weren't so bad long ago. Or maybe I'm just overthinking this and making excuses for them.

My mind won't be quiet. "Oh my god, Kiah. Shut up!" I groan, covering my face with a pillow.

I don't want to think about any of this for another second.

I thrash around the bed, angry at myself, at Elion, at his father, at Canaan, at everyone. Whether they deserve it or not, it's there.

Standing up, I yank the door open and walk out. I won't sit in my room wasting one more second on this!

"Mordious?" I call out to him as I wander the desolate halls.

It's a miracle that he hasn't completely lost his mind. Being in this big, old castle on an isolated rock in the middle or treacherous nowhere would make anyone start to question their sanity.

"Mordi–"

"Kiah!" Elion whispers loudly, yanking me into a room as I pass it.

"Holy– what the hell?" I stumble into the large bedroom.

"Come here. I need to talk to you." He looks absolutely frantic. He peeks his head out into the hallway, and his eyes dart around.

"What is the matter with you?" I feel my heart rate spike. Something is obviously very wrong. He's worried. Or worse, scared.

He practically yanks my arm out of the socket as he pulls me through the room and out a set of ornately carved doors. We're in another garden. A tiny little oasis completely enclosed by tall trees and vines.

"Elion." I dig my heels in, forcing him to stop walking. "You're scaring me! What's wrong?"

"Shh," He wraps his hand over my mouth. "Quiet." He looks around again, searching the garden. "You don't know who might be listening."

"Who might be listening?" My voice is muffled against his palm.

"Have you seen Canaan?"

"No, not since..." The dreamweave. "Not since the last time I saw you." He's already completely freaking out. I'm not trying to make it worse. I learned my lesson about opening my big mouth.

"Ok." He sighs, releasing the tight grip he has on my arm.

"What's going on?"

Instead of answering me, he starts pacing around, walking in circles around the small perimeter of the garden.

Minutes pass while he paces and mutters under his breath. His wings twitch and flex.

"Elion, you're making me dizzy. What is going on?"

"I need you to listen to me. This is going to sound crazy, but just," he stops, taking a deep breath. "Promise that you'll listen to what I'm saying."

"I promise."

"If Canaan asks you for blood, you can't give it to him, Kiah."

"What?"

"He'll be convincing, maybe even bringing up Cheyenne. Don't do it. No matter how convincing he is, you can't give in." His hands shake my shoulders slightly.

"Why would he ask me that?" I feel lightheaded.

"He's getting desperate. His power and control are slipping away. He's losing control of the Kingdom. People are questioning his leadership–his abilities, his decisions. Your blood would give him strength." He looks into my eyes, looking through me, into me.

"Why doesn't he just take more from the donated blood?"

He chuckles, a low, humorless laugh. "Sweet human."

That felt more condescending than loving. I'm missing something here.

"Any blood is nourishing, but there is nothing like human blood. If it's true power he's after, your blood, right from the source, is the best thing."

"From the source?" I shudder.

"From the vein." He runs his finger over the vein in my neck.

"Does he need permission?"

"What?" He laughs again, this time clearly finding something very funny. "What do you mean? Does he need permission? Have you seen him, Kiah? If he wanted to take it, he absolutely could."

"I don't know. I thought maybe there was some magic or something that would keep him from biting me unless I allowed it or something." I'm sure I read that in one of my books.

"Wherever did you get a ridiculous idea like that?"

"I was just asking. Forget it." I feel my cheeks heating with a deep blush.

"There is no magic that requires permission." He's still laughing at me.

"Alright." I fold my arms over my chest. "Would he just take it? If he asked and I said no?"

"Ordinarily, I would say, with no hesitation, that he would never. But he is in dire straits. I have never heard him like this." He looks worried again, looking back at the door.

"You said people are doubting him. Why?" I change the subject. I don't want to think about Canaan draining the life out of me.

"It's a combination of everything, really. A portal was opened, and not one but two humans came through it before it closed. Then the Shadowrithes went into hiding, and he can't find them. They're getting more powerful by the day. Since you've been here, there have been four attacks on Noctyra."

"What?" I gasp. "No one told me that!"

He nods solemnly, "Fully formed Shadowrithes attacked the paladines that guard Noctyra's outer edges."

"Shit." I am hit with a wave of awareness—just how small and useless I am here. I'm a liability. My presence here isn't helping anyone. I'm in the way. I'm something that has to be protected. And what's worse, if they fail, my blood will help their enemies gain strength. "Can I help? Is there anything I can do?"

He smiles, the weight of his hands on my shoulders is nice now, not heavy. "The fact that you want to help is a testament to you. When there is something you can do, we will ask you."

I guess that's all I can ask for.

"We should go inside. It's time for dinner." He starts to lead me inside.

"Wait!" I panic and drag my feet. "I don't want to go have dinner with him!"

"Kiah, he's not going to attack you while we're sitting down to a meal. Relax."

"I don't know if I can just sit there with him and act like everything is normal!"

"Everything is normal. He hasn't done anything. He hasn't asked you. Just relax. I just wanted to make sure he hasn't given in to the temptation to try. He's a better man than that." He looks like he genuinely believes in what he's saying.

"Alright." I follow him inside. "Are they even here? I haven't seen anyone but Mordious in days."

"They're here." He looks ahead in the empty hallway like he can see something I can't.

My palms are sweaty as we reach the dining room. There are trays and platters set out on the table. Calais and Mordious are already seated. I can feel Canaan in the room.

Coming around the table, I find him sitting in his high-backed chair. He doesn't look panicked or out of control.

He looks between Elion and me. Whatever he's thinking is impossible to tell. He doesn't speak, but he also doesn't look angry.

Maybe everything is fine.

"When we finish here, we will meet the patrols in the Hollow Valley and at the Colonnade."

I sit up, my heart leaping into my throat. "Why those places?"

Calais narrows her eyes but keeps whatever snarky comment it on the tip of her tongue to herself.

"There were attacks there this morning." Canaan watches me. "Fully formed Shadowrithes."

I nod, my voice trapped in my throat. I don't know the right thing to say. I don't want anyone to get angry.

"I have a task for you if you're willing." He's looking at me the way he did while we were dreamweaved together. It's almost soft or appreciative.

I start to agree without hesitation, but Elon's warning rings out in my head.

"What do you need me to do?"

"Come with me to the library. I'll show you."

THIRTY

"Canaan?" I rush after him. He's at least ten steps ahead of me and only getting faster.

When he doesn't answer, I run to catch up. "We're passing the library." I look inside as he walks purposefully past the door.

I recognize the route. We're walking back toward my room. And his.

"Canaan?" I'm nervous. The conversation with Elion is too fresh. I don't want to be alone with him. Why couldn't he tell me what he wanted me to do in front of everyone else?

He stops abruptly, turning so quickly that I almost collide with him.

Instead of speaking, he just looks at me. Almost like he has something to say, but he doesn't say it. The air between us feels charged, as if the weight of whatever he's about to say is pressing against my chest, pushing on my lungs.

"Come."

When we reach the hallway that our rooms are in, the reality of how far away from everyone else we actually are sinks in.

"In here." He opens his door and steps aside, waiting for me to walk in.

I hesitate, but there isn't any other choice except to go inside. I can't outrun him. No one is here to help me.

He closes the door quickly and turns to me.

"Has anyone asked you for your blood?" His words are clipped, barely above a whisper. He's acting like Elion was earlier, looking around nervously like someone might be in here with us, listening.

"What?" My voice cracks, and my guard snaps up so fast it feels like a slap. "Why would anyone—"

"Kiah." His tone softens, but the intensity in his eyes doesn't waver. "Has anyone asked you?"

"No!" My mind is racing. "I wouldn't," I add quickly, the words tumbling out before I can stop them. "Even if they did—I wouldn't give it."

The room is silent. His eyes pierce into me, holding me down.

"Good." His voice is quiet. He steps closer, and I instinctively step back, but the door behind me keeps me there.

"Canaan," I start, but he's already leaning in, his hand brushing my hair aside to expose my neck. I flinch, heat rushing to my face, but his grip is firm, but still gentle. Every muscle in my body goes rigid. "What are you doing?" My voice trembles. He's just going to take it.

"Checking." His breath brushes my skin, his gaze fixed on my throat.

"For what?" I force the words out, my voice barely above a whisper.

He leans back, his expression unreadable, but his jaw tightens. "Just to make sure."

He's still touching me, his hand pressed flat against my collarbone, his fingers on my throat.

"You said you wouldn't give it to anyone." His voice is quiet, like he's talking it through to himself, not to me.

"I won't."

"No one?"

"No." I shake my head.

"Even Elion?"

"Elion?" My face scrunches. I thought he was talking about himself. "No! Not Elion or anyone else."

It can't be a coincidence that they are both bringing this up within hours of one another. Both seem to think the other is planning something.

"Canaan? Is something going on?"

"I don't know." A flicker of vulnerability shows in his eyes before it disappears.

"How can I help?"

"Don't willingly give your blood to anyone."

My throat is dry, and a ball of emotion is clogging it. I don't trust myself to speak. So I nod.

"Can you do something for me?" He's still looking at me–so heavy I feel myself shrinking back. Pressing into the door, I can barely stay upright.

"Yes." I whisper.

"Keep this conversation between us."

"Who would ask?"

He narrows his eyes. "Just don't tell anyone."

"I'll keep it between us."

"Tonight, there will be another blood ceremony. Lunaris Nocturne. You should stay in my room. It might confuse whoever has connected themselves to you." He looks around the room. "Do not venture out once the sun goes down. Stay here."

"I will." I promise.

He lingers, his hand still on my skin. I don't move, I can't. This feels intimate. He shouldn't be touching me this way, his fingers burning onto my neck.

"Can I ask you something?" I'm sure he can feel my pulse pounding under my skin.

"Yes," the low rumble in his voice vibrates against my ribcage.

"Why are you afraid that I will let someone have my blood but not that someone will just take it against my will?"

His lip twitches, the smallest hint of a smile tugging at the corners. "I am fearful of that. But what concerns me most is that someone might ask you for it, believing that you would give it without a struggle. And if you did that, they would have preyed on your naivete and kindness."

"And you care about my naivete and kindness?"

"I do."

"W-Why?" My breath trembles.

His eyes are deep, almost unfathomable, as though they've seen things most would never dare to witness. When I look into them, there's an unsettling clarity, a piercing awareness that makes me feel utterly seen. It's not just the way they are shaped, dark and intense, but the weight they carry—the wisdom, the weariness, the scars. It's as if every secret, every lie, every unspoken thought that's ever passed through my mind is laid bare before him–cracked wide open for him to inspect.

I try to look away, but it's impossible. They are a quiet judgment, not cruel, but relentless, as though they've witnessed the full spectrum of human nature. They hold no illusions about anyone, including me. I feel vulnerable, like there is nowhere to hide, no walls to build. This is worse than being naked.

So, I stand here, caught in his gaze like a trap. It feels like minutes have passed and his hand is still gently resting on my neck, but something about him is different—softer, almost as if he's unsure of something, or maybe even hesitant. It's as if he's waiting for me to say something. The silence between us stretches an eternity packed into this one moment. There are a thousand things I want to say, a thousand things I feel, but none of them make it to my mouth.

I can't stand it anymore. I lift my hand, my fingers trembling as they brush against his arm, and the contact—just the smallest touch—breaks whatever strange trance we were in. He flinches slightly, pulling his hand away from my neck, and the sudden distance between us feels sharp and cold.

"Stay in here," he says, his voice quieter than usual. It's almost a command, but there's something gentle about it, too.

His hands come down onto my shoulder and he slides me over, physically moving me out of the way to leave me alone, standing here, with a thousand things to say.

THIRTY-ONE

His room reminds me of him. Big and beautiful but sterile. It doesn't feel lived in, just occupied.

I can't sleep. I can't leave.

The minutes are crawling by. I'm starting to feel desperate. The boredom is taking over rational thought.

I move between the fireplace and the window, back and forth, over and over again. There is nothing new to see or do, but I can't stop.

The flames flicker in the fireplace.

"I need some magic." I whisper to them. "Give me something. Anything. Please." I expect the fire to do something. To grow, or change color, or show some kind of fairy magic that other things in this place have shown.

Maybe it's only water that has magic here. Or maybe it's me—maybe I'm too human to draw it out.

Standing, I move back to the window. His room has a view of the bridge. As I sit to stare out at it, a woman sails gracefully over the bridge. Then another figure follows—a man, this time. His wingspan is huge, his movements fluid and precise. Then three more in a group, gliding through the wind.

My breath catches as I press into the glass.

Their wings are strong, gliding in on the wind. It's like magic of its own kind. The fact that they exist.

They look like angels flying in. My heart feels like it's about to beat out of my chest. It's breathtaking in every sense of the word. I'm afraid and awestruck. I can't take my eyes away from them. By the end, I counted thirty-one.

They must be here to watch someone give themselves over to be drained. I wonder which one of them is the volunteer.

The disgust I felt last time is different now. I can't imagine believing in something so deeply that I would be willing to sacrifice myself like that.

Would I die for Cheyenne? If it meant that she would go home safe and sound. Could I do it?

The memories of that night are hazy. They feel like a lifetime ago. But I still remember the honor and the reverence, the way Canaan caressed his cheek and spoke softly to him. It was only scary because I didn't understand it then.

I don't want to die. But there is something so admirable about dying to help your people–to save your people. The power that they are willingly giving to Canaan is giving him the strength to lead them against their enemies. They are within him, a piece of the fight. It's true, unselfish love.

Wiping my eyes, I feel ridiculous for crying.

The sun sinks behind the ridge, leaving the sky pitch black–no stars in sight. Leaning against the glass, I close my eyes. The air feels different. Colder.

It's like a switch. I feel it. It's begun.

Somewhere in the depths of this place, someone is giving the ultimate sacrifice for their people.

A crackle from the fireplace catches my attention.

Standing up slowly, I watch the figures move within the flames. I recognize Canaan right away.

The candles in the room flicker as I inch closer to the hearth.

He's wearing white again. I can tell the difference against his black wings.

The same intense focus is etched into his face. Even in flames, he's beautiful. I can't take my eyes away.

Stepping closer, I worry that he'll be able to see me, or sense me somehow.

I can only see him and the altar, but I can hear the rest of them humming, just like before. It's powerful and low, a chorus that makes my chest vibrate.

Canaan's wings flex, opening wide as he raises his hands in the air.

Even knowing what to expect this time, my breath still feels punched out of my lungs when the bound fae, the sacrifice, comes up to the altar. It's a woman this time. Her long, flowing hair flickers in the flames. Her wings are bound, and a blindfold covers her eyes.

A dagger of light forms in his hands.

He reaches down, holding the dagger in one hand as he touches her softly. The gentle caress on her neck and cheek is almost intimate, loving.

The sound of the humming grows. The melody is so delicate and haunting. It lingers in the air, a soft breeze that blows through the room. It tugs in my chest –a phantom dancing in the halls of this place.

The light drops down, a precise cut into her skin. His other hand never leaves her–comforting her.

Blood runs down into the carved grooves of the altar, draining into a basin at the end.

Canaan waits with her. Leaning down, he whispers something and her body goes limp. Only then does he step down to the overflowing basin.

He takes it and drinks it. This moment feels like it lasts forever.

When he sets down the empty basin, his power is palpable. It radiates a real, pulsating heartbeat that lights up the room.

Backing away slowly, I feel drained of all energy. I don't want to watch the end. I don't want to see the part where she actually dies. I've seen enough horrifying things to last a lifetime.

His bed is large, and it's obvious which side he sleeps on. I'm not sure why, but I crawl into that side, his side, and slip under his soft blanket. I didn't want to sleep, but now I can't keep my eyes open.

I can smell him on the pillows. A soft, powerful smell that makes me feel safe.

I wait in limbo for my tormentor to come. But it never does.

When my eyes open, it feels like only a second, a single blink, but sunlight is streaming into the room, and I'm no longer alone.

Canaan is beside me, lying on the other side of the bed on top of the blankets.

I swallow down a gasp as I shoot up right.

He looks so different in his sleep. Softer. His wings are relaxed, one of them so close I could touch it if I just moved my finger slightly.

Even sleeping, even relaxed—the change in his strength and power is clear.

It's like a glow in his skin.

The muscles in his back and side are relaxed. His chest moves up and down slowly with shallow breaths. For a moment, I consider sweeping my fingers through his hair, just enough to push it back out of his face.

I don't know why I do it. My brain is malfunctioning. I'm possessed. I look down and I'm touching him. It just happened. I don't even remember moving!

My hand is on his wing. Just barely.

His eyes open, finding me immediately. "What are you doing?"

"Nothing!" I release him.

The silence that settles over us is so awkward, I would rather a Shadowrithe comes to kill me.

"I saw the ceremony last night," I whisper, just to fill the emptiness with something.

"I didn't feel you there." He turns to me.

"It wasn't the same. It wasn't a dreamweave." I realize only now that I'm going to have to explain to him that I asked the fire.

"Kiah," he takes a long, slow breath, like he's trying to calm himself, but I can see it in his chest–in the way it tenses–he's angry.

"I didn't leave the room!" I quickly add before he loses his cool.

"Then how?"

"Well." I clear my throat. "I asked the fire for some magic. I didn't specifically ask to see the blood ceremony, I just asked for something. And that's what it gave me."

His mouth closes, and he stares. His head tilts to one side, and his eyes narrow. "You asked the fire for magic?"

"Yes, I did." I smooth the blanket over my lap.

He scoffs, "Why would you do that?"

"I don't know." I shrug. Why did I tell him this?

"You are a strange woman." He's staring at me with an odd look on his face. Like he can't make heads or tails of me. The feeling is mutual.

"You're more powerful again." I'm not sure why I say this out loud. There isn't any question in it. It's just an observation.

"That was the point of the ritual." He sits up, pressing his back to the headboard. His wings are spread open behind him.

"Right. Well, it worked." I slide out of the bed. "I'll go back to my room now."

"Wait." He doesn't move. "Why did you ask the fire for magic?"

"Um," I stare down at the black glass floor. I can't look at him sitting there like that. It's too intimate. He's only wearing pants. Sitting, lounging really, in his bed with tousled hair and bare feet.

We only slept beside each other, but this is too weird.

"I don't really know why I asked. I just wanted to see. I wasn't even sure if there would be magic there. I guess I was checking."

He hums, still sitting back. "It surprises me that the magic would choose to reveal itself to you." There is something about his face and his casual position. He looks too relaxed. Radiating power, but this easy confidence. It reminds me of Elion. It's sexual and so fucking attractive.

"It surprised me, too." I take a backward step toward the door.

"You looked so peaceful, I couldn't bring myself to wake you."

He looked peaceful, too. But I don't say that out loud. Thank God for a filter, no matter how briefly it stays with me. "I slept well."

"So did I."

He looks... what the fuck is happening right now? He's so pretty that it's making me blush.

A slow smile spread over his face, his sharp, white teeth on full display. "You can leave if you're uncomfortable." His hand runs absent-mindedly down his chest.

"Cool, thanks." I turn and run out of the room, leaving him laughing behind me.

In the safety and solitude of my room, I lean against the door. "What the fuck was that?"

THIRTY-TWO

The scent of freshly baked bread greets me as I step into the dining room, the early morning light spilling through the tall windows. The stained glass patterns on the floor are familiar to me now.

"Kiah!" Mordious gives me a wide smile as I come into the dining room. His enthusiasm is so unfiltered, so genuine, it catches me off guard.

I blink at him, and a small smile tugs at my lips. No one's ever this excited to see me. Calais usually looks annoyed by my presence. Canaan is hot and cold. Elion isn't here.

He jumps up from his chair as I take my seat. "I finished it! Who knew not having wings would make you more tricky?"

When he holds it out, my heart does this funny little skip. It's small enough to fit in his palm, and smaller than the others I've seen. It's a perfectly to-scale mini-me.

The details are so intricate. It looks just like me.

Running my fingers over the tiny face, I can't help but smile. "It's adorable." I can't believe he made this. "I love it."

"Your hair was difficult."

"Tell me about it." I can't stop staring at all of the details. My hairline is flawless. My eyebrows are perfect--slightly mismatched but close enough. He even put my freckles in accurately. "I can't get over it. It's perfect."

"Perfect might be a slight exaggeration." Canaan's eyes flick from the figurine, then to me. "But it's not bad. Looks like you."

That's as close to a compliment as I think he can give in regards to these.

"Well, I love it," I say, my voice softer than I intended. "Thank you, Mordious."

He grins, his happiness infectious. "It's nice to have them appreci-ated for once." He gives a sideways glance to Canaan, who returns the sideways glance.

As I sit down, placing the figurine carefully in front of me, I catch Canaan watching us with something almost like amusement. He must think I'm ridiculous, but I can't find it in me to care.

For the first time in a long while, the air around me feels light. Comfortable, even. And that little figurine on the table? It feels like a welcome, not just some little hobby. I'm so flattered that he even cared enough to make one. I know these little figures are just his way to beat the boredom that hangs over this place, but I still appreciate it.

Elion strolls in, casual and calm. Maybe it's the fact that he gets to leave regularly. But he always seems so leisurely.

"Good morning!" There is extra pep in his step today.

"You seem like you slept well." I feel the weight of hardly sleeping at all right behind my eyes.

"And you seem like you didn't." His mouth tilts downward as he takes the seat beside me.

"Did you not?" Canaan looks the opposite of concerned. He looks like he might start laughing.

"I'm fine." I could really use a strong cup of coffee right now.

Sitting between Elion and Canaan, for the first time, I can feel the imbalance of people between them. I know he just drank the blood sacrifice but wow. It's an indescribable shift. Not physically but there is an invisible shift, like Elion is a child standing before a man. Canaan is vibrating with strength.

If they feel it, neither show it. It's just an unspoken presence.

"I am taking Calais to patrol the border between the territories. Anything you need will be taken care of by Elion or Mordious." Canaan seems so relaxed, it's almost unnerving. I can't stop peeking up at him and I'm afraid Elion will notice. It's like he's holding back something too big to fit inside him. It's more than last time. It's more than this morning.

He's different.

Elion is different, too. He strolled in like he usually does, easy and unbothered, but there's something off. He's not making jokes. He's not flashing those sharp, knowing grins.

It makes my stomach twist.

All I can think about are the last conversations we've had. They're both so interested in what is happening with the other. I'm caught in the middle of a secret tug of war.

I push my food around my plate, barely listening to the quiet hum of conversation. When Canaan finally leaves, the tension doesn't. If anything, it grows.

Elion doesn't say a word as he stands, just tilting his head toward the door. I follow.

Back in my room, the second the door shuts behind us, he's on me. His mouth crashes against mine, his hands find my waist, my jaw, my wrists. I melt into it, letting the heat consume the weirdness, the awkwardness.

Maybe we both need this right now.

"What did Canaan say to you?" He whispers against my neck.

I blink. "What?"

He pulls back just enough to look at me, his fingers still gripping my hips. "When he pulled you outside. What did he want?"

"Oh, nothing."

He hums, skeptical, then kisses me again. I sink into it, letting my hands tangle in his hair. He takes the little figurine from my hands and stares at it. "This is cute."

"I think so."

He sets it on the windowsill and turns his attention back to me. Cupping my face, he looks at me almost sweetly. "He didn't ask you for blood, did he?"

"What? No! Of course not!"

"What else could he have wanted?"

"Elion, stop it." I'm more forceful than I mean to be. "He didn't ask me for anything."

"Then why won't you tell me?"

My jaw tenses.

"Elion—"

His grip tightens, not painful, but insistent. "He doesn't pull people aside for nothing, Kiah."

I exhale sharply, pressing my forehead against his. "I told him I wouldn't say anything."

The frustration is rolling off him now.

"So he has you keeping secrets from me now?"

"No, not from you. He just asked me not to say anything to anyone. Please let it go." I kiss him, slow and deep, hoping he'll let it go. But his hands come up to cradle my face, holding me still as he leans in again, this time softer, more deliberate.

"Did he threaten you?"

"No."

"Did he offer you something?"

"Elion, stop."

His jaw tics.

I sigh, stepping back, the space between us suddenly colder than it should be. "I'm not telling you."

His neck muscles flex under his skin. "I can't keep you safe if you don't tell me what's going on."

"I'm as safe as I can be. If you needed to know, I would tell you." My mind races for something to say that would get him to let this go.

"Kiah." He smiles softly, the tension leaving his body. "I just want to know that while I'm away from you, you're safe here. I hate that I can't stay and keep an eye out."

"He wanted me to stay in his room during the ceremony last night. That's all."

He lets out a relieved sigh. "Was that so hard?"

"No." I whisper against his lips. Placing my hands firmly on his shoulders, I let the feeling of fire start to build. Pushing everything else aside, I focus on it. "Let me." I push down, and he gives easily, dropping onto the bed.

Reaching down between us, I unclip his belt.

"Sit back against the headboard."

"Bossy."

"Do it."

He smiles, running his tongue over his teeth. As he sits back, his wings spread out wide. My mind glitches. It happens quickly, almost so fast I don't notice. Elion's face morphs into Canaan's. His wings flicker between black and white. His chest changes, bigger, broader. His hands are adorned with jeweled rings.

Then he's back, his face, his wings, his body.

Shaking my head, I let out the gasp I'm holding.

Shit. What the fuck? My heart hammers in my chest as I force myself to look at him, to forget about Canaan.

Climbing up onto his lap, I let my dress bunch up around my hips, and he quickly slides his hand against my skin.

"Elion." I whisper, grounding myself in this moment with him. "Touch me."

He doesn't waste a second. I'm stripped naked on his lap in one quick sweeping motion. He drops my dress to the ground and runs his hands over my body.

His fingers snake around my neck, with pressure just firm enough to make each breath a struggle.

"Oh, my god." He isn't even touching me anywhere sexually, but I'm putty in his hands.

With each second, the tension grows.

The air between us crackles, electric and alive. Inside my stomach, my muscles coil tighter, the ache beneath my ribs stings with every panted breath.

With his other hand, his fingertips brush my skin, the barely there contact hot and sharp.

We kiss and lick each other, letting our hands roam and explore. He's pressed into my stomach, hard and hot.

Lifting up, I hurry, adjusting him beneath me. I don't want him to stop me—to try to prolong the torture.

Sliding slowly down, I take him to the hilt in one steady motion.

"You look so pretty when you ride me like this." His hand squeezes around my neck again.

Rolling my hips, I let my eyes close and just feel.

I've never felt this kind of connection with anyone. It's like he can read my mind. He moves his hips to meet mine. Every touch is exactly what I need.

"You feel so good." He groans. The desperation in his voice hits me like a firework bursting through my chest.

He's gentle and rough, harsh and soft. The pressure is perfect. When his teeth scratch at my neck, the burning in my stomach, the ball of pressure bursts wide open.

Our bodies take turns. Mine, then his, then mine again. Around us, the world spins, and the day passes as we stay wrapped around each other.

We don't stop until my body gives out, and I can't move.

"You're a magician." I can barely keep my eyes open.

"Rest. When you wake up, I want another round."

THIRTY-THREE

My body is so sore. A deep, delicious, muscular ache that reminds me of all of the times he made me come last night. Over and over again. He would let me sleep for a few hours, then wake me with his tongue between my legs.

Sitting up, I look around the room and pout. I'm alone.

And while I shouldn't be surprised—he's not supposed to be here anyway—there's a hollow ache in my chest. He probably snuck out in the dark hours of the morning to avoid anyone noticing. There would be a lot of explaining to do if anyone caught him in my room. But damn it, it still sucks.

I've never been the type to hide away or sneak around. If Cheyenne were here, I could almost hear her lecturing me, reminding me that I don't do the whole secret relationships thing.

I don't want a part-time love story. I don't do "undercover" girl-friend stuff. Except, for some inexplicable reason, I find myself in the middle of this one. A forbidden, messy, barely understood relationship with a winged fairy prince.

As I roll out of bed, the second my foot touches the cold floor, a sound stops me. I'm frozen—half in and half out of the bed. It sounded like a scream.

It was a scream.

Sharp, raw, and full of fear.

A second later, another echoes through the air, confirming it.

Panic claws at my throat as I scan the room, looking for something
—anything—that could offer some protection. There's nothing. I'm
just me. No wings, no magic. I'm not going to sit here and do nothing.
Not now. Not when someone is screaming for help.

Another scream rips through the air. It's closer now. The sheer
terror sending a shiver down my spine. My feet move before I can even
think.

"Mordious!" A voice cracks through the chaos—high-pitched, filled
with pain. I race to the window, my heart pounding in my chest, hoping
to see something—someone familiar—that can help. But the sky is
empty. No flashes of wings, no signs of anything.

I can't stand here, helpless. I can't.

With nowhere to hide, I sprint out into the hallway. Canaan's door
is closed. It's just me. Alone.

"Shit. Shit. Shit." I turn a corner and then, there it is.

A woman. She's covered in blood and one of her wings is almost
completely ripped off. Forgetting all about self-preservation, I rush to
the big double doors and push them wide open.

She comes in and immediately drops to the ground. "Help me!" She
crawls across the floor. I can't tell if her hair is bright red or covered in
blood.

"Mordious!" I scream, my mouth moving on its own. It just does.
As soon as I say it, he and Calais burst into the room.

I step out of the way; that is the best thing I can do in this situation—just get out of their way.

Mordious gets to her first, lifting her up into his arms with such
gentleness. I feel emotional watching it. Her wing is torn, hanging on
by the thinnest strip of mangled skin. It's carnage. She's been
brutalized.

"I've got you now, darling." He holds her close to his chest.

"M-My sister, Byantha! She's somewhere and she's close! You have
to help her!" She looks around with wild, terrified eyes. "Please! Help
her!"

"I'll find her!" Calais takes to the air, bolting out the door into danger with no hesitation.

I'm not sure what happens inside of me. Maybe it's the chaos. Maybe I was moved by Calais' fierce bravery. Maybe I forgot for a moment that I'm just a human who can't fly or do anything magical whatsoever. But I run out of the room and down the hallway.

As I round the corner and come face to face with the glass doors that lead into the garden.

"What am I doing?" Even if I found her, how could I possibly be of help? Stopping, I look toward the doors, then back over my shoulder.

I'm useless.

Turning, I start to walk back to my room, listening closely for any sounds. My heart is racing, and I'm full of adrenaline.

"Help me!" I hear a soft, trembling voice and freeze mid-step.

"Hello?"

"I'm here!" She groans.

Stepping back, I look into the room I just passed, an enclosed sitting room with views of the waterfall.

Another red-haired woman is leaning against the wrought-iron doors, blood dripping from her mouth.

"Byantha?"

"Yes!" She gasps. "How do you know me? Have you seen my sister?"

"She's with Mordious!"

"Oh, she's safe!" She stumbles, losing her footing and letting her body slide down to the ground.

"Calais is looking for you! Let me get someone to help you!" I turn. "I'll be right back!"

"Wait! Please! Let me come with you! I have to see my sister." She begs, trying to take a step forward but her leg wobbles and her knee buckles.

"Here!" I run toward her. "Lean on me. We'll go together."

She's so heavy, her wings drag across the ground, leaving an ominous red trail behind us.

"So, you're the human." She grunts in pain but tries to smile.

"That's me." I try to smile in return, but I can't make my lips move.

All of my strength is focused on ensuring we don't fall. "What happened?" I don't even care that my voice is strained.

"We were on our way here with a message for Canaan. We were attacked by Shadowrithes. At least four of them in full human form. I underestimated their strength and speed." She shudders. "This is my fault. She wanted to retreat. I thought we could make it."

I don't know what to say. There isn't anything helpful in this situation, so I keep my mouth shut.

It feels like it takes us an eternity to get to the room, and when we step inside, it's empty.

"Fuck." I groan, leaning against the wall for support as she leans on me.

She starts to feel heavier, like her legs are holding less weight by the second. We're going down. I can't support all of her weight alone.

"O-Ok, Byantha. Let's try to sit you down." I struggle to bring us down to the ground without hurting her or crushing myself.

As carefully as I can, I lean her against the wall. Her wings droop, and her mouth has fallen slack.

"Byantha?" I shake her slightly.

Her eyes are open, and I can see her chest moving, but it's like she's not conscious.

"I'm going to go get help! I'll find someone!" I take a step away from her, but something stops me. She looks... strange.

Just a minute ago, she was talking, and now it almost looks like she's dead.

"Byantha?"

The hair on my neck stands on end, and a chill runs the length of my spine.

The overwhelming urge to run takes over —I feel it in every part of my body. My muscles twitch, ready to flee.

Beside her, something moves.

Blood?

Squinting, I watch as the darkness spreads across the ground. It's not blood. It's too dark... too black.

It's not moving like blood. It's creeping...like a shadow.

THIRTY-FOUR

My body is locked in place. Fear has twisted its way into my muscles, freezing me here. I tremble violently, and my teeth clatter, but I can't take a step. I want to scream, to run, to fight for myself but I've never felt anything like this.

The thing creeping toward me looks like something out of the depths of hell. It's a demon. A shifter. Something too evil to stand upright, so it crawls.

It's like lava, a thick, black tar that rolls across the floor.

I think Byantha is dead. Her pale, sweat-slicked skin has lost its glow–she looks cold and gray. Her chest isn't moving. It came out of her. It oozed from her body.

A hand forms in the mass of swirling mist, reaching out as it gets closer to me.

My brain snaps, like a rubber band breaking. The tension in my body releases, and I run. I don't know where to go, but with the paralysis gone, I know I need to.

Darting for the door, I have no plan. I just have to go.

The vastness of this place has never felt more frightening. I'm alone–far from anyone who might save me.

"Canaan!" I scream, running as fast as my legs will carry me. The long, empty hallways are endless.

Looking over my shoulder, the mass of shadow and blood is behind me, almost close enough to reach out and take me. It floats on the air, half-formed feet, exposed bone hovering over the floor.

"Canaan!" I scream again, clinging to nothing but hope. I don't think he's even here, but I have to believe he will find me. He always seems to.

My lungs burn as I force myself forward.

"Kiah." A whisper floats in the air, swirling around me.

The voice slithers through the air, a whisper so soft it shouldn't reach me—but it does. It curls around my ears, threading through the space between my ribs, sinking deep.

"Kiah."

It drags along my spine, coiling like fingers at the base of my neck. The syllables stretch, slow and deliberate, spoken not to be heard, but felt. My pulse stutters. My blood turns to ice. I don't dare look back.

It's closer than it should be.

Rounding the corner at full speed I slam into Canaan so hard it knocks me off my feet. He grabs me, there is no hesitation or confusion. Holding me tightly, he lunges forward, grabbing the Shadowrithe by the throat.

Burying my face in his neck, I pinch my eyes closed.

I feel everything. But I don't want to see it.

He never lets me go—his arm is a steel band around my waist.

My breath comes in short, panicked bursts against his skin. I wish I could block out the sounds.

The Shadowrithe shrieks, a sound that claws through my skull. It's like metal scraping together, grinding, and awful.

Canaan's body tenses, the muscles in his chest flexing as he twists, the sharp crack of impact echoing in my ears. A deep, guttural growl rumbles through his chest, vibrating against mine as he strikes again.

There's a rush of air as he flies higher, faster, his wings beating hard enough that I can feel the force of it against my legs. My stomach lurches with every sharp maneuver, every sudden shift in direction, but his grip on me never falters.

The Shadowrithe hisses, a wet, slithering sound, followed by the sickening crunch of something breaking.

It takes everything in me not to scream.

Canaan exhales sharply and mumbles something against my temple before his hold on me tightens.

"We want her, Canaan." The Shadowrithe laughs, his voice sounds thick and viscous. "We want both of them. We won't stop until we have them."

The sensation of falling, the sheer terror of dropping out of the sky, but we never hit the ground.

Canaan doesn't taunt him. He doesn't let his ego forward to trip him up. Silently, he maneuvers around, stopping this. And he will stop it. I trust that.

I feel the tug of gravity, my legs dangling backward, we're parallel to the floor.

I hear the scrape of claws against something, glass or stone? Then a dull thud of a heavy blow landing, then another shriek. Canaan moves so quickly that it's impossible to tell what he's doing.

We fall again, rushing downward. A gurgling sound—a sick cough thick with blood makes my skin crawl.

Then silence.

My feet touch the ground gently, but his arm stays firmly around me.

Loosening the grip of my arms around his neck, I lean back to look at him. "Well," I don't know what is wobbling more, my voice or my chin. "It looks like I owe you again."

"You're safe." He looks over my shoulder at what I can only guess is a mess.

"That thing..." I can't even speak the words. It came out of her. It killed her.

"I know." He nods. "Close your eyes."

Wrapping my arms around his neck again, I pinch my eyes shut tight.

We're up, off the ground, my hair blows as he flies away from the horror.

"You can open your eyes." He drops down, walking swiftly through the corridor.

He still hasn't put me down. We move from room to room, methodically clearing every corner of the castle.

Calais is ahead of us, checking before we enter. Mordious is behind us.

After three separate checks, I think it's safe to say we didn't miss anything. No one speaks. We move in total silence through each room, looking for monsters under the beds and behind the curtains.

It takes hours, but nothing is left to chance.

When everyone is satisfied that there are no Shadowrithes lying in wait, he carries me into the kitchen. This is the first time during our stay here that I've come to this room. It's big and beautiful, but it looks ancient.

There isn't an oven or a stove. There is a brick dome over a blazing fire. It's like being pulled back in time.

He sets me down on the counter and starts to pull things out of the cabinets.

"What are you doing?" I watch him cut slices from a loaf of bread.

"You need to eat."

"Oh, I'm fine, Canaan. You don't have to—"

"You need to eat." His eyes flick to mine.

"Alright, fine." I am hungry, but with everything else going on, that seemed unimportant.

He places a very heavy, ancient-looking pan on the hooks over the fire.

He butters the bread and piles it high with cheese and meat.

"Are you—" I can't believe what I'm seeing. "Are you making me a grilled cheese sandwich?"

He sets them in the pan and leans back against the counter. "I am making you toasted bread with cheese and meat."

Humming, I choose not to point out the obvious similarities between the two.

"Can I help?"

"With what?"

"I don't know? I can cut fruit or something." I shrug. I hate the way he looks at me.

He hesitates, but plucks a knife from the strip of them hanging on the wall behind him.

"Do you want some?" I look through the baskets at the sweet-smelling fruits.

"Yes." He looks like he's about to break his teeth. If he keeps clenching his jaw like that, he might.

Quickly chopping different fruits, juicy, sweet apples and peaches, I keep my eyes down. He is so confusing. I don't think he hates me. He continually saves my life. But maybe that's just out of a sense of duty. He's the king. It would make him look weak if he couldn't keep his unwanted guest alive.

But it feels like more than just an obligation.

Or it's exactly that, and he's just a hospitable host.

He pulls the buttery, toasted, cheesy non-sandwich from the pan and sets it on the plate.

It smells so good. Grabbing one, I quickly bite into it.

"Kiah!" He practically knocks it out of my hands. "What are you doing? It's too hot!"

"It's so good, though!" I take a deep breath to let some of the heat out of my mouth.

"Wait!" He hands me a glass of water while mumbling under his breath about impulsive humans.

"This is delicious." I take another big bite.

"You won't be able to taste the rest of it." He bites into his.

A deep, heavy guilt settles in my chest. What is wrong with me? Clearing my throat, I stare down at my sandwich. Elion isn't my husband or anything, but it feels wrong to look at Canaan and feel... things.

He saved me. There is probably a psychological term that fits whatever this is.

Quickly finishing my food in silence, I have mixed feelings about what happens next. I need space from him. He's too close. Too present. But I also don't want to be alone.

"It's been a long day." He takes our plates. "You should rest."

"You probably have a lot to do." He's the king, and this fortress was just attacked. He has better things to do than babysit the human liability.

"Come on." He waits for me to walk through the door before following me out.

Walking through the hallways with him now, I can't place how I feel. I'm thoroughly confused. When we reach my door, I hesitate. I want to ask him if he's going to be in his room. Just in case. Just so I know.

"Inside." His voice is low but firm. He pushes the door open and waits.

Then, instead of leaving, he follows, moving with an unhurried confidence that makes my stomach twist. He lowers himself into the chair by the window, his wings shifting behind him, their dark edges catching the dim light.

"Um, I–" I'm frozen, standing in the middle of the room.

"Do whatever you need to do. I'll be here."

That shouldn't feel as grounding as it does. Without another word, I turn and rush into the bathroom and close the door behind me. He's only a few feet away, but at least now he can't see me.

I let out a breath and start the shower, the sound of rushing water drowning out my racing thoughts. I rub my hands over my face. Calm down.

Then I realize—I don't have anything to put on afterward.

"Shit."

Peeking out, I find him still in the same spot. His eyes meet mine instantly.

"I just forgot a robe." I awkwardly shuffle past him.

"Take your time." There is the smallest hint of a smile on his face. He must think I'm such an idiot.

Back in the safety and privacy of the bathroom, I stress about every single decision. I don't want to take too long. But I also don't want it to seem like I'm rushing. Every decision suddenly feels more important than it really is—how long to wash my hair, how quickly to dry off. What is he even doing out there?

When I finally step out, wrapped in my robe, I half expect him to be gone. But he's still there, right where he said he would be.

"So—" Wow, this is uncomfortable.

"Sleep. I'll stay." His voice is softer now–quieter.

I should tell him to go—to handle the situation that I'm sure is waiting for him. But knowing he's close might be the only way I get any sleep tonight.

Crawling into bed, I snuggle down under the soft blankets. It hits me hard and fast—I'm exhausted.

I fall asleep so quickly that I don't even realize it's happening until I startle awake. Bolting upright in the bed, I see his silhouette in the dark, still sitting in the chair.

"I'm still here, Kiah." Something about his low, rumbling voice makes me feel safer than I've ever felt before.

"Thank you." I'm not sure if I really whisper it or if it's part of a dream.

THIRTY-FIVE

I feel his presence like a beacon in the dark. It's something to hold
onto. Soft and warm, he's holding vigil over me, guarding me from
the darkness that creeps around this place.

I feel it immediately. It's nothing more than a tug. Just a light touch
at the edges of my mind. But I know what it is.

"Canaan!" My voice echoes in my mind. It's too late. I can't say it
out loud. I can't alert him.

Pinching my eyes closed tight, I feel myself floating.

I won't let myself cry or beg. This is happening. There is no choice
in whether or not I go, but I can control my reaction.

The air around me gets so cold that eventually my teeth chatter
loudly in the quiet. When I open my eyes, I'm somewhere new. This
looks like a place where monsters would dwell–where things bump in
the night.

White puffs of my breath hang in the air before me as I search the
darkness for a clue. We're in a forest, but it's not lush and green. The
trees are sparse and black, like they've been burnt. But they haven't, at
least I don't think so. They are just gnarled and dead.

All the warmth I felt from Canaan, the safety of knowing he was
close, is gone.

The ground squishes beneath my feet, wet and spongy, but not with water. It clings to my bare feet like rot, the scent of decay curling in my nose. A slow, deliberate drip sounds somewhere close—thick and heavy.

Then I hear something.

A whisper at first, but it grows.

I am not alone.

Each step I take seems to take me further back somehow, like walking on a treadmill. I'm not covering any ground–not forward or back. I'm stuck.

The whispers are getting louder. It's almost imperceptible. With everything going on, they fade into the background until they are so loud and so close, I find myself crouching down to avoid being hit by whatever is making them. But I can't see them.

Covering my head with my arms, I make myself as small as possible as the invisible terrors shriek and swoop down at me from the trees. It's a nightmare. But this is worse, because it's not a nightmare, it's a dreamweave. I can't wake myself up. I can't leave. I'm trapped here in this place.

"Kiah." They taunt me. Laughing and whistling as they call my name in a chorus so loud it makes the ground shake. "Come on, Kiah! We're waiting for you!"

"Leave me alone!" I whisper, pinching my eyes closed and waiting for it to end.

But then I feel a cool, calming presence. It's familiar.

"Shadow!" I gasp, looking at my little shadow friend. "What are you doing here?"

Urging me forward, it runs into the trees, stopping to see if I'm going to follow.

"I'm coming," I whisper, moving through the trees. "Where are we?"

The voices aren't as frightening now. I'm not completely alone.

After several minutes, I feel a sharp pain in my foot. Looking down, I'm standing in a shimmering field of broken glass. The shards sparkle like diamonds, twinkling in different pastel colors.

It's beautiful.

"Wait!" I call out, hoping the shadow will stop. "I can't go through here."

It's not stopping. Fear spikes in my chest. I don't want to be left behind.

Then I hear something. A sound that makes me step forward onto the sharp glass without a second thought or a moment's hesitation.

"Cheyenne?" I scream, the sound of my voice twisting and echoing through the trees. Whatever is here with me taunts me, calling out her name over and over again so loudly that my eardrums ache.

She called my name. I know it was her.

Unless it wasn't.

I stop, my feet ripped open and bleeding. They did this before. Canaan warned me about this very thing.

But it sounds so real.

"Kiah !" She calls again, and my heart lurches in my chest. The small bit of hope that she's actually there spurs me forward.

"I'm coming!" I scream, my eyes darting in every direction, searching for her.

The forest is alive. The gnarled branches twist around, like a cage that's trapping me here. Shadows stretch unnaturally, shifting when they shouldn't. The air is thick, damp, and there is a smell that I can't place. Raw meat or something dead.

The glass is gone, I passed through it like a small stream. A divide in the center of the forest where there should be no glass, yet there it was.

Now, every step I take sinks slightly into the muddy ground, a quiet squelch that makes me feel like I'm being swallowed up.

Cheyenne's screams rip through the silence, a jagged edge of sound that sends a shiver crawling up my spine. I turn wildly, but there's nothing—just endless trees, their bark peeling in strange, intricate patterns.

The little shadow darts ahead of me, flickering between trunks, barely more than a wisp of darkness. My heartbeat pounds in my ears, drowning out my breath.

"Chey!" I scream into the abyss of trees. "Where are you?"

Nothing but the whistle of the wind. Then another scream—closer this time. I lunge forward, dodging low-hanging branches that seem to shift just as I pass, snagging at my clothes with sharp, brittle fingers. The ground slopes downward, slick and sludgy, and suddenly, I'm at the edge of a stream, black as ink beneath the night sky. The water moves sluggishly, thick and slow, reflecting nothing. It feels wrong.

I hold my arm out over it. There is no reflection at all.

Another sob echoes through the trees, and my chest tightens. The sound comes from ahead, somewhere beyond the water.

Walking parallel to the water, I search ahead for a way to cut across. I don't feel anything, there is no pull to step inside. Maybe there isn't anything lurking in there waiting.

Or maybe it isn't water.

The thought makes my stomach queasy.

I push forward, walking along the bank of the water, careful not to touch it. Every sound has me almost jumping out of my skin.

Then I see it.

The stream dead-ends into a wide drainage tunnel, its entrance carved from ancient stone. Above the opening, an insignia looms— faintly illuminated in the moonlight. A fae, its wings spread open like a shield, framed by a crest of mountains and sweeping curves. It looks old and worn by time, but still powerful.

Reaching up, my fingers tremble as I touch it, running my fingers over the wings. There is something scrawled over the top–words–too faded to read.

Another cry rings out, but this time, something's wrong. It's different. There's laughter woven through it now, high-pitched and trembling, a sound that shouldn't belong to Cheyenne at all.

"Chey?" My voice is barely a whisper.

Silence. Then, the laughter again.

I swallow hard. Every instinct tells me to turn back, to run. But I can't. I won't. I step into the water, the coldness biting into my skin, seeping into my bones. The tunnel is dark. I can't see my hand in front of my face.

My steps echo, each one sending ripples through the sludge. The water feels thick, clinging to my legs as I wade forward.

The sound of my own breathing fills my ears, shallow and rapid.

The walls tighten around me as I move deeper inside, pressing in. Then I hear it—movement in the water. Not mine.

A breath behind me. A ripple against my leg.

And then Cheyenne laughs again—low, knowing.

And I realize I'm not alone.

"Cheyenne?" My voice trembles.

"Hurry up, Kiah! You're missing it!" She giggles. Her voice sounds so happy.

As I step forward, the realization hits me that the water is not knee level. The water is rising. I move faster now, trying to make it to the end of the tunnel before I'm swallowed up.

In the distance, a light flickers. The first light I've seen since I was dragged into the dream.

"Hello?"

Nothing.

With the water now up to my elbows, I'm struggling to move. It's so thick and the smell is getting worse.

By the time I reach the light, I'm in neck-deep water. The claustrophobic panic of being trapped is starting to make me frantic. I can't catch a full breath, and my heart is pounding like I'm running at full speed.

There is a hole in the tunnel, but I have to climb up to it.

"Hello?"

"Come on, Kiah!" She calls, still giggling. It's like she's taunting me.

"What the fuck could possibly be so funny?" I growl, reaching up to find somewhere to hold onto. There are jagged stones, edges that have been broken away, just enough to grip it.

My fingers shake, aching under the pressure and weight of my body. The ledge is so small, I'm holding on by sheer willpower.

Climbing up to the hole, I look inside.

She's sitting on a rock on the bank of a slowly moving stream. It's beautiful. Crystal, clear water trickles around her toes. The trees offer shade, and wildflowers are growing all around, leaving soft lavender and jasmine smells in the air. She's wearing a flowing white dress and her hair is long down her back. There are no signs of injury or trauma–there is no fear. She looks peaceful.

"Cheyenne!" I scream to her, but she doesn't look at me. She's looking at the tree line.

That's when I see it.

There is a Shadowrithe standing just inside the cover of the forest. She's laughing and talking with *it*.

"Cheyenne!" I scream, desperately trying to crawl into this little paradise hidden inside of a nightmare.

My little shadow friend is there. I catch sight of it at the same time the Shadowrithe does. It's trying to show me how to get in. It's pointing to another hole in the wall, just around a bend in the tunnel.

I start to move away, but stop. Watching in horror as the Shadowrithe grabs the helpless little shadow and squeezes. The little shadow squirms and thrashes, trying to escape. But it's so small in the Shadowrithe's hands. He squeezes until it turns to ash in his hands.

Clapping my hands over my mouth, I can't hold back my scream.

Jolting upright, I'm back in my room. My chest heaves, sweat slicking my skin as the nightmare's grip refuses to loosen.

"Kiah?"

Canaan is already beside me, kneeling at the edge of my bed. His hand is wrapped around mine, anchoring me to the present. His voice is low, steady. "You're safe. I'm here."

"No!" I scream, panic clawing at my mind. Panic thrashes inside me, sharp claws digging deep. "He killed it!" My breath shudders as I scramble out of bed, the ground swaying beneath me. My legs buckle, but Canaan moves fast—catching me before I can hit the floor.

"Killed who?" His voice is soft, but there's an intensity in his eyes, a patience that doesn't waver. He doesn't pry, doesn't rush me. He just waits, his hands strong but gentle as they steady me.

I turn toward him, and the moment my gaze meets his, something inside me cracks wide open. The concern in his face isn't fleeting or hesitant—it's real, raw, and so impossibly tender it makes my breath stutter. A sob bursts from me, scraping and charring my throat like fire. Falling forward into his body, I let him hold me while all of the hideous things I saw pour out of me. I can't hold them back, and I don't try.

His arms close around me instantly, firm and unwavering. There's no hesitation, no second-guessing. He just holds me, as if he knew I would break and was already braced for it.

I press my face into him, gripping onto the fabric of his shirt like it's the only thing keeping me from falling apart completely. He smells warm, something deep and rich, and the steady rise and fall of his chest grounds me, tethering me to something solid. Something safe.

"It's ok." His fingers tracing slow, calming circles against my back. "I've got you."

Tears soak into his shirt as the nightmare spills from me in broken gasps. Every awful thing I saw, every jagged shard of terror, pours out, and still, he doesn't let go. He doesn't flinch.

"I have a little shadow that follows me around." My voice is hoarse, barely more than a whisper. "I saw it on the first day. It's been like a little friend." I swallow hard, my breath shudders. "And I saw Cheyenne. She seemed happy."

Canaan doesn't speak right away. He just holds me tighter, like he knows the weight of those words, like he understands the grief tangled inside them.

"Why didn't you ever mention it before?"

"I don't know." It wasn't a secret.

"It might have been a bit of loose magic that found you."

"Well, it's dead now." I straighten my back, trying to find some strength. "It showed me how to get to Cheyenne. It led me to her."

"Where was it? Can you describe it?" The tone of his voice is measured. He knows what he's asking.

"I was in a forest at first. There was a river of glass and almost constant screaming. Then I found a tunnel, or a drainage ditch. The water was black, and it smelled–" A shiver runs the length of my spine at the memory. "It was bad."

He hasn't said anything–he nods occasionally as he listens.

"There was a crest or something on the stones at the mouth of the tunnel. It was a fairy with its wings sort of wrapped around like a shield. There were mountains in the back..."

His body tenses. "If I showed you a picture, would you know it?"

"Yes." My heart leaps up into my throat.

"Come with me."

THIRTY-SIX

I jog behind him across the hall. In his bedroom, he goes to his bed, lifting the mattress up and taking something from underneath.

It's a book. It looks small and unassuming, but having it hidden must mean that it's anything but.

He flips through the pages so quickly that it looks like he's about to tear them. Then he stops, staring down at one page.

"Here." He points to a page before spinning it around to show me. "Is this the crest you saw?"

My heart pounds as I step forward to look.

Gasping, my knees wobble. "Yes! That's it!"

"Are you positive?"

"One hundred percent!" I stare down at it again. That's it–without a doubt.

His face falls. Not just upset but truly devastated. Standing here in front of him, I can see his heart breaking. It's so real and immediate that it makes my own chest hurt. I don't know what is happening, but I know it's bad. The look on his face can only mean something bad.

"Canaan-"

"Follow me." He stands straighter.

I hope that he'll explain on the way to wherever we're going, but he's silent. The wall is back up—he's cold and distant. Whatever we had last night, the camaraderie and friendly feeling between us is gone.

He stops in front of a door and bangs on it so loudly it rattles my bones. It jerks open quickly. Calais looks bewildered on the other side. He steps forward, whispering something to her. Whatever he says, it gets no reaction from her. There is no change in her expression at all.

"Come in." She steps aside, making room.

But only I step forward. Stopping, I turn to Canaan.

"I'm leaving you here with her." His voice is low and stern. There isn't any room for negotiation or even conversation.

Nodding, I step into the room and he leaves quickly.

Turning, I stare at Calais, waiting for her to speak first.

"Have a seat." She exhales loudly. Clearly, she isn't thrilled to be spending the day with me, and in true Calais fashion, she isn't going to hide it.

She sits at a table beside her window. Spread out on the table are several reams of fabric.

Taking a step toward her, I casually look at all of the things she has in front of her. It looks like she's sewing intricate crystal beads onto the fabric. It's absolutely stunning.

"So," I teeter on my toes. "You're my babysitter, then?"

"It would appear so." She frowns.

"What are you doing?"

"I'm making my wedding dress." She flicks her eyes at me.

"You're getting married?"

"Yes, to Mordious." Her tone is flat, as if to say 'duh.'

"What?" I gasp and sit down in the chair across from her. I don't think that's what she meant when she told me to sit. There are other chairs, further away ones. But I'm too invested now.

"Yes. Isn't it obvious?"

Not even a little bit!

"Now that I think of it, I guess it was right there all along!" I laugh and hope she believes me.

Her lips twitch, which for her is basically a smile.

"This is incredible." I lean forward to see better while being extra careful not to actually touch it.

"I made everything by hand." She sits taller, pride evident on her face.

"Not the lace!" I gasp.

"Yes." She nods.

"Calais! Oh my God! It's stunning! Cheyenne would absolutely–" I stop myself. I didn't mean to talk about her. I couldn't help myself. She would be overcome by the sight of this. It's so intricate–the lace, the beadwork–she wouldn't be able to tear herself away from it.

"You can talk about her, you know." She arches one of her perfect brows as she threads a needle with silky white string that looks almost like a spider's web.

"She likes to make things. And she's good at it. She would have been really interested in watching you and picking your brain." I smile, but it hurts in my chest.

"In our family, every bride makes their own dress. It's a tradition passed down since the beginning of our bloodline." She slides a piece of fabric over the table. "This design is a nod to our mothers' dress. And this—" she points to a swirl of pearly beads. "My grandmother."

"Wow." I feel like I'm holding my breath. "When is the wedding?"

"When I finish the dress." She looks up with a mischievous smile.

She's being friendly. Maybe it's the subject matter that puts her at ease.

"Are you hungry?"

My eyes jerk up from the dress to meet hers. "Are you...asking me to eat with you?"

Her mouth falls into a line. "Yes."

"I am hungry, very actually." My mind drifts back to the sandwich from last night.

As we walk down the hallway, her breezy pink robe floats behind her. Her wings are relaxed. I've never seen her not poised for flight. It could be that she isn't scowling at me but she looks different.

I've been surrounded by high handed, brooding men since I arrived here.

This moment, however short-lived, is a breath of fresh air.

In the dining room, there is a spread unlike anything I've ever seen. I can't say for certain but I think she might be staging a bit of a rebellion here.

She's stuck here, babysitting the human she's going to feast.

Mordious joins us just as we sit.

I try to watch them stealthily, but there isn't anything to watch. Never in my life have I seen two people who seem less together than them. They barely acknowledge each other when he sits.

"Wine?" She offers me a full glass.

"Yes, please!"

By the time I finish the glass, I feel almost drunk.

"Here!" She refills it before I even have a chance to set it down.

It's only now that I'm realizing that the entire table is dessert. There is no meat, potatoes, or vegetables of any kind. Fruits, tarts, cakes.

"Oh my god! What is this?" I gasp, taking another large bite of a red layered trifle.

Her head tips back, and she laughs. "That's Canaan's favorite. It's a Linberry trifle with vanilla cream. Eat the whole thing."

"Calais." Mordious scolds her.

"Am I missing something here?"

"He had that made for himself specifically." She smiles sweetly. "Please, finish it."

Reaching into the dish, I take another heaping spoonful. It's too delicious to pass up the opportunity.

She giggles and fills her glass again. "More?"

"Absolutely!" I hold it out to her. If we're getting drunk, I might as well go all in. My head is dizzy, and my body feels loose. "I really needed this." I hum, taking a big gulp of the wine that is starting to taste better with each glass.

"Maybe you've had enough." Mordious takes the bottle from her hand. "Both of you."

"You're no fun." She pouts.

"Yeah!" I chime in, but I think he may be right. I am quite possibly the most drunk I have ever been. "What's in the wine here? It's very strong." I plop another spoonful of the trifle onto my plate.

Calais opens her mouth to answer when there is a sound, a loud, clear ring like a bell.

"Someone is on the bridge." Mordious is out of his chair and in the air before the words even register.

"Come with me." Calais looks completely sober suddenly.

I, on the other hand, am so incredibly drunk I can hardly stand.

"Humans," Calais grumbles, hooking her arm under mine to take most of my weight.

By the time we reach the door, Mordious is storming up the hallway with another man right on his heels. They aren't fighting, so for a moment I'm flooded with relief, but it's short-lived.

"Calais, we need to speak urgently. Take her to her room, secure her, and come to the weapons room." Mordious looks terrifying. He's generally so easygoing.

"Wait, can I stay with you, please?" I hear my words slurring, but I can't stop it.

"Absolutely not." She lifts off the ground, pulling my dead weight up with her.

I'm dizzy as she whisks me away.

"Stay here." She plants me harshly on the ground. "I will come check on you when I can."

I nod, my stomach churning. All that wine and dessert are suddenly feeling like a very bad idea.

In my room alone, my mind runs rampant with scenarios, each one worse than the last. Every possible horror plays on repeat–Elion is dead, Canaan is dead, Cheyenne is dead, everyone is dead. Maybe they've been overthrown, and Noctyra belongs to the Shadowrithes now.

He never explained the crest and just rushed away.

I'm dizzy and nauseous and in a full-on panic.

Running into the bathroom, I heave. Sitting on the floor alone, I try not to let my anxiety consume me.

Everything will be fine. Elion will come strolling in with a smirk on his face any minute.

THIRTY-SEVEN

My fingers drum against the table. Each tap is sharp and deliberate—just loud enough to pierce the suffocating silence. Calais flinches every time the thumping sound echoes through the room. I don't care. In fact, I like it.

Let her feel it too—the prickling anxiety, the restless energy coiled tight in my chest. If I'm unraveling, she might as well join me.

It's been five days. Five endless, torturous days. Canaan hasn't returned. Elion is missing in action. She won't say a word.

I tried to ask her about them a few times, but she goes stone cold and clams up. She won't say anything about them. I bet if I asked her if Canaan is her brother, she would deny it. She won't speak about any of them. She won't tell me about the man who arrived or the emergency meeting.

I'm completely in the dark.

It's been too long. Too much time has passed.

Fear and frustration churn inside me, a knot that feels tighter each day. At night, I lie in bed, staring at the ceiling until the darkness warps into something suffocating. My mind spiraling endlessly, haunted by all the things I don't know. There are two possibilities I can't seem to escape —Canaan and Elion are hurt, or worse.

Sleep is just as bad. Nightmares twist in my mind. There is no peace. No escape. Just the weight of their absence—and fear.

When I tap my fingers again, her shoulders shoot up into her ears, and her jaw clenches. "Kiah."

"Yes?" I tap my fingers again, and she jumps to her feet.

"Stop it!"

"Stop what, Calais?" I tilt my head innocently.

This is a dangerous game I'm playing, but this is the most excitement I've had in days. She's wound so tightly she might physically hurt me.

"You know what you're doing!" She narrows her eyes.

"Calais," Mordious' voice is low–cautious. He's a smart man, this is not something he should step in the middle of.

"Stay out of this," she turns her furious gaze on him. "She is being intentionally grating!"

"Just tell me what's going on!" I rise to my feet, resting my hands on the table to lean in closer to her. "It's been *five* days! Where is everyone? Who was that, and what did he have to say? What is happening? Is Cheyenne still alive? Is there a war? Is—"

"This is what happens when we get friendly with a human!" She shouts.

"Friendly? Who? Surely you're not talking about yourself!"

"I have been very friendly!" She snaps.

"Yeah, you have welcomed me with open arms, alright." I roll my eyes as hard as I can. "I'm going crazy here! I might not have magic, but I'm not immune to the feelings in this place! Everyone is tense and on edge. Something is happening! I can feel it in the air."

"Of course something is happening!" She throws her hands in the air. "Obviously, something is happening. But you forget your place, human. My brother will tell you what you need to know when you need to know it."

My mouth snaps shut. "That's...fine." I don't have an argument. She's not wrong. I'm not fae. I'm not from here. Their wars and politics and problems are none of my business.

But I'm trapped here. And I'm woven into the fabric of this thing completely by accident. I can't leave, but I'm not welcomed into the conversation either.

"I'll see you at dinner." Standing, I leave the room quickly. Mordious looks like he wants to say something, but doesn't. Good man. Calais would probably bite his head off.

Walking down the hallway, a sound stops me. Someone, or something, is in the library.

"Hello?" I strain, listening and waiting. The cold, creeping feeling I get in the presence of a Shadowrithe isn't here.

"Hello?" A woman's voice responds, sniffling.

Peeking into the library, I'm met with the mangled, battered woman from the other day.

"Oh, hi." I try not to look at the horrendous bruising on her face, but it's hard to miss when I'm attempting to casually look her in the eye.

"I was hoping to see you again. Thank you for letting me in." She looks like she's attempting to smile, but the swelling in her lips makes it hard to be sure.

"Of course." I shuffle on my feet.

"And then... my sister." Her voice trembles. "They told me that you–" She cracks and covers her face with her hands.

"I'm so sorry that I couldn't—" I swallow down the sob that's moving up my throat. I couldn't save her. By the time we met, it was already too late. Nothing I could have done would have changed the outcome. I keep telling myself, but it hurts all the same.

"I'm Dyinara." She wipes her face.

"Kiah. It's nice to meet you, even under these circumstances."

"Likewise." She nods.

She's holding a book close to her chest. The way she's gripping it, her white knuckled grip on it like it's going to disappear.

"Do you want to go sit in the garden with me?" I feel stupid asking but some sunshine might be good for both of us.

"Yes." She looks surprised. "I would like that."

We move slowly down the hallway. Each step seems like it's a genuine challenge for her, but she doesn't complain.

I'm struck by guilt. I've been complaining about boredom. Her body was ripped apart and her sister was killed.

As slowly as I can, trying not to make her feel rushed, I walk beside her, ready to catch her. She'll crush me but I'll be damned if I let her fall.

"I'll get the door." I scoot around her to hold it open.

As she shuffles past, she lets out a sound that at first I think is a sob. Craning my neck to look at her, I realize she's laughing.

Hunched over, still clutching the book, she hobbles toward the bench swing.

"I'm a shieldmaiden." She wipes the tears of laughter from her eyes. "I am a warrior. I am trained to hunt and fight. My armour bears the crest of one of the oldest families in Noctrya. And now a human woman has to carry me outside."

Wow. I'm two for two today with the 'human' insults.

Her laughter turns to quiet crying as she covers her face with her hands. "I couldn't save her."

"That's not your fault." I wrap my arms around her.

"She was my younger sister. My responsibility. I should have protected her." She sounds almost angry now.

"You tried." The shadows nearly ripped her wing off completely. The bruises and slowly forming scars are a testament to how hard she fought back.

"I wasn't strong enough." She looks at me, her piercing eyes full of pain and fear. "They're back. And they're strong."

A chill runs down my spine.

"Dyinara," I whisper. "Where is Canaan?"

"He–"

"What are you doing out here?" Calais' voice makes me jump.

"Just getting some air." I don't mean to sound suspicious, but my voice is high-pitched and squeaky.

I'm caught.

Shit.

"Dyinara, please give us a moment."

"Of course." She struggles to her feet and slowly disappears into the castle.

"Don't exploit an injured, grieving woman." She snaps at me.

A sharp sting jolts through my chest. She's right. "I just want to know what is happening. I'm not fae, that's true, but I am stuck here. My life is hanging in the balance just like everyone else's."

She looks up at the sky, closing her eyes against the sunlight. "The truth is, I don't know much more than you. Aerol, the messenger, only said that Canaan would be away and that no one is to come beyond the bridge. I don't have the answers you're looking for. Canaan is handling it. He will take care of everything."

"Thank you for telling me that."

Her eyes blink open. "You're welcome."

We stand in silence for a moment, the golden light shining down and the rushing sound of the waterfall in the air.

For the first time ever, I see her uncertainty. But even now, it's clear that any doubt she has is about the situation and not her brother. She believes in him.

She is frustrated, too. Before, I assumed it was boredom, but now I think it's just the same as mine. She wants answers.

"Canaan will come back soon." She looks up at the sky again. Her confidence in him is unwavering.

I am not so sure, so I keep my mouth shut and nod. I hope so.

We stand in silence for a moment, the golden light shining down and the rushing sound of the waterfall in the air.

"How's your dress coming along?"

She perks up slightly. "Very well, actually. It would appear that days on end with nothing to do but sit around in a secluded castle are very productive when it comes to dressmaking."

"Huh, who knew?"

"Would you like to see it?"

"Very much!"

As we walk down the hallway, things feel lighter again. The tightness in my chest isn't gone, but it's less.

It's funny how quickly things change.

In her room, the dress is hanging in front of her large window. The light comes through the lace and beading, leaving a kaleidoscope of rainbow prisms on the ground.

"Wow, Calais." I'm speechless. It's the best dress ever created. I hold my hand up, hovering over the material without actually touching it. I can't believe lace this delicate even exists. It's a spun spider web—one harsh tug and the whole thing would unravel. It's magic. It must be.

"You like it?"

I open my mouth to answer her when I notice something on the table.

A strange sob mixed with a laugh is drawn out of my chest before I can stop it. Cupping my hand over my mouth, I look at her, then back at the table. "Calais!"

Her mouth tugs into a line. She's so much like her brother sometimes.

"He asked me to make it." Her eyes almost roll.

Stepping toward the table, I squeal, bending down to get a better look. A perfect miniature replica. It's exact. She made a dress for her mini figurine. I'm about to cry.

"Does his miniature figure have a wedding outfit, too?"

"Of course." She snaps.

"This is the sweetest, most precious thing I've ever seen in my life."

She lets out a huff of breath. "It will make him happy."

"He'll love it!" I can't wipe the stupid smile off of my face. She cares about him. She's not warm and fuzzy, but she went to the trouble to make this for him.

"Humans." She tuts, but her face doesn't look so cold and distant.

THIRTY-EIGHT

The tension in my body melts away beneath the hot shower. My muscles are relaxed, but my mind is frantic. The wheels are constantly spinning, never stopping, never letting me rest.

It's strange how days on end of absolutely nothing can leave a person feeling run down and exhausted. I've done nothing for so long, my body feels heavy and tired.

I wonder what Calais would think if I did some laps around the castle tomorrow.

It might be worth doing just to see the look of judgment on her face.

Just as I step out, there is a knock.

It comes out of nowhere, and for a moment, I'm sure I'm imagining it.

Then—again. More knocking.

Sharp. Impatient.

I freeze, my heart hammering against my ribs. No one knocks on my door this late. I grab a towel and wrap it tightly around myself as I run on my tiptoes across the floor, dripping. Another knock. Even Louder this time.

My heart pounds, blood coursing in my ears. This has to be something bad.

Pausing for one second, I listen, straining to hear anything—screams, fighting, the chilling whisper of a Shadowrithe.

There's no sound.

I yank the door open.

Elion.

His dark eyes flick over me, taking in my wet hair, and my barely covered skin, before snapping back to my face. He doesn't linger or smirk. There isn't a witty or teasing comment. He just steps inside and closes the door quickly. "Get dressed and come with me."

"What's wrong? Is something happening?" His tone sends a shiver down my spine. He looks different. I can't explain it. He's like an Elion impressionist. It's almost right but something is missing.

"I'll explain on the way."

On the way to where?

I don't argue. I move quickly, throwing on whatever's closest. Then I step outside, shutting the door behind me.

The halls are quiet as we walk. The only sounds are our footsteps. This is good. We're not under attack.

It doesn't seem like anyone else is awake yet.

The knot in my chest loosens slightly. My mind somersaults trying to think of a plausible scenario that doesn't involve danger or darkness.

Elion stays ahead, leading the way out of the castle through the garden and toward the bridge.

I feel torn. This just doesn't feel right. Elion is my— whatever he is... friend? But something about this is off. Why are we creeping around like we're not supposed to be here?

I don't ask questions, not yet. I wait for him to tell me why we're sneaking through the dark.

When we reach the bridge, the pit in my stomach grows. An overwhelming, all-consuming feeling presses down on my chest. I want to turn around and run back.

"Come on, love. Not much further." he places his hand on my shoulder to gently guide me.

Then it happens.

A scream—sharp and so full of pain—rips through the dark behind us. The hair on my neck stands up, and a chill rolls down my spine.

I spin around. "What was that?"

Elion grabs my wrist. "We have to leave. Now."

I try to pull free of his grip. "Why?"

He doesn't let go. "Canaan wants you back in Noctyra."

"Who was screaming?"

No answer.

"Elion." I dig my heels into the bridge, forcing him to stop. "Answer me! Who was it?"

"Kiah, we don't have time. I'll explain it all when you're safe."

I don't have a choice here. Following him across the bridge, my pulse pounds, and my legs wobble with each step. "Where have you been?"

"Oh, here and there." He smirks, increasing his pace. "Did you miss me, darling?"

"No."

"Yes, you did." His eyes twinkle with the mischief that I'm used to.

"Fine. Yes. I did." I swallow down the sudden ball of emotion in my throat. I did miss him. And now that he's here in front of me, I wish he wasn't.

"I missed you too." He squeezes my hand.

Silence settles between us. The scream is still echoing in the back of my mind. I'm trying to forget about it and focus on this, but I can't. I can't force it back. It's their lingering, making each step harder to take.

I'm useless in a fight against a Shadowrithe, I know that. But it still feels wrong to run away and do nothing to help them.

Despite her best efforts, Calais has been kind to me. And Mordious welcomed me with open arms.

"When we get back to Noctyra," I say slowly, still searching for answers. "Will we be together again?"

"As much as possible." he doesn't hesitate or sound unsure.

I narrow my eyes. "I thought—"

"I still have to go out for patrols."

Of course. Patrols.

"Is Canaan there?"

"Sometimes."

I nod, pretending that answer is enough. But something is wrong. The way he's holding my wrist. I've only done this once, but it feels like we're going the wrong way.

He must notice me looking over my shoulder because he tugs me, pulling me faster.

"Elion–"

"Shh," he stands straighter, looking ahead with narrowed eyes.

Rolling my lips into my mouth, I don't even let myself breathe. Whatever he heard, I don't want him to miss it because I'm panting.

"Stay down," he whispers, pulling me further down the trail.

We creep down the trail. I feel small. He doesn't usually make me feel helpless like this. Well–wait. That's not actually true. When I first got here, he was tricky and high-handed. He only gave me information at a cost. It was emotional torture. He hasn't made me feel like this in a long time.

Taking a deep breath, I look around, forcing myself to put together the pieces that I have. They are few and not enough to create a full picture.

We walk in silence, the leaves barely crunching beneath my bare feet. The sky ahead is softening, the first hints of sunrise glowing across the horizon.

I take a few half steps, pulling behind him. If he notices or cares, he doesn't show it.

My mind is churning, thinking on overdrive until I see something that nearly stops my heart. I stumble forward slightly, almost losing my footing. I want to scream. But I cover my mouth to hold it inside.

The flowers.

Small black and purple flowers are growing in little clusters along the tree line on either side of the path.

When he passes by, they shrink away, curling into themselves and pulling back as if recoiling from him.

A shiver runs through me.

My mind runs rampant with thoughts of monsters inside him— oozing and clawing their way out. Hunger and waiting just beneath the surface of his skin.

I keep staring at the back of his head, his golden hair perfectly set, and the way his wings shift with each step. He moves like he owns the ground beneath him like the very air bends to his will.

He feels different. He looks different. The flowers are fearful.

An idea creeps up my spine like tar, settling into the base of my skull. I think I'm going to be sick.

"Elion." My voice shakes.

He stops, looking over his shoulder.

"What was the place called, the one you took me to?"

"Which one, love? I've taken you to more than one place." He chuckles.

"The special one." I clench my hands so he won't notice them trembling.

He trunks around fully now, his brow creased. "Why are you asking me this?"

"Can you just answer the question?"

"I took you to the Colonnade, to my father's tomb." He narrows his eyes.

The tension in my chest eases some.

"Why do you ask?" He pushes.

"I... I thought that maybe you were–"

"Possessed by a Shadowrithe?" He finishes my sentence with a little smirk.

"Yes."

He steps toward me, pulling me into his arms. "It's me, Kiah. Just me." For a second, a brief, fleeting moment, I see him. His eyes flicker, the warmth I've grown used to returning to them.

"Sorry." I let out a huff of air. "I think seeing that traumatized me a little bit."

"Don't apologize. It's better to be safe." He runs his thumb over my lower lip–a gesture he's done many times–but this time it just feels different. "We have to keep going."

"Alright." I straighten up.

Watching the flowers, I walk a step behind him. They're still doing it.

If a flower is afraid of him, I should be, too. But...

War wages in my mind. Do I trust him?

I'm sure of it now. We're going the wrong way.

He told me he was taking me back to Noctyra, but the path curves in the opposite direction. My stomach twists. Why would he lie? And more importantly, where the hell is he taking me?

"Kiah–"

Whatever he's about to say is cut off by the sharp caw of a crow. One. Then many. I'm struck by déjà vu so heavy it makes my head spin.

Looking up, I search the sky. There are no birds.

"Not again!" I clap my hands over my ears.

The sound is deafening. It shakes the ground. A symphony of crow calls echoes in the air. Unending. One after the other until I'm doubled over.

He grabs me, lifting me into his arms and shooting up into the sky. We're above the canopy of trees in a second flat, above the noise.

I can still hear them in the distance. Five calls, then a break, then three more.

Is that the same pattern as before?

"What the fuck was that?" My entire body shakes, trembling almost violently.

"They may have seen something up ahead. Or maybe they were just spooked by something." He is completely calm–unrattled.

"Elion," my voice cracks, a sob ripping its way up my throat. "What is happening?"

"You'll understand everything soon, love."

"Why can't you just explain it now?"

He kisses my temple. "We're almost to the river."

THIRTY-NINE

"The river?" I cringe. I never want to see that river again as long as I live.

"You'll be alright." He laughs, squeezing me tighter.

"Sure." I'm trying to play this aloof. That's not how I feel inside.

Far in the distance, beyond the dense canopy of trees, I see it. From here, it's just a sliver—a thin, dark ribbon slicing through the forest. As we get closer, it grows.

I don't realize I'm shaking until his grip adjusts, fingers pressing into my ribs. "Kiah, the river isn't going to get you."

My eyes jerk up to meet his. The river isn't. But something else is...

He drops down, his feet hitting the ground hard. "Get in the boat." He points to a small dock, sitting in the middle of nowhere. The water is peaceful; it flows calmly, a smooth, slow current.

"Get in," he repeats, his voice filled with amusement at my expense.

I don't want to.

But I do it anyway. Out here in the middle of nowhere, I don't feel like I have much of a choice.

Sitting in the boat, he is as serene as can be. It's unsettling.

"Elion?"

"Yes, darling?"

"Who screamed? Do you know?" I can't let it go. The memory claws at me, a constant whisper in the back of my mind. Was it Calais?

He smiles. A slimy, tricky smile that makes bile rise in my throat.

Is this place playing tricks on me? Is it playing on my fears?

His eyes look different.

This smile is different—it's one I remember from the first day he took me out, the kind that makes me feel small, like a puppet dangling from his fingers.

"Please." I hate myself for begging. "I'm afraid."

"Of what, love?" His head tilts slightly.

"Everything." You.

He doesn't speak for a long time. I ask him occasional questions. Where are we going? What happened? Is Canaan waiting?

My questions are met with silence.

The dense treeline around us starts to change. The shift is slow. It's not immediately noticeable. Eventually, they are not stacked on top of each other but in perfectly orderly rows.

"Are we going back to the Colonnade?" I'm not sure why this makes me feel hopeful. We had a nice time there. We connected.

"We are." He finally speaks.

"Oh, ok." I let out a breath.

The river laps at the sides of the boat as we glide through it. There is a slight breeze–soft, cool relief from the pressure I feel on my chest. It's strange. I don't feel the pull from that water that I normally do. It's so notably absent that I find myself staring down at it. What happened?

I can't say that I miss it. It's just strange.

We reach the same little dock as the last time we came here. This time, we approach from the other side.

He slides up to the dock and holds his hand out for me, the same way he did last time.

My bare feet are starting to get painfully cold.

Walking through the rows of trees. I feel something finally snap.

"Elion. I'm not taking another step until you answer my fucking questions. You said you would. Now do it." I fold my arms over my chest, fully aware that he could easily throw me over his shoulder.

"Well, then." He turns, a crooked smile on his face. "What do you want to know, love?"

"How about we start with the questions I've been asking you all day? Why are we here? Where is Canaan? Who screamed?" I list them on my fingers.

"I assume it was Calais that screamed." The calm in his voice sends a chill down my spine.

"Why? What happened?"

"Let's continue walking, love. It will be dark soon."

My feet stick to the ground. For the first time ever, even with the strange events of today, I'm truly afraid of him.

He's playing with me. He's always been playing with me.

I force my voice to work. "Where is Canaan?"

He doesn't answer, but he stops walking, and his wings twitch slightly–the only sign that he even heard me.

"Did you kill him?" My voice breaks over the words, and I hate myself for it.

"Canaan is very much alive."

"He is?" I breathe a huge sigh of relief.

Elion exhales a laugh, shaking his head. It's not mocking, not exactly. It's worse. It's the sound of someone indulging a child's misguided fears, someone who already knows the ending to a tragic story and takes pleasure in watching the pieces fall into place.

"Oh, sweet girl. I'm sorry you're here for this. You shouldn't be. You fell through that opening in the ether completely by accident. Just out searching for your friend!"

I don't know what to say to that.

Each step feels like a battle. I could try to run, but where would I go? There are miles of trees in every direction.

"When Chey hears about your fate—when she finds out what's happened to you—it's going to crush her."

"W-What?"

He leans against a tree. The usual glint in his eyes is purely wicked now.

"Do you have her? Where is she? Let her go!" I rush forward, my fist balled up–ready to swing.

"Oh, darling," he hums. "You misunderstand."

I don't realize the huge mistake I've made until it's too late. I'm too close to him.

He reaches out and grabs me, spinning so that I'm against the tree now. My mind races. Not very long ago, we were in this position, against a tree in the Colonnade, just like this one. And he kissed me.

He's not going to kiss me now.

"She loves me," he smiles, his voice smooth, effortless. "My little pet. There is nothing she wouldn't do to help me get my throne back from the evils of the realm. From the ones who stole it."

Something inside me cracks, and a sob rips through me. It happens so fast that even I'm taken by surprise. My hands clench into fists–nails digging into my palms. "You're lying."

But he's not. I can see it. The truth is in his eyes.

Truth and raw fury. It flows from him, a suffocating pressure that grinds me down and forces me to my knees. His wings jerk sharply, the movement violent and unchecked, his usual grace slipping. The air around him crackles with barely restrained rage.

He's a monster.

"Come."

Before I can protest, he throws me over his shoulder like I weigh nothing. The movement is so fast, so effortless, that my breath is knocked from my lungs. The world blurs past in streaks of green and brown as he moves through the trees at dizzying speed.

I try to thrash and fight against it, but he's too fast and strong. My feeble attempts aren't even slowing him down–let alone stopping him.

"Elion, please." My voice shakes as I try to plead with him. To appeal to the good nature, I believed he had. "You don't have to do this. Please."

He lets out a breathy chuckle. "You're a vital piece of my plan, darling. You don't even realize how helpful you're being just by existing." He shifts me higher on his shoulder. "I almost hate to do this to you. We had some good times, didn't we?"

Bile rises in my throat at his mockery, the casual way he dismantles everything I thought was real between us. "What are you going to do to me?"

The answer comes in the form of a groaning creak.

A creaking sound makes my blood run cold. Before I can react, I'm dropped from his shoulder and quickly, roughly, shoved backward. The impact is jarring. I hit the back and fall onto the cold, unforgiving metal floor hanging above the ground.

"Elion!" He slams the door to a rusty metal cage closed. A lock clicks into place. Final.

Wrapping my fingers around the bars, I pull myself up to be face to face with him.

"Why are you doing this?"

He leans in slightly, just enough for me to see the glint of amusement in his eyes and the cruel tilt of his mouth. "I don't have a choice, love. Don't take it personally. Canaan will be here soon."

Canaan. The cruelty in his smile makes me physically ill. Hunching over, I retch, my mostly empty stomach cramping into a tight ball.

He turns to walk away, leaving me caged and trembling.

"Wait! Please!" Deep down, I know this won't work. He doesn't care. It was all fake, a means to an end. "Please don't leave me here alone, Elion!"

He turns back, looking over his shoulder. "You won't be alone, love."

A chill rolls down my spine as the darkness around me shifts. The trees seem taller now, their shadows stretching unnaturally, coiling and moving-whispering.

"They're going to watch you." His voice is almost gentle. Then, louder, as he turns his attention to them. "Watch her. No touching. Not even a little taste."

The shadows shift around me-restless-but they do not touch me. They listen.

I shrink back, pressing myself against the bars, my breath coming too fast. My pulse pounds so loudly I can barely hear anything over it.

Elion's expression shifts, something unreadable flickering behind his eyes as he looks at me. His wings twitch again, the only sign of the fury still simmering beneath his composed exterior.

"Rest, darling," he whispers. "You'll need your strength."

Then he's gone.

FORTY

My throat is raw, every swallow is like sandpaper against an open wound. I'm so dehydrated that there aren't tears when I cry. And that's all I can do. Sit alone and sob.

The sun set hours ago.

It's dark and cold. I'm caged here.

I feel like an animal caught in a trap.

My teeth chatter violently, the cold burrowing into my bones deeper than it should. It's the kind of cold that feels permanent, the kind that makes me wonder if I'll ever be warm again. If I'll ever feel anything good again.

Maybe I won't. Maybe I won't live long enough to.

My mind races, spiraling in endless, frantic loops.

Elion.

I was here. He said it. But I still don't believe it.

His name is like salt to a festering wound.

The shadows taunt me—curling and moving around me, wisping through my hair, whispering in my ears.

His taunting voice plays on repeat in my head. It echoes in my brain, pinging off my skull. I can't escape it.

He has Cheyenne?

I circle through every emotion on a loop, one after the other, and then start again.

Denial. This isn't real. It's a dream–a hallucination. I can't accept it. I never will. He cared about me. I saw it, I felt it in his touch. There weren't any signs–not a single indication that this was coming.

Anger. He lied. How could I have been so stupid and naïve? The signs were all there. I saw the fucking book with the fucking picture of his fucking father! How did I ignore it? How did I let him touch me, hold me, make me believe in something that was never real?

Bargaining. When he comes back, I'll talk to him. It's not too late to fix this.

Depression. Sadness. Loneliness. Despair. It is too late. The hurt runs so deep I think it's splitting me open. I'm being ripped apart–hands curling into my ribcage and pulling until I'm torn in half. The shadows seem to enjoy this one the most. They swirl around my cage when this one hits.

Humiliation. Regret. Self-loathing.

Every touch–every conversation–every glance. The moments we shared play again and again until they don't seem real anymore. I'm questioning everything.

The day I was pulled into the water. He seemed so concerned–so genuine. None of it was real.

He kissed me. I let him inside of me. I trusted him.

I hate him. I hate myself.

He made me nervous and suspicious of Canaan.

Canaan.

Each moment spent with him looks different now, too. Was he trying to save me? Did he know? This betrayal is so much bigger than me.

They both warned me–who had my best interest in mind? Neither? Just Canaan? Were they both self-interested in their own agendas?

And Cheyenne—God, Chey. What lies is he feeding her? She would never be party to anything that involves hurting anyone, let alone me. He will never convince me that she knows the truth of what is happening here. He's been lying to her, to me, to all of us.

The scream I heard is haunting me. Who was it? Why?

I can't reconcile that Elion would truly hurt anyone.

Closing my eyes, I lean against the cage.

"Hello?" I call out in the dark. I have questions. If I'm going to be exsanguinated, I would like to know a few things first.

The shadows creep around, lurking.

"Are you at the bottom of the ranks? The expendable ones that have to stay here all night and babysit." I taunt them. "The bottom feeders."

A hiss floats on the wind, disappearing in the dark.

"Oh, you don't like that?" I exaggerate the pity in my voice. "Well, I don't fucking like this!" The cage rattles on the chain.

They're agitated now. Curling and shifting in the air.

I don't know what's coming next.

But I know it's going to hurt.

There is a sound in the dark—a snarl. It's different. The shadows hiss and whisper, but they haven't done that.

It's not the creaking of trees or the rustling of leaves. It's something else.

Holding onto the bars, I squint in the dark, searching.

Again—closer this time.

Oh, shit. Oh, god.

Something is coming. Slowly, almost leisurely, it moves across the ground—floats.

The tall form of a person, long and lean, emerges from between the rows of trees.

I am quite literally a sitting duck. I can't move. Even if I could outrun this thing, I'm trapped.

With nothing to do but wait, I watch as it comes closer and closer by the second.

My lungs feel like they're collapsing under the weight of my fear.

Pinching my eyes closed, I force myself not to watch anymore. A monster is coming for me.

I'm shaking so hard the cage is rattling on the chain. Death is coming for me, and I don't even have a fighting chance.

The beautiful moments of my life flash through my mind. My mom. Cheyenne. The times I felt truly loved, special, and seen.

Soaring high above the trees with Canaan.

He was injured, and I was terrified, but it meant something.

My biggest regret is not giving him my blood freely. If I could go back, that would be the only thing I would change. The rest of my life led me here, for some reason.

I should have given him my blood–made him stronger. He deserves it. Elion on the throne feels like death to a lot of us, not just me–and probably Canaan.

"I've been waiting weeks for this." The slow, raspy drawl of his voice pulls a whimper out of my chest. I don't mean to. I don't want to give him any more pleasure from this, but it slips out. "My delicious little pet."

The cage moves, and my stomach drops.

He hums, a low, terrifying sound that no man could ever make. The sound takes a piece of my soul and floats away into the dark.

"W-Wait." I blink my eyes open.

"I've waited long enough." He smiles, rows of razor-sharp teeth dripping with something I hope isn't blood.

It's the vilest smile I've ever seen. My breath is caught in my throat as he clicks the lock open.

"I'm going to take my time with you." He moans, sniffing the air. "I can smell your fear. It's delicious."

His hand, bone and exposed muscle with bloody stripes of flesh hanging from it, takes my arm and yanks me forward.

There is a whoosh. A sound from above me. Then I'm knocked roughly to the ground. I drop from the cage onto the hard dirt.

Spinning around, I catch strong, black wings.

Canaan.

FORTY-ONE

The Shadowrithe shrieks, a sound so vile it forces me to my knees, my hands clamping over my ears as I rock back and forth to soothe myself. It's a sound out of the depths of hell. It drills into my brain–a frequency that shouldn't exist.

Then I hear it. It wasn't just a scream.

It was a summons.

The shadows surge upward, thick and viscous, as if the ground itself is bleeding darkness. They're spilling out of hell, rolling and twisting like ink in water. The gates of hell are flung wide open, and they're taking the opportunity to rush out.

Curled on the ground, I can only watch as they rise from the ground, a sea of smoke. But it's not smoke. It moves with intention and purpose. It's living.

"Kiah!" Canaan's voice cuts through the chaos. The sharpness of it strikes fear into my heart in a way that I didn't know was possible. I thought I was as afraid as is actually possible, but no. Now I am. The tightness in his voice–the fear. "Run!"

The shadows devour him.

They swallow him whole, his entire body disappearing into a misty black fog. One moment, he's there—strong, unyielding, fighting. The next, he vanished into a writhing mass of mist.

Jumping up, I turn and sprint, bolting in between the trees as fast as I can.

My bare feet pound against the ground–my instinct to get as far away as possible coursing through me. Run. Run. Run.

But then, it hits me.

I skid to a stop, stumbling against the uneven ground.

Looking around, I find a rock that looks sharp enough to do some damage and turn back.

This isn't what he said to do. And it's very likely the stupidest thing I've ever done. But I can't leave him there.

He came to save me.

Running back, I take a breath and force myself to be brave.

"Hey!" I scream, using the rock to slice open my hand. I don't even feel it, adrenaline rushing through me.

Blood pools in my palm, and the shadows stop their attack. They smell it. The distraction only works for a split second, but it's enough for him to shoot upright.

He's so bloody I can hardly tell what I'm looking at.

"Run!" He yells again as they turn and come after him.

Covered in blood, he takes on hordes of them. Alone. I'm wingless, powerless–useless.

Whatever he's hitting them with is turning them to ash in the air. The dust blows back toward me, making it hard to breathe. My lungs and throat burn.

Ducking behind the trees, I creep away, fading into the background. My mind scrambles to think of a plan. I could run around and back to the water. Anything I can do is useless. By the time I reach help, Canaan won't need it anymore.

"Wow!" Elion's voice surrounds me. "You smell delicious!"

He swoops down, grabbing me.

In a matter of seconds, he has me so high; the trees look miniature below us. I cling to his shirt, holding on as tightly as I can.

"Canaan!" His voice echoes in the air. He's taunting him. "I've got her!"

"Elion, please! Please, don't do this!" My voice trembles, and my body shakes in his arms.

His golden eyes glimmer with something unreadable—amusement? Pity? Cruelty? I can't tell anymore. I used to think I knew him. This man is a stranger. Every good or kind thing was a lie.

"I'm sorry you got caught up in all of this," his voice smooth as silk– so deceptively soft. It almost sounds like care–but I know better now. "I had to use the situation to my advantage. Imagine my surprise when I opened the Ether and not one, but two very helpful, very lovely little humans came through!"

He smiles—that smile. The one I've seen hundreds of times, the one that used to make my stomach flip, my chest warm. But now, it feels like a knife between my ribs. It feels like a betrayal. His teeth look longer, sharper, like something dangerous when they didn't before.

"Don't hurt me." My chin wobbles. "I'm not too proud to beg for my life. Please, Elion. If any of it, even a single moment, was real–"

"Oh, darling." He exhales dramatically, tilting his head as if he was looking at a foolish child. His lips dip into a mock frown before curling back up– all wicked delight. "I guess I was too convincing. You thought it was real, didn't you?"

The breath catches in my throat, stuck behind a painful ball of emotion. My ribs feel like they're caving in, pressing against my heart, making it hard to breathe.

"I—" My voice falters.

There isn't anything to say. He's right. I thought it was real. He tricked me. I fell for it. I believed him.

"Oh, don't cry now, love," he coos.

A pendant hanging from his neck catches my eye. It's the crest. A fae, its wings spread open like a shield, framed by mountains on each side.

I'm not sure why, but seeing that cracks my heart in half. My little shadow. Cheyenne. Canaan.

Tears spill over onto my cheeks, dripping down my chin.

"I hope Canaan kills you," I whisper. My voice isn't strong, but I mean every word. "You're as weak as your father was. And you will lose the kingdom, just like he did. You don't deserve it."

His expression shifts in an instant, the easy smirk vanishing. His eyes flicker with something violent. Rage. His grip on me tightens painfully. "If only he would have been strong enough to ask you for the one thing that would have helped him." His expression is so cold.

My blood. My blood could have helped Canaan, and now it's too late.

"Put her down, Elion!" Canaan's voice cuts through his murderous stare.

Elion's grip tightens again for a second before his lips pull into a sneer. "You want her? Come get her."

Then—he lets go.

And I drop out of the sky.

I fall through the air, the wind whipping through my hair. My scream is cut short by an arm hooking around my waist.

The force punches the air from my lungs. My body jerks, and I gasp, but no breath comes. My chest seizes, a sharp, desperate pain shooting through my ribs.

Before I can get my bearings, we're hit hard. A full-body tackle that sends me careening toward the ground again.

My body slams into the dirt, and I know it's bad immediately. A searing, white-hot pain shoots from my head, down into my limbs. Opening my eyes, I watch their blurry bodies fight. Dark and light, battling in the sky.

With each breath, a cackling sound creeps out of my lungs. It's getting harder and harder to get air, like I'm sinking, like water is rushing into my lungs, pulling me under.

I try to sit up, but suddenly, my body is so weak. I can't do it. Digging my fingers into the dirt, I try to keep my eyes open.

Something is really wrong.

In the distance, high above me, the clash of metal hitting metal and shouting ripple in the air.

The coppery taste of blood fills my mouth.

I think my head is bleeding.

Little by little, the fight above me fades. The sky blurs, the sounds dull to a distant hum. My body is so heavy, sinking deeper and deeper into the earth.

I think I'm dying.

The ground beside me shakes, and I force my eyes open. Elion is bloody and battered, standing above me. He has his sword and Canaan's.

He smiles down at me–it's almost sweet. "Hey, love."

I cough, but I can't make any words come out.

"It's such a shame that you both have to die. You know, your blood could save him." He taunts me.

Who?

My mind swims. Save who?

Turning my head, I see Canaan. He's on the ground in the distance, his bloody body completely motionless.

Oh, Canaan. Even dead–or dying–he's beautiful. He looks like a fallen angel lying in the dirt. His wings spread out below him.

I move my hand across the dirt, reaching for him.

"Poor little darling." His voice starts to echo, pinging around in my mind.

Closing my eyes, I ignore him, pretending he's gone.

"What a pity."

Then, silence.

Opening my eyes, I use every ounce of strength I have to roll onto my stomach. With my face in the dirt, I plead. "Please help me. You've given me magic before. Help me now."

The ground shifts, just barely, but enough to help me pull myself toward him.

"Canaan?" I cough, blood dripping out of my mouth. He doesn't move.

Pressing my ear to his chest, I listen for the beating of his heart.

Bringing my arm up to his mouth, I press the crook of my elbow against his teeth. "Take whatever I have left. Don't let him win." I whisper. "Go make him pay for it."

My eyes get heavy, and everything fades away. The pain, the cold–it's gone.

His heartbeat is getting stronger. He'll live.

The thought makes me feel warm as the edges of my vision get dark. Black spreads in, taking over. I feel peaceful.

It's strange—dying. Maybe if it happens quickly, it's like a blink, but this feels slow. My body is easing into it. Losing a piece at a time.

It's not sad—not really. Just like falling asleep or the sun setting. It's natural. It's right.

All the shadows are gone, a distant memory that can't hurt me now.

There is something on the horizon. White and warm. The bright light shines down on my skin, and I feel safe.

"Kiah."

I'm floating.

FORTY-TWO

"Open your eyes, Kiah."

I hear the command, but my body isn't responding. It can't. I feel dull, like I'm underwater. A slight pressure against my skin holds me down. It's not harsh or painful–just there.

Time weaves in and out, an intangible thing that just slips by me. I can't hold on to it or make it stay.

A touch on my arm, gentle but firm, stirs me further. I try to open my eyes again.

Something tugs in my chest. Like my heart is trying to burst out from behind my ribs. I'm being drawn in by something. My blood, my bones, they're reaching out, searching.

"Wake up, Kiah." He says it again. This time, there is slightly more desperation in his voice. It vibrates in my chest.

His voice is a beacon of light, pulling me out of the shadows. A string tied around my heart and his, guiding me through the water up to the surface.

My body aches like I was dropped out of the sky.

Oh, right.

The memory of free-falling, weightless but full of terror, comes back into my mind. I don't actually remember hitting the ground. It's a gap in my mind that I can't see past–a block that only hides the moment of impact.

Canaan caught me. I didn't hit the ground.

But then I fell again.

I'm lost in my mind, trapped here under the weight of my own limbs.

I try to say something, but all that comes out is a croaky groan.

Something—someone—touches my hand. It feels strange. Warmth spreads through me. "Wake up."

When I finally make my eyelids work, I'm in a dark room. Low lights flicker on one wall.

"Kiah."

Everything hits me at once as the recognition of his voice finally settles in my mind. Every memory–the fear, the betrayal, the hurt–physical and emotional pain.

"Canaan?" I gasp, lurching forward, but my chest hurts too much to sit up completely.

"Don't try to move too quickly. Your ribs are still healing."

"You're alive!" My eyes well up with tears. Not just alive, but looking incredibly well. Last time I saw him, there wasn't a place on his body that wasn't bleeding. Now...

"So are you." He doesn't smile, but there is a softness about his face.

"How?" I run my fingers over my arm. I can't place this feeling. I'm sore, but not weak–not frail. My body is different. I can feel my blood coursing through my veins. More than just the pulse of my heartbeat. It's like moving a muscle–the contraction–my blood is alive, it's aware.

"Well," He looks down at the floor. "I healed you." He looks guilty.

"How?" I'm suspicious of his lack of eye contact.

"I gave you my blood."

"I beg your pardon?" I choke. That was the last thing I expected to hear.

My head spins, and a second heartbeat joins mine. It's a rhythm of two beats, just a step behind each other. One, then the other, alternating repeatedly. Mine, and a shadow behind it.

"Oh, my god! What is this?" I press my hands to my ears. I can't escape it.

"You're probably hearing your heartbeat. And maybe mine." His voice dips down for that last part. There's that guilt again. I've never been able to read him this well before. It's like his expressions are accompanied by subtitles.

"Yours?"

"You'll get used to it. I don't even notice anymore."

"Notice what?"

He doesn't answer. His jaw clenches, though.

There are too many things happening at once.

"Where is Elion? Did you get him? Did you find Cheyenne?" All of my questions spill out at once.

"He's gone, Kiah."

Shit. Everything inside of me rolls and churns, a frantic boil of too many things for one person to feel at once.

I feel calmer suddenly–an instantaneous release of something soft in my mind. Like an internal hug.

His hand is on my foot. Just touching it, barely.

I shake the chaos from my mind. "Can you just start from the beginning? Just fill it all in for me?"

He sighs and sits on the edge of the bed. "Where should I start?"

I don't even know. I don't know anything anymore.

"I suspected Elion when you showed me his family crest. I left to get confirmation, but was pulled into a situation with Shadowrithes. I know now that it was a distraction. It was my weakness. I didn't want to believe it. I gave him too much time. He has had your friend all along. He opened the portal beyond the ether and has been drinking from her —not enough to raise suspicions, but enough. Using her blood, he made an army of Shadowrithes in full human form."

"Oh, Cheyenne." I knit my trembling fingers together.

"I should have found her. This is my fault." His voice is hollow. I can feel the vast, unending self-loathing coming from him. This isn't just lip service, he truly blames himself. He hates himself for it.

"No," I reach for him. "You–"

His eyes flick to mine, and I feel suddenly breathless–pinned to the bed. Rage. I expected that. But there are other things there–things I didn't expect. Possession. Fear. Longing.

"I am responsible." His features turn stone cold as he pulls himself back, hiding behind a wall of icy, stoic detachment.

"How could you have known? Don't do that to yourself." My voice cracks. I should have known. I was sleeping with him for fuck's sake. I feel sick to my stomach. "He betrayed you." He betrayed me.

"They attacked the city. Nineteen dead. Twelve wounded. The blood of the elders stolen. Then they disappeared again." He stops, watching me. I feel his concern in my chest.

Looking at him, I have this understanding now that I didn't before. His face isn't unreadable. I know what he's thinking—what he's feeling. It's like I'm inside of him—or he's inside of me.

I nod, trying to blink back tears. "Keep going."

"I'll find him, Kiah. I'll make this right."

"You were blindsided. You can't—"

"I am the king. I should have been more vigilant. A king should not be blindsided. It never should have happened. The signs were there, but I ignored them for the brotherhood that disguised deceit and treachery."

He won't take any comfort or sympathy. Nothing I say will make him see that the only person truly at fault here is Elion.

I know how much he loves his people–the lengths that he will go to for their safety.

"Mordious." He barely whispers.

"What?" I heard him. But I can't accept it. I won't. "No." I shake my head so violently it hurts in my ribs. "No! He–but...Oh, god! Calais!" The full weight of everything drops on me and I sob. It's ugly and awful, but I can't stop it.

Covering my face with my hands, the bed moves, dipping down beside me. He lifts me up against his chest, lying down on the bed beneath me.

His wings wrap around us, shielding me from the world while I cry every tear my body can produce. Not just for Mordious, but for all of them. How could Elion do that? He knew them–lived beside them.

Flashes of Calais, curled over her table, making her wedding dress flash into my mind. I can't even imagine her pain. I'm so selfish. Elion used me, so what? People died.

The tension in his arms is tight. He isn't speaking, but he doesn't have to. I know. Fury. Rage. Violence.

For someone so filled with wrath, he's so calm. Outwardly, he's unwavering. Inside, he's boiling.

A paper-thin restraint sits between us. He's holding it back, but whatever is itching beneath his skin is growing by the second.

Why and how do I possibly know that I don't understand?

As soon as my breathing evens out and the sniffling stops, the air in the room gets thicker–hot, and suffocating.

The tips of his fingers flex against my hip. "Now is not the time. I know that. But I can't..." he stops a low, rumbling breath from his chest vibrating through mine. "You were in a relationship with him. When I asked, you lied."

Wiping my eyes, I swallow the urge to cry out in pain as I sit up to look at him.

"I'm sorry. He told me it was forbidden. I didn't want him to get into trouble."

"It is forbidden." He growls, his eyes flashing almost red.

"I—"

"It's forbidden because a human's blood can be used as a weapon against our kind! Especially when all of us are not partaking!" The volume of his voice rises with each word.

"He never drank from me!" I scream back, wincing as my ribs expand.

"Be careful, Kiah! You're actually being truthful. You wouldn't want to make a habit of that now!" He snarls.

With unexpected gentleness for this situation, he carefully moves me off his chest and stands.

"Hey, fuck you! I didn't know, ok?" I already feel guilty enough without this. "I only lied because I thought I was protecting him! If you recall, you asked me to keep things from him, too! And I did it!"

"So you lie to your lovers, too. Wonderful."

"Why the fuck do you care, anyway?"

"I don't. I just don't appreciate being lied to, and it seems everyone has been doing a lot of that lately." He grits his teeth. "That's probably when he established the connection to pull you into the dreamweaves."

"Oh, shit." All the fight goes out of me.

The silence is painful—stretching around us and swallowing up everything.

"He dropped me, Canaan. Out of the sky. He left me on the ground beside your dead body, coughing up blood—dying." My chin trembles as I suck in a painful breath, trying to hold back the sadness. "I'm sorry I lied to you. I wish I could take it all back. He made me believe..."

"I should not have started this argument. Now is not the time."

He runs his hands through his hair and sits at the end of the bed.

"Where are we?"

"Noctyra."

"We are?" I look around.

"This is my room."

"Oh." I try to swallow, but my throat is dry. Maybe that explains why I feel so completely surrounded by him.

"It's been three days." He clears his throat.

"Has it?" I pick at my cuticles. "Have you been...here?"

I don't have to ask. I know he's been here beside me. I can just feel it. It's part of my memory—the feeling of his body beside mine.

"I never left you."

I feel open. Exposed. I can't hide anything. The way he looks at me is physical, he's touching me, he's peeling back the layers.

His blood is in my veins, flowing, feeling, touching everything.

He looks different now. The distance I always felt stood between us is gone. It's just us now.

And the way he looks at me.

It's so personal. It's almost like...

"Canaan." I don't mean to whimper, but that's what comes out. My insides are twisted into knots.

"You should eat. Even with my blood, you'll be weak after giving so much to me." He reaches out and tucks a strand of wayward hair behind my ear.

My heart stops beating as his fingers graze my cheek.

Why does it feel like he's done that a million times before? It's so familiar and comfortable.

"Right, yeah." I pull back. We need distance between us.

"A ceremony will be held tomorrow for Mordious. No one expects you to be there—"

"I'll be there!" I gasp. "I wouldn't miss it!" I don't care if I have to crawl there—I'll make it.

He nods his head, lingering beside the bed. "I'll bring you something to wear."

"Thank you."

He doesn't leave right away. He stays, watching me.

"Canaan." My cheeks heat.

"Sorry." He clears his throat. "Don't try to go anywhere."

"I won't," I promise. "I'll be right here."

As soon as I'm alone, I coil into myself, hugging my body tight. I need to shower—to wash any traces of Elion off my skin. I hate that he's touched me. That his mouth and tongue have been on my skin.

Tears prick in my eyes again as all the things we lost settle into my brain to torment me.

FORTY-THREE

"Um, Canaan?"

"Yes?" He perks up as if he'd been waiting for me to say something.

"I would really like to shower." I hesitate, unsure of how to phrase it without triggering whatever has him so irritable. I can't explain to him why I feel the need so desperately—why the idea of standing under hot water, scrubbing away any traces of Elion's touch on my skin is so necessary.

A moment of privacy will be dual purpose here. Both to feel free of Elion, but also to have a moment alone.

Since he brought me my dinner last night, he's just sitting there at the end of the bed. Watching me. It's incredibly unsettling. Some space would be really appreciated.

I fell asleep, and when I woke up, he was still there.

I'm feeling like an animal in a zoo, a spectacle. Stop staring at me.

"I'll wash your hair."

"What?" I choke on the ill-timed sip of water in my mouth. Coughing, I glare at him. He can't be serious.

"You won't be able to lift your arms above your head because of your ribs." He stands, offering me his hand.

"Ok. Wait. Stop right now." I don't move. "What the fuck is happening? Why are you being so nice to me?"

"I'm not being particularly nice to you." A crease forms between his brows. "No more than usual."

"Oh, bullshit!" I'm not imagining this! "You've been sitting there like a statue all night!"

"At no point during your stay here have I mistreated you."

I narrow my eyes. "I mean, you accused me of masterminding the dreamweaves, so there's that. But otherwise? No. You haven't mistreated me. But that's not the point. Why are you acting like this?"

"I'm not acting any differently," he snaps, his jaw tightening.

But he is. And we both know it.

I feel it every time he looks at me. He's acting like nothing is happening, but my body is reacting to his.

"Right. Fine. This is completely normal." I take a breath and hold it, bracing myself for the pain in my ribs when I stand.

Gasping, my eyes jerk open as his hands come under my arms, supporting me as I inch my feet toward the ground.

"Canaan."

God, why is my voice so breathy and weird?

My feet land on top of his, and we freeze.

His chest is pressed to mine, I'm standing on his feet, and his arms are wrapped around me. I feel drunk. My head is dizzy in a loose, free, euphoric way.

"Let me wash your hair."

"Ok." I don't know what I'm saying until I hear the answer spoken aloud. I can't say no. Even thinking it feels like a betrayal somehow.

"Kiah," his fingertips graze my jawline.

"You smell so good." The words spill out of my mouth.

He stares down at me, and I'm filled with this overwhelming energy —a deeply rooted need to touch him more. My hands plant themselves on his chest. I have no say in the matter. My brain is turned off, and my body is doing things I have no control over.

"Let's go." He's the first to break the trance that's woven through my head.

I exhume to put me down, but he carries me, lifting me in too intimate a way.

Outside of his room, the hallway is dark and somber. The weight of grief and loss is oppressing. This place was always dark, a heavy, ancient feeling in the air, but now it's worse. I wonder how I ever smiled here. Or how I ever slept a single night that wasn't consumed by nightmares.

The double doors leading into the bathhouse are open as we approach. A lump of nervous energy rises in my throat. Fear and shame, guilt and unease, it hits me hard–all at once. If I never saw this place again, it would be too soon.

"It's going to be alright." His voice is steady–calm.

My mind races. He doesn't know everything that has happened here–the things I've done. I want to keep it that way.

Inside, he sets me on my feet with so much care it makes my knees feel wobbly. The way he's carrying me, the softness in his hands– I feel like a most treasured possession.

"I'll turn so that you can change and get in. I won't watch you."

He spins around and pulls his shirt off, his back straight. When he steps into the water, my breaths turn shallow and quick.

Slipping slowly out of my clothes, I watch him. He doesn't peek. Elion would have.

Standing at the edge of the gradual slope into the water, I cover myself with my hands.

"Come in." He hasn't turned around, but somehow he knows.

I hesitate still. Fear and anticipation battling inside, holding me hostage here on the edge. I swallow hard and step forward, slipping into the water.

The warm water feels so good. The pain in my body is instantly soothed.

The trickling from the fountain at the center is the only sound.

I wade out until my chest is covered, the darkness doing the rest. His wings are relaxed behind him in the water. They're so large. Much larger than...

I need to stop thinking about him. I never want to think about him again.

When I reach him. I don't dare look. Just stare at the water, where it's safe.

"How are you feeling?" He steps behind me, and his fingers brush my hair, gathering it, pulling it over my shoulder. "You're tense."

No shit.

"The water feels good."

From the fountain, he pulls a handle like a handheld shower head.

"Hey!" I look over my shoulder.

"No one ever showed you that?" He brings it up and carefully wets my hair.

The scent of the shampoo fills the humid air. Clean and soft—slightly familiar.

When he slides his hands into my hair, my breath catches. His fingers massage my scalp, and I let my eyes drift closed.

It's too gentle, too intimate. I can feel his strength in every touch, but he's holding back, careful, as if I might break.

He walks around me, moving to stand in front of me, but I keep my eyes pinched closed.

He presses closer, not quite touching, but I can feel him there. The heat from his body is close enough to seep into my skin.

I swear I hear his breath hitch, but when I open my eyes, his face is calm, his expression unreadable.

There is a scar on his chest, a big gash carved into his skin. I open my mouth to ask him about it, but stop myself.

"You're alright." He whispers.

A bolt of something dark and dangerous shoots through me. My fingers curl into fists beneath the water. "What?"

He makes a low sound, something almost like a laugh. "I didn't say anything."

"You—you did!"

"No." He brings the water up to rinse the shampoo out of my hair.

"I heard you." I grit my teeth. "Don't play games with me, please."

"Kiah." He stops what he's doing to meet my eyes. "I didn't say anything. I swear. What did you hear?"

"You said 'you're alright,' I know I heard it." I'm questioning my sanity.

"It's just memories." He looks past me, over my shoulder. "I hear them too."

"What do you hear?" I'm afraid to ask, but I have to know.

"Take whatever I have left."

It doesn't hit me all at once. At first, it doesn't make sense.

"Oh!" I clap my hand over my mouth. The memory floods my brain and sends me into a dizzying spiral. The blood.

"It's just a memory." He assures me, but his voice is too raspy and low. "I'm almost finished."

Shutting my mouth, I try to keep myself silent. I don't need to say anything else.

His hands run through my hair again, and goosebumps run over my skin. My insides are fluttering and rolling around.

"Canaan?" There goes my mouth, talking without permission again.

"Kiah?" He actually sounds like he's smiling.

"Do you feel it too?"

"It?"

"This." I move my hand in the space between us, "This feeling."

His hands stop moving. "I do." He clears his throat.

It helps that he seems as nervous and weirded-out as I do. If he were completely unaffected, this would be much worse.

"What is it?"

"It's just the blood."

"Oh." That sounds reasonable. I can accept that. We shared blood, we healed each other. This is just a temporary consequence of that. It makes complete sense—we feel close because we are. We shared something profound with one another.

"Wrap yourself in a robe." He takes my hand and gently guides me toward the edge.

I move as quickly as my body will allow, wrapping myself up before he has a chance to look. But he doesn't even try.

He's not Elion.

I have to remember that.

"Stand still." He runs his fingers through my hair, gathering it up. It takes a moment to realize that he's braiding it. He works quickly, his fingers weaving my hair into an intricate plait. When he's finished, he lays it over my shoulder. "There."

"Thank you." My throat is too dry to speak. I know it must be the blood, but...no one has ever taken such careful and purposeful care of me.

"We have to leave now. We have a monument to honor." He nods.

FORTY-FOUR

"Kiah, take a breath." This is the tenth reminder he's given.

"I'm sorry."

My stomach is in knots.

This all makes sense. The Falls is the location of their memorials. Mordious spent all of his time guarding it. It's fitting that his service is there. All of these things are perfectly rationalized in my brain, but I can't make my body relax.

I don't want to go back there.

It doesn't help that he insists on flying with me in his arms. Not that I was particularly interested in taking the monster-filled river again.

"Can you distract me?" I realize my fingernails are digging into his shoulder.

"How?" He flies up higher, bursting through the clouds with ease.

"Tell me something true."

He hums, tightening his grip on my body. "I will tell you a truth. But first, tell me what you know of the war that resulted in my reign over the entirety of the fae realm."

"He said it was a disagreement between your father and his." I won't speak his name.

He huffs. "A disagreement."

"Yeah."

"Did he tell you what they disagreed about?"

"He didn't." I swallow hard. The clipped tone in his voice sets me on edge.

"The Rimfae, King Esren, and Thaloin, King of the Shadowrithes, were allies in the war. They fought against us to keep the portals open, to allow easy access to humans. We stood guard at the gate and held the line." His eyes flick to mine.

So many things make sense now.

"They lost, and you became the king over everything." Elion made it seem like Canaan took it without cause.

The canyon of guilt in my chest cracks and splinters, growing wider and more painful.

"He claimed to understand. I wonder how long he spent plotting." There is a strange thoughtfulness in his voice where I thought I would find anger.

"Can I ask you a question?"

"Yes."

"Why were you willing to go to war to protect humans?"

"Because someone had to protect you."

I know he means "you" in the general sense, but holy shit. My blood is on fire.

"Oh," I whisper.

"Centuries ago, there were no barriers between realms. The gates were open. Humans and fae lived side by side. Our magic is stronger when you are present. Your blood gives us power and strength. We lived in peace. Then humans began disappearing. It started slowly, then it became more and more frequent. They were abusing their power and strength." He dips down below the clouds, and the ground below us opens to the road up the mountain.

We're almost there.

"If a human gives their life's blood, the last drop, it makes us temporarily euphoric; the power is addictive. They had to be stopped, and the realms had to separate." His arms tighten around me, but this time I appreciate it.

"So with nothing to gain and at great personal cost, you kept humans safe?" I can hardly wrap my head around it. The selflessness is almost shocking.

"Life is a precious thing. Fae or human, it doesn't matter. We are strong, so we had to stand up for good."

What does swooning actually feel like? I'm fairly certain I'm doing it. My heart feels like it's beating too fast and too slow at the same time.

Was he always like this? Or did I mistake his intensity for contrarianism or maybe pretentiousness? He is good to his core–noble even.

I wish I had told him everything.

Maybe he would have put the pieces together faster.

"Don't do that." He whispers. "Don't blame yourself."

"You're blaming yourself, too."

"Yes." His lips twitch. "But that's because this was my responsibility. It's sort of the cornerstone of my job–making sure this kind of thing doesn't happen."

"But you were betrayed."

"I should have seen it coming. He used you as a shield. I thought he was just being secretive about you. At least I was right about one thing."

"I'm sorry." The look on his face makes me swallow a hard lump in my throat.

"Hindsight is one of life's greatest cruelties." His gaze moves over my face.

This blood-sharing thing is a kick in the teeth.

The weight of his stare is staggering. It makes my stomach clench. He looks at me like I'm something precious, something rare—like I'm worth everything.

His eyes, dark and piercing, hold a tenderness I don't know what to do with. It's not just attraction. It's reverence, devotion.

It feels real.

He's not a stranger, he's someone I've shared things with—intimate things—every thing.

But we haven't.

I don't know how long I've wanted to be seen like this, to be known like this. It makes me ache, makes me almost desperate for him, because I know deep down—he is so good.

Not just good-looking, steady in a way that feels like gravity—he won't let me fall. And for some impossible reason, that goodness is wrapped around me.

"Calais has something for you to wear to the ceremony. It's in my bedroom." He cuts through the emotions scrambling my brain.

Calais. I haven't seen her. A flicker of guilt crawls up my spine. I doubt she wants me to hug her, but the urge to reach out, to do something, eats at me.

Mist hangs in the air all around us. I know we're getting closer to The Falls, but the curtain of fog is shielding it from view.

"Ready?" He whispers.

No. "Yeah."

His grip on me tightens, and we burst through the fog. We're so much closer than I was expecting. Halfway over the bridge and getting closer by the second.

"We're going to avoid the foyer. I'm dropping into the courtyard beside my room."

I have questions but I don't ask them.

As his feet hit the ground, I realize how tightly I'm holding onto him. His shirt is balled up in my fists.

"Sorry about that." I smooth out the wrinkles I made.

"There are extra patrols here today. They won't risk attacking. There will be too many here." He reassures me before I can even express my concerns.

He brings me into his room. Unsurprisingly, it looks the same. But it doesn't feel the same.

Last time we were here, I ran out of the room while he was spread out in bed. I was so nervous and uncomfortable. Maybe things haven't changed as much as I thought.

That day feels so close and so far away.

After I ran out of here, Elion came. He pestered and bothered, asking over and over again about what Canaan said in our private conversation.

It was more than concern—he tried to mask it—to make it seem like he was only asking for my safety, but it was more than that. I felt it then; I know it now.

Then I slept with him again.

Shame. Guilt. Regret. Disgust.

"This is for you." He hands me a long blue dress. "I'm going to check on Calais. Stay here." He looks angry. The softness–the tenderness he had in his eyes for me the whole way here is gone.

"Canaan?"

"Just get ready. I'll be back for you soon. The ceremony is going to begin at dusk." He doesn't even look at me as he speaks. Half the words are mumbled as he's walking toward the door. Then he's gone.

The sudden shift in his demeanour is so stark it has me feeling anxious.

He couldn't have known what I was thinking about. We have a blood bond. He's not a mind reader. It probably has nothing to do with me. He's stressed too. More than me.

Shaking off the tension in my shoulders, I stare at the dress in my hands.

It's going to be too long for me, made for a fae woman. But the fabric is buttery soft, and there are beads across the bodice. It's beautiful.

I don't feel beautiful.

Even as I slip it on. I can't ignore this weight in my stomach, tugging me down.

I'm an idiot. I actually thought we had a deep connection. Sometimes he would look at me, and I would feel like the only woman in the world.

I have to get to Chey before he breaks her heart.

Pulling the dress on, I stare at myself in the mirror. I feel undeserving of something so lovely.

Pulling up the train, I walk over to the window and push it open. I wish my little shadow were here.

A soft breeze blows in through the open window, carrying the scent of the flowers growing outside. This is really a Hail Mary–my desperation grasping at straws, but I lean out, looking at the bushes and plants.

"Hey," I whisper, my cheeks growing warmer. "I don't know if anyone is listening, but this worked before. Um, Magic, I'm not sure how to address you. Do you think you could do something today? I don't even know what." I cover my face with my hands. "I'm not even sure what I'm asking, really. Just anything you can do. If you can make Calais feel peace or give Canaan a sign." I feel like a child writing a wish-list to Santa. "Maybe you don't do that kind of thing, but..."

"Kiah." His voice behind me makes me scream. My fear is immediately replaced with deep embarrassment.

"Hey." I clear my throat.

"Ready?" He doesn't ask any questions about what he just walked in on–and I'm grateful–but the way he rolls his lips into his mouth lets me know he absolutely heard me.

We walk down the hallway, taking a staircase that I never knew existed. His grip on my wrist is tight but not painful–just enough to keep me close.

An angry, guttural scream stops us both.

He closes his eyes for a second, exhaling slowly. I feel the tension change in his posture, and his muscles clench.

"Come on." His voice is tight. Resigned.

Whatever is happening, he already knows.

He turns us around, retracing our steps toward the foyer.

"Stop doing that! Leave it there!" Calais's voice cracks, sharp with grief and rage. "No one touches this! It stays!"

"Calais!" Canaan calls, but she doesn't respond. She either doesn't hear him or she doesn't care.

"If you don't like it, walk another way! It—"

We step into the foyer, and I freeze.

She's pacing, her chest heaving. Two fae, both I don't recognize, are on their hands and knees, scrubbing feverishly at the stones. A bucket sits beside them, the water inside murky red.

Blood.

A thick, dark stain is spread across the floor and seeped into the cracks.

My stomach turns.

"This mark stays until I rip Elion's head from his body." She grits her teeth. "Don't erase him!"

"I'm sorry." One of them has his hands up in surrender. "We didn't know."

"Go!" She shouts, her voice echoing off the walls.

They scramble up and leave quickly, rushing past us.

"Calais." His voice is low and steady.

She whirls on him, her entire body trembling. "No, Canaan. This stays until Elion has paid for what he did!"

For a moment, silence hangs between them, thick and suffocating.

"It stays," he finally says, he promises. "I'll make sure no one touches it."

I can't take my eyes off the stain.

It's so big. He was a big man.

"I was bringing you these." Her shoulders straighten, her chin raising up slightly—more like herself.

She holds out her hand, the miniature figurines of Canaan, and it hits me like a brick to the face. My knees wobble, but Canaan wraps his arm around my waist.

"Thank you." He reaches out, taking them from her gently.

She nods. "I'll see you outside."

When I'm sure she's gone, I crumple slightly, covering my face with my hands. That little doll.

"Fuck." I wipe my eyes as quickly as I can.

"He is with his father now, and his father's father. He has found his way into the arms of our ancestors, and they hold him. He is surrounding us from beyond the eternal veil."

That... is comforting.

"His blood will be added to the casks when Calais is ready to give it. He will strengthen all of us, even from beyond."

That...is creepy.

Rolling my shoulders back, I tip my chin up, mimicking the strength of the woman who just lost her future husband. If she can be strong, I can.

Walking side by side, we are greeted in the garden by several people dressed in white. They look peaceful—if not slightly worse for wear. They're battle-scarred and healing.

"Your Majesty." One of them bows, and the rest follow suit.

"Stand here." He directs me to a spot.

In the center of the courtyard, a huge fire is blazing, but it's giving off no heat. Lifting my hand toward it, I study the flames.

"That is a current of magic." He leans in, explaining quietly. "His spirit is moving on to white shores."

Streaks of orange paint the sky, and the sun melts behind the mountains. The rushing sound of the waterfalls hums in the background as we wait.

"Just do what I do. Repeat after me." He whispers.

The door swings open, and Calais steps out.

An audible gasp moves through the crowd. She is wrath and heartbreak.

She's wearing her wedding dress, dipped in red. She looks like an enraged goddess, ready to burn the world to ashes.

The delicate lace she made by hand looks like freshly drawn blood. The wind blows through the hem of her skirt, pulling it up into the air as she walks.

Her face is stone cold, but the crack in her voice from earlier plays in my head. She isn't going to let anyone see it.

With her head high, she takes her place on the other side of Canaan.

"Mordious." His voice booms like he spoke it into a microphone.

"Mordious!" Everyone repeats.

"Mordious!" Calais calls, her voice shaking.

"Mordious!" We all chant after her.

Everyone drops at once, kneeling before the fire. I quickly get down. With bowed heads, they place one palm against the ground.

When I place my hand on the ground, I jerk it back in surprise. A cool current pulses up from the dirt. It's alive.

Placing my hand down, I let it swirl around me. It feels like magic.

The silence engulfs me like it's alive, too. It moves around me, wrapping me up in it. It's cool and calming.

Suddenly, the wind whips around us, harsh and furious. A million tiny flower petals whirl through the crowd, a swarm, a flurry of fragrant pieces.

Calais holds her hands up. Closing her eyes as the petals land all over her. A laugh bursts from her chest, and a tear rolls down her cheek.

They catch in our hair and clothes, and float around before the wind carries them away, blowing into the current and disappearing.

"There was your magic," Canaan whispers. A lopsided smile pulling at his lips.

A NOTE FROM THE AUTHOR

Dear Reader,

I wanted to take this opportunity to thank you. Writing books is my dream, and knowing that you've taken the time to read them means everything to me. I can't express enough how grateful I am for your support. If you enjoyed the story, it would mean the world if you left a review. Your thoughts help other readers discover the book. Even a few words make a huge difference! If you're not able to, that's okay—I'm just happy you're here. Thank you for being a part of this journey with me. I appreciate you more than you know.

With gratitude,

Myranda

ABOUT THE AUTHOR

A bonafide motha' to five kids under the age of eight, Myranda requires no fewer than 2 cups of black coffee (2 sugars) each day to support her habits and has finally built up the courage to publish her work. She enjoys noise-cancelling headphones and long waits in school pick-up lines and can change a diaper one-handed while blindfolded.

Also by Myranda Rae

SERIALS

🐺 👹 **fantasy/shifter**

Beyond the Ether

1 Blood of the Innocent

2 *Blood of the King

The Fairytales series

1 Captivated, Cursed

2 Love You Anyway

3 Finding Iris

4 Sucker for You

5 The Lost Girl

The Playlist series

1 Fix You

2 Beloved

3 Cherry

4 A Warrior's Heart

Sons of Sorsha (The Playlist) mini-series

1 Jack

2 Lucas

3 Samuel

4 Asher

👽 🛸 **scifi / aliens**

Coiled Throne Series

1 The Coiled Throne pt. 1

2 The Queen Trials pt. 2

The Astrynian Warriors Series

1 The Destroyer's Little Pet

2 Havoc

An'eo Chronicles

1 Callisto

2 Proximus

3 Nyon

4 Kieran

5 Loide

Tribute to the Alphagods

1 Wrath

2 Pride

3 Envy

4 Lust

🌿🔥 **contemporary**

The Underworld duology

1 What's Done in the Dark

2 Will Come to Light

3 Zion (bonus mini-short)

STANDALONES

🐺👑 **fantasy/shifter**

• Alpha's, Kings & Play-things

• BEAST: Destined to the Hellhound

- Mark of the Damned
- Bound: Mates at War
- The Queen in Shadows
- Suck Me Slowly

🫦🔥 contemporary

- Enemies Closer
- Unplanned: A One Night Stand
- PINK
- Lewd & Lascivious
- The Other Side
- When I Whisper His Name
- Just the Two of Us
- Going for Gold
- The Void He Feels
- *Bound to Break

* Indicates Work in Progress

www.ingramcontent.com/pod-product-compliance
Lightning Source LLC
Chambersburg PA
CBHW070337260626
47160CB00003B/1070